Praise for *New York Times* bestselling author Rachel Lee

"A mix of angst and humor delivered in a vividly imaginative, soulful narrative."
—*RT Book Reviews* on *A Cowboy for Christmas* (Top Pick!)

"While the relationship-building excels, it is the heroine's strength in the face of such personal adversities that is the real scene-stealer."
—*RT Book Reviews* on *A Conard County Baby*

"Lee's poignant, tragic tale of loss brings to light the suffering of many returning vets; her anguish-filled dialogue makes it real."
—*RT Book Reviews* on *The Widow of Conard County* (Top Pick!, Winner of the Best Harlequin Special Edition, 2013)

"A dramatic suspenseful tale about moving forward with your life when interruptions occur."
—*Fresh Fiction* on *Conard County Marine*

"*Defending the Eyewitness* is a page-turner full of mystery and suspense, keeping the reader engaged every step of the way."
—*Fresh Fiction*

Dear Reader,

My first real foray into archaeology was a dig I participated in when I was fourteen. Volunteers were needed and I was eager. I learned a lot from crawling around on hard ground, using tweezers to pull pieces of charcoal and pollen and seeds out of the ground. I also learned about time pressure. We had three months before the bulldozers returned to finish putting the road through.

Then came the glorious summer visiting my uncle Bill in Montana. He was a geology grad student, and he shared his love of those mountains with me, but more importantly, he took me into an isolated area to show me an ancient rock painting, faded and weathered over the years. Once it had shared a message of some kind, but even now, though it was impenetrable and hard to see, it still caused my breath to catch, thinking of the ancient hands that had painted it.

One of the things I saw in my uncle's geology lab was a bunch of carefully laid out fossils. A whole new window into the past and far, far different from a museum. These had just emerged from the ground and still needed to be identified. Magical. These magical memories gave life to this story.

My uncle Bill, who passed away just recently, opened windows in my mind. Those windows have never closed, nor was the passion he shared ever lost.

Rachel Lee

CONARD COUNTY WATCH

Rachel Lee

HARLEQUIN® ROMANTIC SUSPENSE

Recycling programs
for this product may
not exist in your area.

ISBN-13: 978-1-335-45655-7

Conard County Watch

Rachel Lee was hooked on writing by the age of twelve and practiced her craft as she moved from place to place all over the United States. This *New York Times* bestselling author now resides in Florida and has the joy of writing full-time.

Books by Rachel Lee

Harlequin Romantic Suspense

Conard County: The Next Generation

Visit the Author Profile page at Harlequin.com for more titles.

For Butchie.

Chapter 1

The rosy, early-morning sunlight struck the cliff face in Wyoming at an angle, heightening shadows and shapes. The mystical moment between night and day, when secrets revealed themselves to eyes trained to see.

The cracks and lines in the rock face were mostly sharp, barely weathered in the year since Thunder Mountain had shaken to open up this fresh cleft in its lower slope. Rock had been exposed for the first time in millennia, and with it treasures untold.

Paleontologist Renee Dubois stood somewhat precariously on broken and tumbled rocks at the base of the cliff. The cleft was narrow, one side a thirty-foot-high rock face, the other what she thought of as the tooth, shorter and thinner. The part that had broken away. The narrow space between them gave just enough room in which to work.

With her digital camera, she took photos every fifteen seconds or so, but her eyes were far busier than her camera. Watching the shadows shift as the sun rose revealed an ever-changing view that brought out some shapes as others faded slowly into the background, and filled her with constantly freshening amazement.

Excitement fluttered in the pit of her stomach. When Gray Cloud, an old family friend, had brought her out here last fall to see what the mountain had revealed, she had known in her gut that this was wondrous. Now she looked forward to a whole summer to work on it with the tribe's permission as long as she took care to observe that this ground was sacred, and as long as she promised to return any human bones to the tribe.

Sixty-five million years at least, she thought, staring at the lower layers that yielded only bits of their secrets. Secrets that may well allow her to prove her pet theory…or that might dash it by the end of the summer. Either way, the outcome would be important. Either way she would learn. Either way she would make some marvelous discoveries with her team.

She shifted a bit on the unsteady stones and balanced herself again, taking photos from a slightly different angle. The light was still changing, but only at times like this could human eyes begin to appreciate just how fast this planet was spinning. In no time at all, full daylight would be born, the shadows would reveal so much less, and the mystery would retreat behind the ordinary.

When Denise arrived, Renee would have her come out here at dawn and sketch this all onto a grid, then match it to the photos. Only when the search area was perfectly documented could they begin to brush away rock and loose dirt.

But something caught her attention, and even though she knew better, she let the camera dangle from its neck strap and pulled a three-inch paintbrush from the rear pocket of her jeans. The bristles were a bit stiff, not too soft to accomplish anything, and she stepped toward the cliff. That little group of straight lines might be an accident, but to her it looked like more.

Brushing gently at them, removing a light layer of grit to bring them into the foreground, she had to force herself to stop as excitement caused her heart to pound. An egg? A cracked one with the fetal tissue showing? My God.

She shoved the paintbrush back into her pocket and took quick photographs, hoping to get a few before the daylight washed it out.

Her hands trembled just a little with her exhilaration and she had to tamp down her eagerness. Every step of this must be done just right or it would all become meaningless. Restraint. She had practiced a lot of it in her career, but for some reason this site endangered her patience.

Hardly noticed, some small rocks tumbled down from above. She wasn't surprised. This cleft probably still had some settling to do, but she was glad of her hard hat.

She drew a couple of deep breaths, reminding herself of the importance of method and methodology. Man, she'd been doing this work long enough that it kind of surprised her that she wanted to get ahead of herself. Giving in to her urge could simply ruin it all.

The light had begun to turn flatter as the sun rose

higher. The minutes of magic had passed. Looking at her feet, she stepped to a firmer perch, ready to resume her study of the revelations.

Gray Cloud was an elder of the local tribe, but he was also known as the Guardian of Thunder Mountain among his people. This was all sacred space to them, and even though her second cousin was married to the man, she had been astonished by the invitation to investigate. This was not a place the local tribe wanted too many outsiders to visit.

Just then, a shadow fell across her and the rock face in front of her. Turning quickly, she saw Gray Cloud. The years and the weather had worn his striking face to a dignified set of lines that emphasized his heritage. The years hadn't diminished his powerful frame, however. Right now he wore a blue Western shirt with his blue jeans and heavy work boots. His long hair was caught in a tie at the base of his skull.

"Hey," she said.

He smiled. "Excited still?"

"Beyond words. It's all I can do to keep my hands to myself."

"We're as excited as you are," he told her. "This history predates our people by millions of years but we're fascinated, too. That which comes before is a guide to what will come after."

An interesting perspective, Renee thought, turning her gaze to the rock cliff again. Usually her work didn't give her the opportunity to indulge in such thoughts. She had to be focused on details, because details added up to the big picture. But this big picture had been followed by a massive extinction event that no one yet fully comprehended. Some had survived. Others had not. Why the differences?

Maybe this site would lend some answers to that. "I'm just so thrilled you showed me this and asked me to work on it. Was that a fight for you?" She understood all the good reasons the tribal elders were reluctant to grant access to sacred areas. Perhaps most importantly, non-natives had a way of disrespecting them. Surely the invitation Gray Cloud had extended to her hadn't come without some disagreement.

"You are the cousin of my wife," he said. "I trust you. I know you understand and will make everyone else understand the respect this place requires."

She nodded and looked at him once again. "Most of my team will be students in training for this. We're all taught to be respectful of local culture, and I'll remind them again if necessary. We don't want to cause you or your people any upset."

He nodded, then looked up toward the top of the mountain. It was, of course, pretty much concealed by trees, but Renee could have sworn she *felt* it like a brooding presence.

Her cousin Mercy had warned her. All those years ago she had come to this area to study the returning wolf pack. Here she'd met Gray Cloud. Anyway, Mercy had felt the mountain's brooding presence, and had spoken of it more than once. Just before Renee came out here, Mercy had called to remind her again. "I swear that mountain is alive."

Renee wasn't ready to go that far, but standing here in its shadow beside Gray Cloud, she found it easier to believe. Too bad Mercy was on a field trip in Mexico, because she'd have loved to have her older cousin here.

"You know," said Gray Cloud, his voice reminding her that she wasn't alone with the mountain, "understanding is often a matter of perspective. The mountain shook and opened its slope to reveal secrets. You can believe that was a mere accident or you can believe there was purpose. My people believe there was purpose. I don't think it's a coincidence that my wife is your cousin, either. How convenient to have a paleontologist in the family."

She let a small laugh escape. "Very convenient. I'm not going to argue with you, Gray Cloud. As a scientist, I subscribe to a different set of beliefs."

"I know, but to some extent they're still beliefs. This cleft wasn't part of an earthquake. It just split open." He shrugged one shoulder. "Make of that what you will. It's going to be an exciting journey of discovery regardless of what either of us believes about the cause of the cleft."

She couldn't disagree with that. Nor did she want to be disrespectful. Gray Cloud had shown her an extraordinary amount of trust by bringing her here and giving her permission to pull together a team and start peeling back the layers in that rock face. Her fellow professionals dreamed of such opportunities.

"Did you notice anything yet?" he asked.

Her excitement level rose again as she pointed. "That looks like an egg with the fetus still in it. When we work it out, we'll know."

"It could help prove your theory."

"That these saurians actually lived in family groups? It could. Either way we're going to learn an awful lot." She raised her gaze, scanning the rock yet again. "There's so much here, Gray Cloud. I'll have to figure out what happened here long ago to leave so many fossils behind."

"Maybe the mountain swallowed them."

Her gaze snapped toward him and she saw that he was smiling, but behind that smile were worlds of possibilities she didn't accept. Before she came to paleontology, as an undergrad she'd studied quite a bit of anthropology. She had some grasp of how important mysticism was to the human race. She wasn't going to question his. Still, the mysteries those dark eyes seemed to offer made her aware that there might be some things missing in her logic-oriented life.

Then, almost abruptly, she realized she'd been missing an important part of the morning. Closing her eyes, she listened to the breeze ruffle the treetops so far above, and to a chorus of birdsong that sounded happy to be alive.

Excited as she was to be here, the natural world reminded her that it still existed and that it was beautiful.

"Renee?"

A distant cry floated up the side of the mountain. She recognized the voice. "Up here, Cope. Do you need me to come down?"

"Nah, I can find you."

Carter Copeland was a college professor of history who'd been a friend of hers since he left the Marine Corps behind over a year before. They'd met at a conference and had kept in touch with irregular emails. The instant she told him about this project, he volunteered. Not exactly a paleontologist, but he said he learned fast, and he was willing to do the most menial of jobs. Better yet, he'd told her with a laugh, he was free so she could apply her grant money to more important matters. Considering how small most grants were, she felt no urge to look a gift horse in the mouth. Anyway, most of her interns would need to learn a lot, too.

Waiting for him, she allowed her eyes to look higher than the rock face, into the sunlight-dappled trees that swayed so gently, catching sight of a small bird winging from one branch to another. Idyllic. Soon to become an active swarm of people at work.

At last she could hear the sound of feet on the scree just below, then Carter Copeland emerged into the clearing.

The Marine Corps had put him in a physical condition that any man would have envied. Broad shoulders, narrow flanks, flat belly. Even in khaki work clothes he looked damn sexy. A cowboy hat rode his head, shadowing his face, but Renee didn't need a clear view to fill it in. A strong jaw, a straight nose, cheeks carved by his past experiences. Amazingly blue eyes. He was only in his late thirties, but experience at war sometimes made him seem far older. Right now, however, he was smiling and looking as if he'd enjoyed the steep climb.

As he stepped farther into the clearing, he paused and stared at the rock face. "My God. That's incredible! And you said it just opened up? It's like something out of *Aladdin*."

Then he caught himself and turned to Gray Cloud, offering his hand. "We've met a few times before. Good to see you again, Gray Cloud. As you can tell, Renee's been kind enough to let me do some basic tasks around here."

Gray Cloud smiled and shook his hand.

"You're Renee's cousin by marriage, right? And the wonder worker who got her permission to explore this."

Gray Cloud nodded and Cope returned his attention to the vertical fossil bed.

"Incredible," he said again. "To think that no one's laid eyes on this for millions of years. Well, obviously." He laughed, his blue eyes dancing a bit. "Weren't any humans around in the Late Cretaceous. But what an opportunity! It's like the mountain swallowed up a chunk of history and then decided to spit it out for exploration."

Renee's gaze jumped to Gray Cloud and saw the humor in his dark eyes. "My thought exactly," he said.

"Two against one," Renee said lightly.

"What do you mean?" Cope asked.

Gray Cloud answered. "She doesn't believe the mountain has purpose. Or sentience."

"Ah." Cope looked at her. "In theory, neither to do I. But can you think of a better way to explain this?"

Renee sighed, letting go of a difference of opinion that would have no resolution. "I'll let you know. In the meantime, all I can say is that Mercy, my cousin, would agree that this mountain is…"

"Sentient," said Gray Cloud.

Renee fake-scowled at him, making him laugh. He patted her shoulder. "I'll see you tomorrow, Renee. That's when you should be bringing your team up here, yes?"

"Yes," she agreed. "We're supposed to gather at the diner in Conard City this evening and plan our next steps."

"Then I'll see you in the morning. Nice to meet you, Cope."

Then Gray Cloud strode away, melting into the forest's shadows quite quickly.

Cope looked at her from those amazing blue eyes. "Were you two having a disagreement?"

She shook her head. "He's a mystic, I'm a scientist. Those disagreements don't mean much as long as we treat his and his tribe's beliefs with total respect."

"I don't have a problem with that. When I was overseas in the Corps, I saw plenty of disrespect for people's monuments and treasures. I hated it. And I might as well disappoint you and tell you that in the mountains of Afghanistan I sometimes felt those towering rocks were *aware*."

He moved, and for the first time she realized he was wearing a backpack. He swung it from his shoulders and set it on the ground. "So we can't touch yet, only look, right?"

"Right. All the groundwork has to be laid."

"Well, it's early. In the military I learned to eat whenever I had the opportunity, and I just happened to have a bunch of goodies in my pack. Join me?"

She'd been in such a hurry to get up here before dawn this morning she hadn't brought any food or beverages with her. After all, she figured she'd be here for a couple of hours at most, taking photos.

But Cope opened a tall insulated bottle and the aroma of coffee won the day. "That smells so good."

"And I just happen to have two cups. Grab a stone to sit on, Renee."

Five minutes later he'd found another flat rock to use as a table. She watched with delight as he laid out two cups of coffee from his bottle and some paper containers from the bakery that held offerings of cinnamon rolls and croissants. Pats of butter lined the containers and plastic knives waited to help.

"This is so neat," she said honestly. "You thought of everything."

"I try. Anyway, about this site. I gather that it's sacred and secret?"

"I'm not sure how secret it is, but I don't think Gray Cloud wants it headlined. It *is* sacred ground to his people, and they don't want it being trampled by lookie-loos." She waved her arm. "Look how narrow this space is. We're going to have trouble working in here, never mind having outsiders trampling through. Then, there's a river below. All this rock couldn't have moved without throwing detritus to the bottom. That'll all have to be checked out, too."

He swallowed a mouthful of roll. "I can see that. It's weird how this split, though." He looked along the length of the cleft in both directions. "I'm guessing years of freezing water in some crack eventually levered it apart. But it feels like something is missing right in the middle."

She gave him props for noticing. Narrow as the cleft was, there was still enough flat ledge to stand on and work. Rockfall must have filled in the space between the wall and what she thought of as the "tooth." Her geologist could figure that out, though.

"Apart from that, you want to protect the cliff face. Are you going to have any kind of security?"

Her head jerked up a little. "Security? Why in the world?"

He looked down a moment, then grabbed a paper napkin and wiped his mouth. After some noticeable seconds, he answered. "You haven't had a whole lot of time to get to know me, so maybe I'll sound paranoid. Maybe I am. I saw too much of this kind of thing wantonly destroyed during my time in Iraq and Afghanistan. I'm not saying someone is going to have a religious objection to these fossils—although it's possible—but there could also be looters. You don't want folks coming up here to scavenge a dinosaur tooth or bone."

He had a point. It wasn't something she'd considered because of the comparative secrecy of this site, but once her team started arriving, word was going to get around this underpopulated area. Most would probably just accept it as interesting, but it was easy enough to imagine those who'd want a piece of it. And all they'd have to do would be to follow one of her team up here.

Now she felt careless not to think of it. How many sites of this nature often needed some kind of protection? Many, because Cope was correct: an awful lot of people wanted a fossil, especially if it might be unique in some way.

"My grant doesn't run to full-time security," she said reluctantly.

"I don't suppose it does." He sighed, popped the last of his roll into his mouth and wiped his hands on the napkin. "I'm probably needlessly worried. Consider where I came from not so long ago."

But he'd caused her to think along a whole new line, and when she looked up at that rock face, she could all too easily imagine how much damage could be done to it by a careless and uncaring person. "I'd better mention this to Gray Cloud. He can probably keep an eye out better than my team could."

"He may already be doing it. Sacred ground is an important thing."

There was that, she agreed silently. But she'd still mention the concern to Gray Cloud. In one way they were completely united: this site mustn't be disrespected.

"I didn't mean to cast a cloud over the day," Cope remarked. "Enjoy your roll and enjoy the view. That rock face is breathtaking."

"You should have seen it in the minutes after dawn," she answered, willing to change the subject and let her enthusiasm grow again. "The march of the shadows revealed so much. I have a bunch of photos I can show you later, if you want. And someone is sure going to be out here in the morning to start laying out a grid. Her name's Denise. She should arrive this afternoon. Anyway, she's a great artist, and by the time she finishes we'll have a fantastic drawing as well as a grid to work from."

"So everything has to be labeled as to where it comes from?"

"Totally. The rock layers will help date everything. I'm hoping they'll also tell me why so many fossils are here in this place. You know Wyoming is full of marvelous fossil beds, but this find…it looks rather sudden. Too many bones too close together."

"Some kind of catastrophe," he mused, reaching for another roll.

"I'm wondering." The coffee was staying warm in the insulated mug he'd poured it into, and she settled more comfortably, savoring it and savoring her view of the cliff. "I think I'm obsessed."

"Hard not to be obsessed with a mystery like this."

He scooted around a little on his rock to give himself a better view, staring straight at it. "When you described it to me, I had a mental image, of course. It wasn't anywhere near as grand as this."

"It keeps taking my breath away, again and again." She placed her remaining piece of roll on the edge of the container, wiped her fingers on her jeans and raised her camera again. Photographing this throughout the day today was rapidly becoming a compulsion, almost as if she was afraid it would disappear overnight. Well, it probably could, if the mountain moved again.

"How stable is this cleft?" Cope asked, practically reading her mind.

"Gray Cloud brought me to see it last autumn when I was visiting my cousin up here. It's been stable that long. But one of our team is a geologist. She'll be better able to tell me the situation with the matrix."

"Matrix?"

"The rock the fossils are buried in. What kind of rock, how hard it is, whether it's going to crumble if we use dental tools or defy us so much we need a jackhammer."

That elicited a laugh from him, a pleasant sound on the warming morning air. "A jackhammer, huh?"

She lowered the camera, smiling. "Wouldn't be the first time. You just have to take out huge slabs without troubling anything else. But this scene is so different, everything so close together. We'd better be able to use brushes and small tools or we're just going to have to cover it with a protective sealant and study it from the face only."

"That would be disappointing."

"To say the least. Preservation first, however." She

paused, then added, "Speaking of stability, however, everyone needs to wear hard hats up here. While I was taking photos this morning, some small rocks fell from above. I'd hate for anyone to get beaned by something bigger."

"Of course. It's a simple precaution." He leaned back a bit, propping himself on one arm as she helped herself to more coffee. "I'm the historian, right? I'll be the first to admit I don't know a whole lot about paleontology or archaeology. What I *do* know is how many travesties occurred in the past thanks to the first explorers around the world who saw these kinds of sites, and tombs and ancient cities, as a treasure trove to be taken and carelessly cataloged."

She nodded, liking him more by the minute. "Sadly true. Egypt is still trying to recover artifacts from private owners and museums."

"I know. Trying to reassemble an impressive history." He smiled, his blue eyes bright. "So I'm glad to work with someone like you who understands how wrong that would be, sacred site or no. I saw enough looting in the Middle East to jam in my craw. I get people are poor, but the history they're digging up and selling will never be replaced. And finding items in situ is so important to understanding them."

"Amen to that." She turned a bit on her rock, looking toward the other side of the cleft. Considering the tall rock face behind it, it seemed odd there was just that thin wall of rock, maybe ten feet high, facing it. Small, but it might hold treasures. Some of the split must have tumbled downward to a stream some thirty feet below, which was lined on the far side with trees. More rock had probably crumbled into the fill layer on which she was sitting. The stream below would be useful in their attempts to screen for tiny artifacts, and of course they'd have to study the tumbled rock for remnants. But still the geography appeared odd. She'd have to ask Claudia about that when she arrived. The geologist could probably explain what had happened here.

Maybe a cleft hadn't really opened up. Maybe there'd been a rockfall on just this side only. But Gray Cloud had talked about it opening. As she sat there studying the terrain, she wondered briefly if Gray Cloud was right, if this was more than just a happy chance. Again the sense of the mountain looming over her tickled her deep inside, a sort of uneasy fluttery feeling.

But no, she wasn't about to go down that path. This whole expedition had to be based on science, not strange feelings.

"You look troubled," Cope remarked.

She glanced at him, realizing she had forgotten about him for so long that the hot coffee in her insulated mug had begun to cool noticeably. The air had warmed from the rising sun as well. Not enough to make her shed her jacket yet, but it wouldn't be long.

"I'm not troubled, exactly," she answered. "It's just that this cleft is odd. I'll need to ask Claudia about it when she gets here. Or maybe it's nothing unusual at all, just a problem with my understanding of how Gray Cloud described it."

"That's possible. Different cultures and all that."

He sat up and poured himself some more coffee, taking one of the remaining rolls.

Curiosity about something besides old bones awoke in her. "How much did you immerse yourself in the local cultures when you were…over there?"

"As much as I could." His gaze grew distant. "Know your enemy and all that. Except most of the people weren't our enemies at all. They were ordinary people who were trying to live an ordinary life in the midst of chaos. I was lucky to have a facility with languages so I could even make some friends." He seemed to shake himself, then his gaze fixed on her again. "Ever seen a goat climb a vertical rock face?"

The change of subject was startling. She guessed he was trying to shake off memories he'd awakened. "Can't say I have."

"They're amazing. They'd climb up and down those rocks as if they were level. Even the smallest of them are good at it. There was a day when I was an outpost, and I watched them for hours. Walking and jumping like it was nothing at all. A human rock climber wouldn't be able to do it like that on his or her best day."

That turned her attention back to the rock face. "I wonder if the mountain goats will try that wall?" The idea worried her. So much possible damage.

"I think they stay at higher elevations. Anyway, there's nothing they'd want on that rock. Nothing growing, and probably not enough salt to make it appealing. It just reminded me of them."

She smiled at him, glad she'd allowed herself to invite him to join her team. They might not have a crying need for a historian, but he probably had a lot of good stories to tell, and his perspective on the past could be useful.

Impatience began to tickle her again. God, how she wanted to start excavating those bones. It would be such a painstaking process, to do it correctly, that she couldn't imagine being very far along by the end of the summer. Almost before she would know it, they'd be covering up all that history to protect it from snow, wind and rain. To keep it pristine. To prevent site contamination.

It had survived the past winter with little protection, if any. No reason to get worked up about next winter. "Dang," she said suddenly. "I'm such a worrywart. Already planning how we're going to protect this face from next winter. Heck, it made it through the last winter."

"Unless the mountain decides to shake, I doubt it's going anywhere."

She returned her attention to him. "You're an odd man, Carter Copeland."

He flashed a charming grin. "Blame it on my past. I'll never be ordinary again. So much the better if I deal with life with humor. So." He paused. "Who all is going to be part of this team?"

"Claudia Alexander I already mentioned. She's a geology postdoc who's curious to find out why there are so many fossils here."

"How come? Apart from a disaster happening all at once."

"Fossilization is a rare thing, believe it or not. Special conditions are required, and nothing can disturb them for a long, long time. That's why we actually have so few fossils, although you probably wouldn't believe it when you go to a museum. In fact, when you go to a museum and look at those big statues of, say, a tyrannosaur, you're seeing a lot of fake bones. Partly because we don't have complete skeletons, and partly because the real fossilized bones are usually radioactive from all the centuries buried in the ground. When we display a genuine bone, we give it a coating of lead paint."

Oh, she had his interest now. His gaze became piercing and she could almost sense the thoughts running around inside his head. "I never guessed that."

"Most people don't." She set down her cup, pulled the band from her ponytail, and scooped her long auburn hair into a fresh one beneath the bottom of her yellow hard hat. "People think of the ground beneath their feet as this totally benign floor. But you dig deeper into it and you start to find all kinds of poisonous heavy metals. Some are very useful to us, but few of them are safe for extended exposure. For an example, I've seen tailings piles from mines that were over a century old where not even a blade of grass could grow."

He nodded. "So we shouldn't stand too close to that rock face."

She laughed quietly. "Open air and all that. But yeah, you should shower at night, and when we start working on it, we'll wear dust masks as a precaution. I doubt any part of that is radioactive enough to make someone sick, but why chance it when we're going to be exposed all summer?"

"I agree." He drained his coffee cup, then asked, "Okay, a geologist is joining the team. Any other paleontologists?"

"For right now, interns. Mostly grad students, some of them mine."

At that moment her attention was drawn by a sound at the east end of the cleft, from within the trees. Gray Cloud? Not likely. That man moved with enviable silence. Who then?

After a half minute or so, a figure emerged from

the trees into the clearing not far from the rock face. Renee wasn't certain anyone else was allowed here, so she stood at once.

Cope apparently picked up on her unease and stood too, calling out, "Could you hold it there, please?"

The rider stopped. "Sorry if I'm disturbing. I'm Loren Butler from the ranch to the south. I heard something was going on up here and wanted to check it out."

Renee chewed her lip. Was she going to have to defend this site from everybody who decided to take a ride?

"This is tribal land," she called back. "Sacred. We have permission to work here. Do you?"

The man chuckled. He tipped back his head a little, revealing a pleasant face as the sun slipped beneath the brim of his cowboy hat. "Nope," he said frankly. "I heard there was some kind of rockslide up here last summer. Frankly, it's a weird-looking one. Not exactly a cleft like Gray Cloud said. Or maybe part of the cleft is broken. Guess I won't find out today. You can tell the elders I was here. I prefer to stay on good terms with my neighbors. But you can also tell them I was curious about what exactly happened."

He paused, then added, "Just a couple miles south of me, on Thunder Mountain, they had rockslides a few years back ago that put a halt to building a ski resort. Makes you wonder if Gray Cloud ain't right about this mountain having a brain. See ya."

He turned his horse with a few clucks of his tongue and rode slowly back into the woods.

"I guess he has a reason to be curious," Cope remarked. "If the mountain's going to get busy making rockfalls, he might have something to worry about."

But Renee's thought had turned in a different direction. "It *was* a cleft."

Cope turned to face her. "Was?"

"Last fall I was visiting my cousin and Gray Cloud brought me up here to show me." She turned, taking care with the placement of her feet. "Right now it looks like a slide," she said, pointing toward the rock face, "but when he showed it to me last fall, there was a narrow cleft in the rock, just enough for one person to walk through. The part to this side, where you can see the creek below, was thin but still tall and upright. It didn't contain anything interesting I could see, so I wasn't upset when I came back this year to discover that part of the top of the narrow piece had apparently crumbled. Gives us more room for work." She shrugged. "But we're still going to have to check all the stuff that fell below as well as what's beneath us in the cleft."

"Obviously," he agreed. "What about farther up, like that guy just mentioned?"

"He's right. It's more of a cleft beyond those trees there, but you can't tell if it all happened at once. Maybe Claudia will be able to. Regardless, I looked at it last fall and it didn't appear promising. Which doesn't mean I won't check it out anyway."

Cope fell silent, and Renee continued to stare at the rock face, but her thoughts were moving through time, not space. "You know," she said after a minute, "it's really weird that part of that narrow wall of rock collapsed like that."

She fixed her gaze on Cope. "It's almost as if someone deliberately knocked it down. As if they wanted samples and disturbed more than they intended."

She watched Cope's face darken, but he didn't respond. Of course not. He was the one who had suggested security that she couldn't afford. On the other hand, who the hell would want anything from here other than a cool fossil? And freeing something from the rock would take many hours. The most any trophy hunter could have hope of finding was something that was already loose.

That hardly required full-time rent-a-cops.

Another bunch of small rocks tumbled down from above. "Let's get your hard hat," she said. "Then I need to think about how we can stabilize the top of that wall."

"I've got some ideas."

She didn't doubt it for a moment.

Chapter 2

The plan was to start off small, but the group didn't feel all that small when they gathered at Maude's diner that night, some meeting others for the first time.

There were Larry, Maddie and Carlos, all undergrad interns. Then there were Bets, Mason and Denise, her three graduate interns. And last but not least, Claudia Alexander, the geology postdoc, a woman with short, no-nonsense dark hair and huge gray eyes that seemed almost too big for her face. She stuck out among a group of young people who seemed almost blended in their similarities. That would change as Renee got to know them all better, but for now she hoped no one expected to be called by name.

"Okay." She decided some honesty might be helpful up front. "I'm terrible with names. I'll recognize your faces for the rest of my life, but give me time with your names. I'm better at identifying fossils."

Laughter rolled around the tables that had been pulled together with the permission of the diner's owner, Maude. In fact, Maude was already pouring coffee all around with a great deal of clatter and frowning. A couple of Renee's interns looked intimidated by this, but once Cope ordered a dinner for himself, suggesting they all do the same if they were hungry, they relaxed. Maude, he told them sotto voce, was a local character.

Renee had met the woman last summer and was prepared for the graceless service they were receiving. Still, it was nice to know everyone was a target.

Soon they had ordered a meal from the menus. Young, active, with healthy appetites. Not surprising. Renee ordered a steak sandwich along with the majority, knowing it would probably be too much to eat, but once the dig got under way they'd all be working long hours, most of them physical. In her experience, on a dig like this, most people lost a bit of weight. You ate while you could. Soon enough they'd all be sick of beans heated on the portable stoves.

"I'm going to run over the basics again," she said when everyone was served and eating. Playful conversation had been rather desultory as the interns tried cautiously to feel one another out. "We're guests on tribal lands. Invited guests. That invitation will last only as long as we honor our hosts and their customs. Only as long as we treat the land as sacred, because believe me, the tribe believes that mountain is sacred. Tomorrow you'll probably meet Gray Cloud, who is the Guardian of the Mountain in their culture, and one of the tribal elders."

She paused, looking around the table, assessing the expressions on the many youthful faces. At this point she saw nothing to trouble her.

"I'm sure you all studied enough anthropology to know that the beliefs of local people are always to be respected, and your personal opinion of them does not matter. The local indigenous believe that Thunder Mountain, the mountain we'll be working on, is sentient. You don't have to believe that. You *must* respect it as if it is true, however. If one of the local tribe members tells you not to do something, stop at once. We can always talk with them if it's something necessary, but in the meantime just stop. Trust me, when you see the rock face and fossils that are visible right now, you'll fully understand what a tragedy it would be to find ourselves shut down because we were careless of their beliefs. Got it?"

Heads around the table nodded. All those earnest young faces. She sincerely hoped their youth wouldn't result in any kind of hijinks. "It's time to act like the professionals you want to be. I'm counting on you. Questions?"

The youngest guy at the table, Larry, she thought, waggled his hand for her attention as he finished chewing a mouthful of food. She waited patiently.

He took a swallow of cola, then spoke. "How can a mountain be alive?"

"The essence is really quite simple. The indigenous people believe that consciousness exists in everything, from the trees to the stones. It's not limited to animals that run around. While the consciousness may be different from what we know ourselves, it still exists. Mother Earth, for example, is a living being, too."

"Okay," Larry answered slowly.

"Always give thanks for the gifts of nature."

She smiled. "Think about that before we go out to the site in the morning. The very stones will hear you, according to local tradition. The stones, the trees, the birds, the running water. If you at least make an effort to respect that, we might get through the summer."

The group fell silent as they pondered what she had said and thought about the summer ahead. Good. This was their last chance to change their minds while she could possibly find replacements. Plus, she wanted them to be very aware of the delicacy of their situation here. It would kill her if this expedition fell apart because they thought she was exaggerating the cultural limitations.

At least no one argued with her, and no one tried to play "rules lawyer" by looking for a loophole in what she had said. That might be very promising.

Conversation shifted to what they hoped they might see tomorrow, and what kind of discoveries might await them. Renee let them ramble and build up their own excitement, but didn't join in. She hadn't told very many about the potential size of this find lest she wind up with the paleontological equivalent of "claim jumpers." Yeah, really, other professionals might try to grab the site for themselves.

So for now she remained mostly mum and not even the members of her team had any real idea of what was out there. Tomorrow, when they saw that rock face for the first time, they'd probably light up like the Fourth of July. Not many got an opportunity like this.

Enjoying her secret for the last few hours, Renee smiled and listened to the conversation. After they'd all finished eating and the bills began to arrive, she reminded them that they'd meet here at seven in the morning.

Watching them scatter in the general direction of the La-Z-Rest Motel, which was clean if outdated, Renee remarked to Cope, "I hope we have enough four-by-fours to get them up there."

"We can sort it out in the morning," he said reassuringly. "Make two trips if necessary. How early will you be going?"

"Well before dawn. I'll take Denise to start drawing. The shadows reveal so many mysteries."

"I'll see you then."

She watched him drive off, wondering vaguely where he lived, then climbed into her own battered vehicle and headed for the motel.

She pondered if she should take her camping gear with her tomorrow and just plan on staying on the mountain. She hadn't much worried about it before, but that unexpected visit from a neighbor had bothered her a bit.

Word was getting around Conard County, and from what Mercy had told her over the years, news spread like wildfire around here. Maybe they needed to have someone there all the time. Mentally she began to calculate their budget, and whether it would run to enough tents and sleeping bags. They already had folding tables, propane stoves, lanterns... Well, half a camp, anyway.

Yeah, maybe she should leave her camping equipment in the back of her truck and get some help hauling it up the mountain tomorrow. Then she could shepherd them all through filling in their own blanks for camping out there.

Then, making a final decision could wait for tomorrow. She headed toward her room at the motel and tried not to think too much about Cope.

Nice guy, but every time she looked at him her thoughts wanted to wander far away from her purpose. She was here to collect dinosaur bones, not a gorgeous hunk.

But man, he was definitely a *hunk*.

Laughing at herself, she parked in front of the motel.

Cope headed back to the apartment he rented in the complex on the edge of town. There'd been a small building boom when the semiconductor plant had arrived years ago. Then the plant had picked up stakes, a lot of people had moved away, and these days you could pretty much have your choice of apartments in these four buildings. Not that there was a whole lot of difference among the units. One- and two-bedrooms were the most common, with a few three-bedrooms being the biggest. He'd chosen a two-bedroom with two baths and was content.

He especially enjoyed standing under the hot spray of the shower. It was his first goal when he came home tonight. The fossil site had been dusty and the grit had clung to his skin in places. He supposed he was going to get used to that. He had in his former life with the Marines.

Which was exactly what made a hot shower one of the greatest luxuries in his life now. To be able to stand under hot water and wash himself clean? Heck, he was probably an addict.

As he stood under the spray letting soap and shampoo rinse off him, his thoughts turned to the fossil site and most especially Renee Dubois. She was a pistol, that one. Not a shy bone in her body, and he suspected she'd protect the dig site like a mother bear with a cub.

Pretty, too. Well, more than pretty. He'd always liked auburn hair, but hers was accompanied by a pair of green eyes that seemed to be lit from within. Totally unusual.

From what he'd seen today, she was strong and determined. She'd even been ready to face down that curious neighbor and had flatly told him he was on tribal land without permission.

Yeah, a lot of people might have been reluctant to do that. However, the guy's arrival had seemed odd. It was Renee's first day at the site, and surely the man who owned the neighboring ranch had better things to do with his time, and surely the news of the excavation couldn't have traveled the grapevine this fast? After a bit more than a year here, Cope had no trouble grasping how fast interesting news could make the rounds in this county, but this beat all. A day? Usually it took a death or a major fire to hit warp speed on the rumor mill. Unless a tribal member had mentioned it a while back. Or maybe the motel owner. They'd surely rented enough rooms for the group.

Still it seemed a bit strange, although Butler had left easily enough.

But being a fairly normal man, he soon forgot his inventory of Renee as a potential warrior and returned to his inventory of her as a woman. He suspected she'd object mightily to such thoughts, with every right. But he neither needed to act on them, nor needed to reveal them.

Instead as he stood in his hot shower, he could remember her lifting her arms to regroup her hair. Her breasts had been suggestively outlined by the T-shirt she wore under her unzipped jacket. Full, but not too full. Nicely rounded. Inviting.

All of her was female, though. He'd walked behind her on her way down the mountain and had been able to tell she wasn't afflicted by the need to be so thin it had to be unhealthy. No, she had a good set of hips, a nicely rounded bottom and a bit of a sway to her step.

She was also graceful as she navigated the broken and unsteady terrain. A woman in command of her body.

He liked that. Hell, he liked her. And if he were smart, he'd just leave it at that. He'd volunteered to work this dig because of a huge curiosity and a desire for the experience. What he didn't want to do was blow himself out of the water by expressing too much interest in the team leader. By making her uncomfortable.

The Marines had taught him self-control. Time to use it.

But then his thoughts drifted toward that unexpected visitor again. The neighbor. The man on horseback continued to trouble Cope, though he had no reason to explain it. It was just so soon after Renee's arrival. Too soon.

Maybe Butler had just wandered that way out of curiosity, not knowing whether anyone was there, having heard about the new cleft. It was possible.

But Cope had spent too many years in a uniform in

dangerous places to just dismiss the guy. He couldn't imagine any reason the man could become a problem, but that didn't mean there wasn't a reason.

If he showed up again… Cope told himself to let it drop unless something else happened. He'd spent too long at war, and didn't even trust his own suspiciousness any longer. Paranoia, he told himself.

Cope reached out and reluctantly turned off the water and reached for a towel. Renee planned to get out there before dawn. He'd better get his sleep so he could follow along and be useful.

Over at the motel, Renee had taken Denise to her own room to talk. The room itself was pleasant enough, although it showed its age. The days when rough wood paneling on walls had been charming were long ago. The blue-checked curtains looked nearly worn out over the mini blinds; the chair and table in one corner might have been used as modern in a 1950s sitcom. The bedspread was a brown-and-blue plaid. But, Renee admitted, it was spotlessly clean as far as she could tell.

Denise followed her in and perched on the edge of the bed.

Renee spoke as she closed the door. "In the morning, before dawn, I want you to come up with me to the site. I don't have to tell you what the early light does to shadows."

"Heck no," said Denise. Her artistic ability was one of her biggest entrées into this world. "Got any photos for me?"

Renee handed over her camera and flipped it to begin a slide show. Then she went to the bathroom and used the motel's cheap coffeemaker to brew some for the two of them. At least there was more than one packet of coffee on the counter.

"Wow," she heard Denise breathe. "Renee, you gave me no idea!"

"I didn't want too much information getting out. You know of Dr. Bradley?"

Denise glanced up. "The site thief? Everyone's heard of him. I'm sure he's not the only one."

"Exactly. Once we're established I won't feel it's as important to keep a shroud over all this, but in the meantime… I'm thinking of camping out there."

Denise nodded as she continued to watch the slide show. "This looks revolutionary, Renee. Maybe we *all* ought to camp out there."

Renee gave a quiet laugh. "Nice idea, but once we start working we're not going to have a whole lot of extra room. Maybe we can establish a base camp farther down the mountain. I'll have to ask Gray Cloud."

The slide show came to an end and Denise looked at her. "Gray Cloud is really your cousin?"

"By marriage. My cousin Mercy is a wildlife biologist. She met him on Thunder Mountain a couple of decades ago when she was studying the wolf pack up there. If you ask her if the mountain is sentient, I'm pretty sure she'll say yes."

"And you?"

Renee shrugged. "I'm not here to judge. I'm here in the hope that I can prove a theory of mine. Or disprove it, as the case may be. And that fossil bed is so rich it ought to provide a whole lot of answers, plus new questions."

Denise nodded and put the camera down. "So you want me to sketch all this before we start poking around? With measurements and a grid so every find can be localized?"

"Exactly," Renee said, filling two cups with coffee and walking through the door to perch on the edge of the bed.

Denise accepted the coffee and sat cross-legged, clearly thinking. Her gray sweater and blue jeans signified she was used to a far warmer climate. Renee was happy in her T-shirt and jeans.

"Okay," Denise said presently. "You've got your whole team here, right?"

"At least for the start, yes. We may need more later, depending."

"How would it be if you choose the part of the face where you'd most like to start working? Then I can start the grid there and work outward, so you can get started quickly. All I'd need to do is take a quick survey of the entire face, measurements and so on, so I'd know where I'll eventually be heading."

Renee felt her excitement bubbling up again. "I didn't think we'd be able to start so soon!"

Denise grinned. "It might still be a couple of days. It's just that the whole grid doesn't need to be done first."

Renee felt lighter somehow, as if realizing she might be able to get to work sooner had lifted some kind of load.

Denise picked up the camera again and restarted the slide show. "This is amazing, Renee. Just amazing. Early-morning light?"

"To get the best use of shadows."

Denise nodded. "Can you get me out there before dawn tomorrow? You can show me where you want to start, and I can begin sketching until we've got enough light to do measurements."

Renee wanted to agree immediately, but she had a slight problem, namely seven members of her team who were planning to meet for breakfast and follow her out to the site. Then she thought of Cope. "Just a sec."

She had his phone number filed on her laptop because she'd talked to him maybe a half dozen times in the planning stages. Gray Cloud had approved of him when she mentioned Cope wanted to participate, which she took as a good sign.

She picked up her cell and called Cope. "This is Renee. Sorry to bother you but I need a small favor."

"Sure," he answered. On the phone his voice sounded smooth and warm.

"I need to go out to the site before dawn in the morning with Denise. The rest of the team is supposed to meet at the diner at seven for breakfast and then follow me. Can you gather them up and show them the way?"

"Oh, I think I can do that," he drawled, a hint of laughter in his voice. "But man, it'll be so hard to corral all that youthful energy."

"Like you don't do it in a classroom all the time."

"That's why I have my doubts." Then his tone turned serious. "No problem, Renee. I'm the gofer on this job. If you think of anything else, let me know."

"Gallons of coffee?"

He laughed. "I'll see what I can do."

"Oh, and Cope? I have hard hats for everyone in the back of my car, so when you get them out there, make sure everyone wears one."

"Now that I *can* do."

She disconnected and looked at a grinning Denise.

"Done. We'll have to leave about three tomorrow morning, though. Bring a warm jacket and get as much sleep as you can."

Denise unfolded and stood. "I was excited when you asked me to do this, but after looking at your photos I'm so impatient I can hardly tell you. Maybe you'll be rewriting the textbooks."

Renee hadn't thought of anything so grand. A paper or three, yes, but rewriting the texts on the Late Cretaceous era?

Whcn she climbed into bed after Denise left, it wasn't sugarplums dancing in her head. Dinosaurs followed her into her dreams.

Chapter 3

The night still ruled the land when Renee and Denise arrived at the foot of the gorge in the morning. Renee was impatient because she wanted to get to the rock face before the first glow of dawn began to light it, but she was extremely aware that either one of them could have an accident and be stuck on the mountainside until Cope happened on them.

They both had heavy-duty flashlights with strong beams to light their way, but even as the path before them was revealed, the woods became darker. Creepier. A thought that wasn't familiar to Renee.

She tried to ignore the feeling, wondering where it came from, but she couldn't escape the sense that from the corners of her eyes she could see shapes flitting among the trees, dark shapes. It almost felt like they were being paced on both sides by something.

Maybe Gray Cloud had some of his people out here, keeping an eye on matters. That would be okay, but she'd like to know about it.

On the other hand, she remembered the guy who'd ridden up there just yesterday, unheralded and curious. He'd said he was a neighbor. Was he?

But who besides another paleontologist could be interested in this area? Sure, you could make money from some dinosaur bones, but you were more likely to have them confiscated the minute the state found out what you were doing if they were in any way unique.

Deliberately, she tried to shake off the feeling that they weren't alone on this part of the mountain. Dang, maybe Gray Cloud was right. Maybe the mountain itself was watching them.

She reined that thought in immediately. No craziness. For this job she had to remain firmly centered in science.

She glanced around, though, and decided if anything was dancing among the trees following them, it must be the shades of the newly revealed saurian bones. They might be interested in how their discovery was handled. The thought drew a small laugh from her.

"What's so funny?" Denise asked.

"I'm having early-morning crazy thoughts. Don't worry, I just need to finish waking up."

Denise gave an answering laugh. "I hear you. I half feel like I'm still dreaming. The woods are encouraging some nutty images. Too dark under some of those trees."

Glad to know that she wasn't the only one with a runaway imagination, Renee said, "Not much farther now."

"Good, because I'm beginning to see some predawn lightening to the east. I want to see this place the way you did when you took those photos."

Denise got her wish. A dozen yards later they emerged onto the ledge that had been left behind by the rockfall. There was just barely enough light to see the face of it, but nothing more because the predawn twilight was still so flat.

"It's weird," Renee said as she slipped off her backpack and lowered it to the ground. "This was originally a narrow cleft. When Gray Cloud brought me here last year it really *was* a cleft so narrow we nearly had to move sideways to get into it. Then over the winter the other side thinned out and part of it fell, probably down to the stream below. We'll have to check all the rubble, but first..." She pointed. "First I wanna get at that."

"I can see why," Denise answered as the light strengthened and shadows began to appear. "My God," she breathed. She hunted quickly for a central position and pulled out her large tablet. On the screen the rock face grew steadily more visible as the light brightened slowly and the shadows grew. Denise wasted no time using a stylus to start a grid.

"Where did you want to begin?"

Renee hesitated only a moment before pointing. "There's an egg here. I realize I'm going to have to move a whole lot of mountain above it to reveal it, but it's too promising to pass up."

"That's where the grid will start then. But if you change your mind, it's okay. By the time I'm done, everything will have coordinates on the x and y axes. We also need some GPS to back us up."

"I can do that," Renee answered, although she didn't

jump to it. She was growing mesmerized again as the morning light painted the shadows that revealed darn near everything.

"My tablet will get the coordinates," Denise said. "Just enjoy."

Renee found a place to settle beside Denise and just drink in the wonder before her.

"It's amazing," Denise murmured. "Has there ever been a fossil bed like this?"

"Yeah, there are some good ones. The whole area of Montana, Wyoming and the Dakotas is loaded with fossils, and there are some parks devoted to them."

"So what is it about this one?"

"It's there?"

Denise laughed. "I'm serious."

"So am I. The fact that it's here would be enough. But the density of the fossils makes it especially interesting. So many packed in like this raises a bunch of interesting questions."

And that egg, Renee thought. That egg. If there were more of them, if most of the fossils appeared to be the same species…well.

While Denise worked, Renee continued her study of the rock face and the fall around it. Soon, unable to hold still for long, she began moving along the ledge, studying the spoil beneath her feet. Every so often she spotted what appeared to be some bone poking out of a rock, but she left it alone.

Then, as she stood staring down at it, she remembered the hundred pin flags poking out of her backpack. Hurrying over to it, she pulled a handful out and made her way cautiously back to the bones she had noted. A bright orange pin flag soon marked each spot. There would be plenty of others, she was sure, and now that she had spotted these, she realized she'd better get to it before the team started arriving and important things might inadvertently get stepped on or buried before they were noticed.

The richness of the fossil bed probably extended to the rubble at the bottom of the rock face. They'd need to take extra care so as not to crush something.

The dynamics of this dig were beginning to sink in. They wouldn't only be removing the large fossils from the rock, but they'd have to scour every inch of this ledge for items they'd never want to miss. In her initial bliss at the big find, she'd forgotten to think about all the minor details.

She almost laughed at herself. This wasn't her first rodeo. She'd let her enthusiasm override her sense, but that had to stop immediately.

"Give it a rest," Denise said eventually. "You've covered the whole ledge and you're distracting me by moving."

So Renee plopped down behind her on a larger boulder and waited patiently.

"And don't look over my shoulder. It drives me nuts for some reason."

"I'm not." Nor was she. The shifting shadows on the fossil bed entranced her. She kept picking out new shadows that suggested great wonders. If this proved at all as productive as it appeared now, she'd probably work this site for the rest of her career. Happy thought.

The rest of the team arrived around nine. Renee had begun helping Denise measure out the area and place red pin flags for each point there would be a vertical line in the grid.

Before long, she'd sent most of the students below to hunt through the rubble beside the river. Fortunately, getting down there proved to be reasonably easy. A short way up the gorge, there was a narrow path leading down to the stream. The team went ahead with flag pins and soon their excited voices could be heard rising up from the stream.

Cope remained on the ledge with her and Denise. For a few minutes, Renee allowed herself to be distracted, thinking that he drew her interest almost as much as the fossils. Almost. Grinning inwardly, she decided to enjoy the unusual attraction.

She noted, however, that he seemed to be extremely alert, and his gaze never stopped wandering the woods around them, above them and below them.

Finally, she stepped over beside him, speaking in a voice that couldn't easily be overheard because of the rush of the stream below.

"Is something wrong?"

"I don't know." His blue eyes snapped to her face. "Did you feel strange coming up here?"

"Like someone was hiking along with us?"

"That's what you felt? Close enough. There are eyes on us, Renee. I can't imagine why anyone would want to just watch. That Butler guy wasn't shy about coming forward to ask what we were doing, after all."

She had believed she was feeling weird when the thought crossed her mind that the mountain was aware of them. But now, for the first time, there was an icy trickle down her spine. "You're sure someone is there?"

"No, I'm not. I didn't see anyone, but I learned not

to disregard this sensation." All of a sudden, he smiled at her. "Ignore me and go back to what you were doing. I'll play sentry for a while just to ease my mind."

She nodded and returned to a rock where she'd been sitting with her large tablet, using a stylus to overlay outlines on some of the photos she'd taken yesterday. The egg continued to grab her attention, and it amused her to note how many photos she had taken of it yesterday morning. Carried away.

But as she outlined it, using the setting to give her fine lines resembling a sharp black pen, she pulled more detail out of it. She was definitely not losing her curiosity about it.

She lifted her head after a bit, noticing that the stream was louder today than yesterday. Much louder. It nearly swamped the voices of her team below. Had it rained up higher on the mountain? She could still faintly hear the voices. They called to one another and sounded as if they were having a good time poring through the rubble.

She lifted her gaze to Cope, and found him walking slowly around, his attention fixed on the dark places beneath the trees. The same dark places that had bothered her earlier.

He moved with remarkable grace considering the surface was rough and unstable, but his feet came down lightly and didn't seem to disturb much when they landed. He was wearing desert boots, she realized. Probably left over from the Marine Corps days that he'd briefly mentioned. The limestone and sandstone dust that seemed to be everywhere disappeared on those boots.

She looked down at her jeans and wished they had the same ability. But mostly she wished Cope hadn't confirmed her uneasiness by saying he felt there was a watcher.

In the first place, she couldn't imagine why anyone would want to do that. In the second, she didn't need to be on guard all the time. Every bit of her mind needed to focus on the job at hand. Even a small mistake could cause problems down the road if something was overlooked.

Cope's voice interrupted her rambling thoughts as her hand continued to sketch. He squatted down beside her. "Why are you sketching over your photos?"

"To bring out some of the details, the stuff the shadows didn't pull out from the rock. Did you see anything?"

"Not a soul." The corners of his eyes creased a little, a hint of a smile. "I don't usually get unnerved this easily."

"Frankly, I was unnerved all the way up here. I kind of wish I'd been the only one."

She blew dust off the screen of her tablet and tucked it into its case. "I need to see how they're getting on down below."

"They sound like they're having a good time." He straightened and offered a hand to help pull her to her feet. "Let's go see?"

Along with the heap of items the team had brought up here, they had a couple of empty five-gallon water jugs. Cope grabbed both of them before leading the way to the steep path down to the stream. "I'll bring you some water, Denise," he said as he walked behind her.

"Thanks. My camel pack is getting low."

Renee's had emptied more than half an hour ago. The mountain air was dry and her tongue was beginning to feel sticky. Behind Cope, she slid and climbed down the steep path to the stream bank. Claudia was using her geology pick and hammer to pull small pieces of the bank loose. The other five were setting out pin flags to mark items of interest, and she could see that some of the finds had been washed in the stream already, glistening and dark and standing out from the surrounding rubble.

Smiling faces greeted her. "This is very cool," Larry—she thought it was Larry, anyway—said. "I think I found half a trilobite." He held a wet rock up to her and she looked.

"Now that's old," she told him. "And you're right about what it appears to be. We'll need to study it more closely to peg it exactly in terms of species and probable age."

He nodded, taking the rock back and gazing at it. "My first find."

She was tempted to tell him to keep it, but she couldn't do that until she was sure it was just another trilobite, of which there were a whole lot. If it proved to be perfectly ordinary and offered no insights, she'd tell him to take it home and begin a collection for himself.

But right now, they didn't know enough to let anything slip by.

Cope had moved upstream, to a point where the water fell from a slightly higher ledge, and was filling both five-gallon bottles with fresh stream water. She saw him pop in the purification tablets so at least they wouldn't have to boil it to safely drink it.

She decided he could be a very useful guy to have around.

It was starting to get dark here in the gorge, though. Night always came early in parts of the mountain, and she needed to get these students safely out. In a week or two they'd have an easily traversable path from below, carved by their own feet, but not yet.

She looked at Cope. "You want to lead them down and back to town? We're losing light."

"Not without you and Denise." He called out to the others. "You can drink the water in this bottle in thirty minutes, not before. Unless you want to adopt some little amoebas."

Laughs answered him. "Meet us above just after you have a good drink. Renee thinks we need to beat the light down, and she's right."

"We ought to camp out," one of them said. "It would save a lot of time."

"I have to talk with Gray Cloud about that first," she replied. "I told you, we have to walk softly here." And she'd been trying not to test the limits of their permission to be here, not until they'd had a chance to prove themselves to be respectful. But maybe camping was an idea she could check out right away.

Then she turned toward the path they needed to climb. "Cope?" she asked quietly.

"Yeah?"

"Are you still uneasy?"

"Yup."

She paused, her hand on a rock she planned to use to steady herself. "You see something?"

"It would be easier if I had." Then, without another word, he lugged the other water bottle up the narrow, steep path behind her.

Nice view, Cope thought as he climbed behind Renee, then gave himself a mental slap for the thought. Shame, shame, they were working together.

He was just trying to distract himself anyway. Under other circumstances he'd be trying to get a date with her. Not under these.

He hated the skin-crawling feeling he couldn't shake. Someone was out there watching. Why? He couldn't dash off into the woods to look around, and it wouldn't make any difference anyway. If there was a threat out there, he needed to be close to Renee and her team. Wandering the woods wouldn't make him much help.

He wished Gray Cloud had shown up today. He'd have liked to question the man about whether any of his people might be watching them. If someone objected to this dig on sacred land, someone he needed to worry about.

If this continued, he was going to have to get some answers one way or another.

Maybe the worst part for him was not knowing how much of this was PTSD. He'd been luckier with that than many of his fellows, but that didn't mean he didn't have any at all. This creeping suspicion of someone watching was too similar to experiences from his time at war. How could he be sure he wasn't just dragging that out of his past, given that he was in the mountains and among the forest again?

But Renee had claimed to feel it as well. Maybe just jitters about a new and unfamiliar area. Even now the shadows under the tree were deepening, promising invisibility and hiding places for evil, if there was any out there.

Up top, he glanced at his watch and waited until it was safe for Denise and Renee to drink. They needed to plan this entire project better. No one should go without water up here the better part of the day. Tomorrow, those jugs and a couple more were going to be filled first thing. Excitement couldn't be allowed to get in the way of health.

Yeah, he saw the so-called camel packs they were all wearing. He'd worn them himself countless times, but the taste of the water didn't encourage drinking. That might make the supply last longer, but it wasn't good for anyone to ride the edge of thirst.

The group from below drank as much water as they could, then emptied the bottle and collapsed it before bringing it up. Good thinking. Meanwhile he began to make a mental list. He was fairly certain that among this group he was the only one with the background to deal with extended periods in the mountains. If they decided they didn't want to drive back to Conard City every night, they were going to need some help dealing with the conditions.

He knew one thing for certain: he was not going to leave this site unguarded unless he found out from Gray Cloud that his own men were watching it.

Because after this day, he had a strong feeling that

someone else had an interest in this mountain, and it didn't necessarily involve dinosaurs.

Just as they were about to begin the trek back down to their vehicles, Gray Cloud appeared, emerging seamlessly from the deepening shadows.

"Hi," Renee said warmly, and shared a brief hug with him. "Are we doing okay?"

"It seems so." The man smiled, then glanced at Cope. "Someone has some questions for me?"

"We'd like to camp, a little way down the mountain, so we don't have to drive out every day," Renee said before Cope could utter a sound. "Is there somewhere you could permit us to do so?"

"Of course. I'll show you the place. Makes more sense than driving that distance. It'll give you more time to work as well." He paused, his dark eyes shifting to Cope. "Yes?"

Cope turned to Renee. "You head on down with the others. I won't be far behind, okay?"

She hesitated a moment, then nodded, picking up her backpack. "Let's go, gang."

Gray Cloud waited, his arms folded, for Cope to speak.

"Since we got here this morning," Cope said presently, "I've been feeling watched. Renee and Denise evidently saw shadows moving under the trees and tried to talk themselves into believing it was their imagination. I'm not certain Renee believes that. Anyway, I wanted to know if you have some people keeping an eye on us. Or people you know of who might not want us here."

Gray Cloud lifted his gaze to the woods around. "No

one is shadowing you. Not of my people. That doesn't mean no one else is." He turned his gaze to Cope, a piercing look. "And the mountain may be paying attention. Don't laugh."

"I'm not laughing," Cope admitted. "I spent enough time in the mountains of Afghanistan to get the feeling that mountains aren't dead heaps of rock. But Gray Cloud, would the mountain's attention feel like human eyes?"

Gray Cloud shook his head without hesitation. "It's a very different kind of awareness. All right, I'll have some men scour the area to see if there are any other outsiders prowling around. I understand this fossil bed could be very valuable."

"Probably more valuable if it's properly dug up." Cope rubbed his chin, wishing he could rub away the feeling that something was wrong. "We had a visitor yesterday from a ranch south of here. Loren Butler. You familiar with him?"

"Yes."

Something in Gray Cloud's tone wasn't exactly warm.

"Is he a problem?"

"Not overtly, but he doesn't much respect our ways, although he claims to. If he comes back, I want to know."

Cope smiled faintly. "I think Renee told him off."

At that, Gray Cloud laughed. "She would. The heart of a wolf resides in that woman. Powerful but loving. Like her cousin. All right, I'll have some of my people check out the area so you can concentrate on this work. It needs to be done before the mountain slides again, or shrugs it off. Too much would be lost."

Cope agreed with that as he and Gray Cloud began to follow the others down.

Gray Cloud spoke again while the voices below were still distant. He spoke quietly, as if he didn't want his voice to travel. "You're a warrior, Carter Copeland."

Cope almost missed a step. "A part of my life," he admitted. "So?"

"I mean you're a warrior in the right way. You don't seek a fight, but you *will* protect those in your care. That's a true warrior. I'm glad you're here with Renee. I'm glad she invited you. I saw enough of you since you started teaching at the college to know you're a good choice to keep an eye on this team of hers."

"Nice compliment but…"

"No buts," Gray Cloud interrupted. "You have a strong sense of duty to those in your care. That's a good trait, the defining trait of a true warrior." Gray Cloud flashed him a grin. "You know you'll do what's right. Renee has some experience on projects like this, but she and her team are innocents in the woods."

Now that *did* draw Cope up short. He knew instinctively that Gray Cloud wasn't using the word *woods* to refer to the trees. "What do you mean? Do you know something I should be worried about? That *we* should be worried about?"

He watched as Gray Cloud's gaze grew distant. "I don't know what I know," the man said finally. "Right now, like your sensation of being watched, I have a feeling, nothing more. All is not well on this mountain."

Great. Wonderful. That was so damn helpful, Cope thought as they drew closer to the team.

By late the following afternoon, after a trip to Conard City's sporting goods supply, a camp had been created on a patch of level forest land. Tents had sprung up, tarps hung from tree trunks, metal folding tables held cookstoves and other gear, and ice chests were full of food. Most everyone on the team had some camping experience, so the setup went smoothly.

This possible expenditure had been planned for in Renee's budget, so her credit card smarted only a bit. Keeping the team in town would have been so much more expensive in every regard.

Denise and Renee marched up the path to the cliff face to continue mapping the area, and Cope added his shoulders and arms to the effort. As they measured, he tapped small pins lightly into the rock around which black twine was twisted to mark the verticals of the grid.

Another day, Renee figured, and they'd be ready to start work up here.

It was nearly six by the time they marched down again to join the rest of the group, who'd been putting the finishing touches on the camp. Most importantly, they'd brewed coffee and tea on the camp stoves, which were hooked up to large bottles of propane. Renee was more than ready for that coffee. Its aroma had practically dragged her down the last half of the trail.

Larry handed her a cup before she could even ask and waved her into one of the camp chairs. "Gray Cloud said we could build a fire tonight if we want."

That surprised her. "Really?" she asked as she sat. She hadn't expected that, but rather that they'd be warned not to have any fires at all because of the dangers of wildfire.

"Yup. There's a fire ring over there. He said not to build it too big and keep plenty of water nearby to put it out. Bets and Mason ran back to town to get some sandbags for smothering the fire just in case, and Carlos and I hiked to the bottom of the stream over there to get water to use if things got out of hand."

She settled into her chair and smiled at him. "How many of you were Scouts?"

That caused some laughter, but it seemed some of them had been. Prepared for just about everything.

She was glad when Cope chose a chair near hers. She liked being able to glance at him and watch his face. As far as she could tell, nothing had troubled him today, but he wasn't completely relaxed. Tension, or possibly vigilance, appeared to remain with him. Maybe he never relaxed. How would she know?

But he was still some pretty good eye candy. A pleasant warmth filled her whenever she looked his way.

Within an hour, her team had made her feel pretty special. Some of them were apparently masters of camp cooking, and soon they'd offered a meal of biscuits, bratwurst and mixed veggies.

"No reason we have to live on canned baked beans," Mason said. "Although we'll probably get there as we get busier. What's the plan for tomorrow?"

"Before we get into that," Renee said, "we need to talk about basic precautions. I don't want anyone going off on their own, understood? It's too easy to get hurt. Twist an ankle, fall and break a leg. Everyone keep your hard hats on all the time. That rock is still shedding pieces from above. And I'm not being a nanny, okay?" Not being a nanny but unable to forget the creeped-out feeling she'd gotten up there only yesterday, the growing conviction that they were being watched. Cope had felt it, too, and she'd go with his judgment as well.

Everyone nodded, as if they got it. She hoped they had, because she couldn't help worrying that something worse might be out there than an accident.

"Then there's the wildlife. You all received the information on the animals around here. You're not likely to encounter them if you just stay within our area and keep making noise. And that's the last I have to say about that unless someone has questions."

After supper, she wasn't even allowed to help with the cleanup. It seemed, she thought wryly, that there might be some brownnosing going on here. She wondered how long that would last.

As Bets took her plate from her and poured her more coffee out of the huge speckled blue coffeepot, she glanced at Cope and what she saw disturbed her.

He looked as tightly wound as a spring, and he was staring into the dark woods as if he could see something there.

She followed his gaze, but couldn't see anything beyond the tight circle of their camp, which was getting darker by the minute. Overhead stars wheeled in their courses, visible wherever there was an opening in the forest canopy. Gray Cloud had put them in a clearing, so the view of the sky was superlative.

But she didn't care about that. The shadows were deepening under the trees around them and they seemed to be a growing threat.

While the others chattered and made short work of cleaning up, she rose and walked over to Cope. His blue eyes snapped up to her.

"What's wrong?" she asked quietly.

"Someone's watching again. Maybe Gray Cloud's men."

It struck Renee that Gray Cloud would be unlikely to put men out here to guard them without at least introducing them so there'd be no misunderstanding.

"God," she said quietly.

"What?"

"My cousin Mercy spent a summer on this mountain while she was researching her dissertation. Like Gray Cloud, she came to believe it's alive."

His face was set in stone. He didn't disagree with her, but his gaze returned to the woods. "It's gone now. And whether the mountain's alive, this was no mountain I was sensing."

She squatted beside him, holding her cup in both hands. "Do you think we're in danger?"

The bold question popped out of her, and she wasn't sure why she had asked it. Dinosaur digs weren't the kind of things to result in murder or mayhem for any reason.

He sighed, relaxing visibly one muscle at a time. "No," he said finally. "But I don't like it when someone's curious and won't just come and say howdy, like that Butler guy did two days ago. That's all."

He had a point. She straightened and pulled her chair over closer to his. She didn't care if her team wanted to talk about them. Nothing was going to come of it, and she and Cope were natural friends being so much older than the others.

Renee stuck her hand into the pocket of her jacket and pulled out her cell phone. No signal. Sighing, she stuffed it back in. "I can't call Gray Cloud from here. There's no signal at all. I don't think it's likely he'd ask some people to keep an eye out without letting us know who they are."

"I'm not so sure. He said he was going to have a couple of men check the area out to see if anyone had been hanging around, so maybe that's all that happened. No reason for formal introductions if they're just going to slip by. Who knows? Maybe a wolf was checking us out. The curiosity wouldn't be surprising."

"I guess not."

Then he turned a smile on her. "Regardless, it's gone and my reactions may be a little exaggerated because of Afghanistan. This place reminds me of some of the places I served."

She turned in her chair to look at him better. "Is this situation causing you trouble? Maybe you don't want to be here with us."

He held up his thumb and forefinger, indicating a small space. "It's giving me that much trouble. Not worth thinking about. I'm just doing a self-check on my reactions is all. Always a good thing to do."

Probably a good thing for her to do as well, Renee thought. She had a way of letting her enthusiasm take over. "You're remarkable," she said after a few moments. "How many tours over there?"

"Four."

"Definitely remarkable. You make it sound like it was nothing."

He laughed. "Only because you haven't heard me rant yet. So what's the plan for tomorrow?"

"We've got to finish laying out the grid and tacking twine to the rock face as well as we can without damaging anything. Everything has to be accurately sited in order to interpret our discoveries. Then we'll be ready to begin releasing the fossils."

"I like that term, releasing the fossils."

It was her turn to laugh. "I like it, too. I'm sure it's not accepted terminology, but I always think of the fossils as having been imprisoned for millions of years, and we're bringing them into the light again."

"I like the term, too," said Mason, wandering over to join them. "A fire while we chat?"

It was getting chillier by the moment, and the idea of gathering around a campfire appealed to Renee. Besides, she couldn't imagine that her conversation with Cope had anywhere else to go.

"I'm in," Renee answered. "Cope?"

"Nicest thing on a chilly night. God knows I spent enough cold nights without one. I'll help."

Far back in the woods, from where the campfire could be only dimly seen, eyes watched and noted. He thought he had enough information now. With so few members of the team, there would be ample opportunity to disrupt the work and scare them off. The people he worked for needed some time to complete their plan.

And complete it they would. Those rocks held far more of value than some damn fossils.

Satisfied, he slipped away into the darker shadows, careful not to make so much noise that he disturbed animals and birds into making frightened sounds. A night forest coming suddenly to life would be a warning to that guy down there, the one who used to be a soldier. He'd be aware of all the things to pay attention to.

Yeah, it might take a bit of time, but he and the others would put a stop to this dig until all the pieces were in place. They were close now. Very close.

He also had a great idea how to use this mountain to his advantage. By the time he got done, the damn tribe would be calling the dig off. The ultimate success.

Chapter 4

The campfire gathering had been fun last night, Renee thought, as she and the team hiked to their assigned places on the mountain. Lots of funny stories from her team, who seemed to have reached the blessed age where they could laugh at their own childhood antics.

Today they all wore hard hats colored international yellow for visibility, no exceptions. They'd been a bit careless yesterday, but there was a very real danger of some rock falling off the side of this cleft, and while a bruised or even broken shoulder was a relatively easy injury to deal with, a blow to the head would not be.

Denise hurried ahead. She was clearly excited about finishing her grid and putting all the GPS markings on it. They might not be able to lay a twine grid everywhere without damaging parts of the site, but they could sure as heck use the GPS.

"Why do you need the grid?" Cope asked, climbing alongside her, having heard her explanation. "I mean, wouldn't GPS be enough?"

"It will be for locating the fossils, but having a grid to work…that keeps people in a confined area with their work, not rambling all over. I suspect we're going to find more fossils deeper in, so controlling the areas of digging will be useful. It'll help keep us within the time line on those fossils. Every layer of sediment and rock marks time, like rings on a tree."

"I can see that. I hadn't thought about it, though." He took her elbow, steadying her over an especially rough part of the trail.

"This isn't much of a path yet," she remarked. "I wonder how many times we'll go up and down it to flatten it out." She also wondered why his mere touch on her sleeve-covered elbow felt like the brush of an electric wire. Nobody's touch had ever done that to her before. Cope might prove to be dangerous in a totally unexpected way.

"Ask your geologist," he said from behind her. "That'll depend on the underlying rock."

For a minute or so, the only sounds were their boots on the trail, the breeze in the treetops and occasional birdsong. Then she heard him say, "I shouldn't have said that."

"What? Why not?"

"Your operation, boss. You don't need my useless advice. You sure didn't need me to suggest you ask Claudia about the underlying rock here. Guess I wore brass too long. Old habits die hard."

She reached a level spot on the trail and waited for

him to finish the last three feet and catch up. "What made you so sensitive to such things?"

"My sister."

"Oh." The things she didn't know about him. "What does she do?"

"She teaches English at the university in Heidelberg, Germany. She's always complaining that European men are chauvinistic. Listening to that for a couple of years has taught me to be a bit more cautious about what I say to the boss lady." He gave her a half smile. "Not working too well, I guess."

She laughed quietly. "If only you knew how accustomed I am to men contradicting me or trying to take charge. It gets so I hardly notice, it's so common. Like a fish swimming in water."

"Well, if I annoy you, tell me so. Callie would. That's my sister, by the way."

"I hope I get a chance to meet her someday." Still smiling, she turned and started climbing again. The path was steep, but not so steep she couldn't do most of it without having to hang on with her hands. Not much farther and they'd be on the ledge.

The ledge. It had been a dream-space for her since Gray Cloud had first shown it to her. She'd spent months gathering grants based on her first survey, and now she had arrived, ready for the undertaking. Years of exciting research and study probably awaited her, the fulfillment of lifelong ambitions.

With each of the last few steps, she felt as if she were growing lighter. The steep path no longer seemed too steep. She was here, and she might even be able to start releasing some of the fossils today.

From below she heard the cheery voices of her students. Just ahead she heard Denise and Claudia talking. The moment had truly arrived.

Which explained the big grin on her face as she at last joined the others. Her fingertips nearly tingled with the desire to get at it.

Denise had done a great job, isolating the area Renee most wanted to get at first. Claudia was busy measuring rock layers, chipping them lightly with her geologist hammer and studying the qualities.

"What do you think?" Renee asked her.

"It's looking good for Late Cretaceous where the egg is. I'm noticing we're not seeing any sign of large fossils much above it. There must have been some kind of catastrophe, a sudden wipeout."

"That would actually be useful to me."

Claudia smiled. "I thought so. Listen, I'm going to do some sampling from all around. Maybe the layers of rock will tell us what happened to that egg and the other things poking out around the same level."

"That's why I called you."

Looking over the edge of the cliff, she saw her other interns busily sifting through the rock below, occasionally pulling out a piece they put on a separate table. Then she looked down at the remains of the slab that had partially fallen over the winter, the tooth as she thought of it. There was still about ten feet of good rock that would need examining, but that egg called to her like a siren. Finding an egg with a fetus still in it was even rarer than finding other bones from the long reign of dinosaurs.

But she still had to wait a bit before she could dig in. Denise was almost done, but not completely. She perched on a rock and Cope sat beside her. "So tell me," he said, "why is it so hard to find fossils?"

"Because most organic material, if left exposed, rots pretty quickly. A primatologist once remarked to me that if they hadn't seen chimpanzees with their own eyes, they wouldn't have known they existed. They searched an area of about 150 square kilometers before they found a partial skeleton. Nature's very efficient in cleaning up remains."

"Really?" He fell into thought, looking bemused. "I never would have guessed. I mean, I know about vultures and other carrion eaters. I've certainly seen enough in action. But I never thought of it in quite this way."

"Fossilization requires perfect conditions. Or nearly perfect conditions. You need remains that predators don't rip apart and scatter all over dozens of miles, stripped of all flesh, bones broken. Plenty of bacteria and insects will finish the job. That means we need the remains to…oh, maybe fall into tar or a swamp, or to the bottom of a lake bed to be quickly covered with silt. To be buried in ash, or flash-frozen during a quick climate change. Like the woolly mammoths you've probably heard about. A find like this is a treasure trove."

"That's enough to get me excited." He rested his elbows on his knees. "I imagine you can hardly wait to start. I'm getting there."

"Yeah." She sighed. "It'll also be fascinating to find out what Claudia learns about the conditions around the fossils. Was there a sudden flood, one that maybe swept all the animals together? Did one of these mountains erupt and asphyxiate them with ash and bury them swiftly? I have a billion questions."

They were dancing around in her head like popping corn. Her tablet held a list of most of them, and she'd studied it for weeks before arriving here, wondering how many she'd be able to answer and if she'd overlooked anything.

"In the end," she remarked to Cope, "this is going to be a lot of slow, dirty work. For every day of excitement there will be lots of days when we come up with nothing. We'll get dirty and sweaty and tired with nothing to show for it. But right now…" She smiled again. "Right now I'm staring at what it's all about. I just hope there's a lot more in there than I can detect out here."

She reached out a hand and he grasped it. She needed a solid touch right now, feeling as if she might float away if not tethered to the ground. Everything she'd wanted was at last coming true right before her eyes. No more waiting, no more hoping for a unique find. Gray Cloud had brought her right to one.

"You said Gray Cloud is married to your…cousin, right?"

"Yes." She turned toward him. "Did I say? Mercy's a wildlife biologist and she met him while she was studying the wolf pack on this mountain. Right now she's down in northern Mexico studying the gray wolves. They're facing some migratory problems because of border fences and she's studying the impact."

Cope stared off into space for a bit before saying, "I never cease to be amazed by the way humans consistently act as if we're the only species on the planet that matters."

In an instant she truly warmed to him. "Too many people don't see beyond their own noses," she agreed.

"I'm not sure we're built to think of long-term consequences," he remarked, returning his gaze to her face. Those blue eyes of his almost made her shiver with pleasure. "We tend to think only a day or two down the road. Sometimes that's useful. Sometimes not so much. But you'd think by now that we could see the impact of short-term thinking."

Crunching on rock drew Renee's attention and she saw Claudia making her way toward them, her hammer tucked into a holder that hung from her waist, a sample case full of glass bottles in her hand.

"I think that's most of what I need for now," she remarked, sitting beside them. At once she began to wrap a padded container around the samples, zipping it into place. "If there's anything unusual here, I'll find it."

She smiled at Renee, her gray eyes dancing. "This could be exciting. I know we'll find some uranium. That's everywhere on the planet, usually deep enough that we don't run into it without mining, but who knows. Quite a bit of rock sheared away. A lot of sandstone that indicates sediment, but there's granite and some quartz as well. So a mix of sedimentary, indicating lots of water, and igneous, indicating that this mountain may have erupted far in the past. There used to be gold mining up around here, yeah?"

"I think so. Farther up and over to the south there's a gold-mining camp, abandoned long ago. My cousin told me about it. Apparently, they didn't find much ore."

Claudia nodded, her eyes still sparkling. "Quartz is a good indicator there might be gold around. But I'll keep my mouth shut about it. The important thing is fossils, not some slim chance of finding a small vein of gold. Probably wouldn't be worth the effort of trying to extract it."

Cope spoke. "What are you going to learn from those samples?"

"I hope to find out why there's a layer of fossils all together here." She pointed to the rock face. "Not all of them are as obvious as the egg, but when the shadows catch them right, you can tell quite a few dinosaurs died right there at about the same depth. Renee has a bunch of great photos on her tablet taken during sunrise. Anyway, something had to have happened and it's my job to try to find out what. And if I can, what helped the fossilization along. Dang, what a find!"

Later, Renee went below to where her other interns were busily looking through the debris on the creek bank.

"Small rocks are still falling," Bets remarked as Renee joined them. A young woman with fine blond hair she could never keep in a tie, and a plump body, she stood with her hands on her hips, eyeing Renee from beneath her hard hat. "Maybe pieces that were shaken loose when part of that wall above tumbled. Or maybe the ground is moving very slightly. This entire place is geologically active, I believe, from what Claudia said the other night. But aside from that, we're finding a lot of smaller fossil pieces."

"What are your thoughts?"

The others gathered around, eager to join Bets and Renee. "Some of them may have been damaged in the fall. Not many pieces seem complete, but we've got a whole lot more to look through."

"Not as good as what you have on the ledge above," Mason added. "At least not yet." Even under a hard hat he looked too young to be a college student. Fresh-faced.

"Still important," Renee reminded them. "I hope I might be able to get started on the rock face before we lose light, but I'm not counting on it. When we get to that point, two of you can come up to help, but we've got to keep working this debris. Sometimes the most important information can come from the smallest pieces."

And again that feeling returned, the feeling of being watched. Despite herself, she turned around to look. The forest shadows, dappled still with light before the sun sank behind the peak, offered nothing. If anything out there was watching, it knew how to avoid detection.

"Remember," she said before she climbed back to the ledge, "stay together. I mean it."

A couple of them looked a little surprised by the reminder, but didn't argue. They were going back to work, Mason and Carlos lifting buckets of the fallen rock and dumping them on the sifter where Larry and Maddie started shaking them while Bets ran water from the stream over them to highlight their shapes and remove loose dirt.

They were doing a good job, Renee thought as she climbed back up to the ledge. So far, she could only count herself damn lucky.

Denise was practically rocking as she worked at her tablet. Cope was scoping out broken rock on the ground using her pin flags whenever he saw something of interest. For just an instant she felt like an unnecessary wheel at her own site.

"I'm getting excited," Denise said, still rocking, her voice rising. "The more I diagram, the more I'm seeing. Renee, you've got your life's work looking down on you."

"I'll second that," said Claudia. She was brushing at the exposed rock face with an artist's brush, urging fine dust into a sample bottle. "I think Cope is finding stuff, too."

"They're doing good below, too," Renee answered. "Dang, this is like walking into a museum."

"A very important museum," said the familiar voice of Gray Cloud from up the mountain a short distance. Renee whirled and saw him picking his way over some talus and around shrubs and trees in the company of two younger men in jeans and plain chambray shirts. They wore their tribal heritage proudly in their faces, and gently in their smiles of greeting.

"My nephews," Gray Cloud announced as they reached the ledge. "Short and Tall." He shook hands with Denise and introduced himself to Claudia.

Renee had heard the story years ago, so she didn't ask. However, Denise bubbled over with curiosity. "Short and Tall, really? You both look the same height."

The young men laughed and sat cross-legged on the rocky ledge with them.

"We're twins," Tall said. "Our mother had a dream just before we were born in which there were two bear cubs standing on their hind legs, and one was shorter."

"Oh!" Claudia said, expressing delight.

"So, Short here was one inch shorter at birth. He got named Short Bear and I got named Tall Bear, and we also go by Sam and Tim, if you prefer."

"What a neat story," Claudia enthused. "I love it!"

Short gave a wry smile. "I don't mind it until someone calls me Short Rib."

"Oh, no," said Denise, turning enough that she could look at them instead of the wall.

"Oh, yes," said Short. "Not so much since I got bigger, though."

"And came back from the Rangers," Gray Cloud remarked. "Cope?"

"Yo."

"Short and Tall are under your orders if needed. Meantime, they're going to wander by here every now and then just to make sure everything is going well. If they use their training wisely, you won't know they're here. Anyway, I don't want to interrupt the work you're doing so I'll bring my nephews down to your campfire tonight so everyone can meet them and know they're safe."

"Thank you," said Renee and Cope at the same instant.

There was a pause. Then Gray Cloud indicated he wanted to talk to Renee and Cope alone. "About tribal stuff," he said, apparently so Claudia and Denise wouldn't become offended. Although that wasn't very likely, since the two of them had fallen into conversation with Short and Tall.

"There's more," said Gray Cloud in a low voice when the three of them stood apart from the others. "You felt the eyes. That wasn't the mountain. The mountain is hardly aware of you, busy with its own dreams. But my nephews could find no sign of anyone having been up here except this group. As near as they can tell, no one is showing any interest in this dig."

Renee felt a bubble of tension she'd hardly been aware of seep away. "Thank goodness. Nothing to worry about then."

"I didn't exactly say that. I listen to the mountain. The fact that we can't find anyone nosing around doesn't mean no one is interested. I asked the sheriff to keep his ear to the ground."

Renee hesitated, not sure of how to respond. Even feeling slightly embarrassed to have caused such a stir. "I hate to put you out, Gray Cloud. I'm probably over-reacting to something minor, like a raccoon."

"You weren't the only one overreacting," Cope reminded her.

Gray Cloud didn't answer directly. "You should probably know that my nephews are tribal law officers. If you need help, they'll be more than willing. But right now, it appears you're all alone out here, which is what you want."

Gray Cloud walked back over to where his nephews were laughing with Denise and Claudia, then squatted. He looked at Claudia. "You're the geologist?"

She nodded.

"This land has never been mined. But that doesn't mean it hasn't been mapped. I'll bring you a map to-night. It might be useful."

He and his nephews bade them farewell, then marched up the slope to disappear once again.

Renee hadn't gotten to any work on the rock face that day, and Cope could tell she was disappointed. The findings of the group working down near the creek had been interesting, certainly not a waste of time, but didn't deliver the kind of news she hoped for.

"Most of these will wind up in boxes in a museum basement," she remarked to him as the interns insisted on cooking while she and Cope enjoyed cof-fee. "I didn't see anything that seemed to provide new knowledge, not yet, but they need to be more closely examined. I've been wrong before."

He nodded and smiled at her. "When was that?"

"When what?" Then she caught on and he enjoyed seeing the laugh roll out of her. "Lots of whens. I got started in excavations while I was still in high school. We had a funded dig about thirty miles from my home-town, and they were desperate for hands, however in-experienced, because a road was coming through and they had a limited amount of time to gather artifacts."

"Really? Why limited?"

"Because the road was coming through and all that has a timetable with dollar signs attached. They liter-ally used bulldozers to clear off the top five or ten feet of soil for us and then we went to work. My first day I discovered charcoal from a fire pit and a small piece of bone. I was so dang thrilled. And I screwed up by touching them with my hands." She shook her head. "I learned a hard lesson that day, although after I got scolded they told me they had enough samples that my mess-up wouldn't be critical. And that was only my first mistake."

He nodded and gestured toward the rock face. "Do those have to be protected from human contact, too?"

She shook her head. "Fossils like this can be washed to get rid of contaminants." Then she smiled. "I hope there's still some viable DNA in some of those bones."

"That happens?"

"A number of years ago, a paleontologist got to won-dering why the bones in her lab all had such a distinc-tive, unpleasant odor. She checked it out and found that all those millennia hadn't been enough to kill all the life inside those bones. DNA remained."

Cope sat quietly for a while, thinking that he'd known a whole lot less about Renee's work than he'd thought when he volunteered.

He also found himself wondering why Gray Cloud had pressed him to accept Renee's invitation to help out. He was now a history professor, rediscovering his civilian legs after so many years in the military. That in no way made him more than a useful gofer on this site. Nor was it as if Gray Cloud knew him that well. Their encounters had been few, the most significant a time he had Gray Cloud come in to speak to one of his classes about the indigenous view of the West's settlement.

But now with the feeling of having been watched, and Gray Cloud's readiness to volunteer his nephews as occasional sentries, he wondered what the man had known that he hadn't shared. Was he expecting some kind of trouble?

He didn't like the idea that Gray Cloud wouldn't share such information, nor did the man seem the kind to mislead them. So no, he'd probably just accepted their sense of being watched as a matter worthy of attention.

And maybe he'd just believed that Cope could keep an eye on this group. Certainly, he had a skill set for the mountains.

Tossing the thoughts aside as he ate dinner and listened to the group chat around the small campfire they'd built once again, he realized how much he enjoyed the company of these interns. They were purpose-driven, unlike many of his classroom students who studied history merely because it was part of the general education curriculum. These were good company.

"I think I'll be heading out in the morning," Claudia said. "I want to get some analysis of the samples I took, and a spectrograph would be very handy. I should be back in a day or two."

"Sounds good to me," Renee answered. Then she looked at Denise. "And tomorrow I get to start chipping away at that rock face, right?"

Denise flashed a grin. "If Cope will help me put up some more strings somehow to mark the grid so that everyone behaves themselves, sure."

Cope spoke. "Is there some way to draw the grid on the rock safely? Poking holes in it to hold twine might damage it and that is troubling me. I know we did it earlier, but I'm afraid I might drive a tack right through something important."

"At this point," Denise answered, "we can mark with a carpenter's pencil. I happen to have several. But your height will be an advantage."

He'd busted up his shoulder pretty good in Afghanistan, so it was difficult to reach over his head, but he didn't say anything about it. He'd deal.

Something in the deepening night shifted, an almost atmospheric change that put him on high alert. He looked at Renee and tried to see if she felt anything, but apparently not. She was deep in conversation with Denise and Claudia.

Cope lifted his head and looked around, trying to see beyond the circle of light from the fire. But more importantly, he strained his other senses, seeking a change in the forest sounds or a new odor of some kind. The wind kicked up suddenly, rustling the nearby treetops, causing a branch or two in the deep forest to crack. The flames of the fire danced wildly now and leaned toward the east.

Well, there went any hope of detecting something from his chair. Rising, he began to circle the edge of the campsite they'd made, peering into the dark shadows, waiting for his eyes to fully adjust.

Maybe he was losing it. No reason to think he'd been luckier than so many of his fellow veterans. Maybe it had just taken longer to set in, or maybe being up on the side of this damn mountain was waking sleeping tigers in his subconsciousness.

Gray Cloud had said that Tall and Short—he got a kick out of those names—hadn't seen signs of trespass out there. They'd check in every so often to keep an eye on the dig. There was absolutely no reason for him to stay on high alert.

Except for instincts he'd lived with so long he was beginning to think they'd never let go.

Finally he'd completed his circumnavigation. It hadn't done much to ease the edginess that plagued him, but that was likely imaginary. He returned to his seat beside Renee and listened with half an ear to the conversation that bubbled up from all the interns. No silence here.

Eventually Renee leaned toward him and asked quietly, "Everything okay?"

"Yeah. Actually. Guess I'm having a touch of PTS."

"Post-traumatic stress?" Her gaze grew intent. "Do you have much of it?"

"No, actually. It's probably the environment here, the mountains. I think I said something about it to you earlier. Anyway, it'll pass, and I need to push it."

She frowned faintly. "Push it why?"

"So it'll quit irritating me. You've heard of immersion?"

She nodded slowly. "Jump into the stimulus until the problem passes. Yeah, I've heard of it, but don't ask me to stick my hand in a jar full of furry spiders."

Laughter began to find its way up from his gut. "Do they have to be furry?"

"Oh, yeah." She tilted her head and looked rueful, but when the laughter escaped him she joined right in. "And no amount of knowing it's silly makes it possible for me to *feel* it's silly. You have more guts than I, Cope."

"I don't know. I'm not dealing with furry spiders."

They both laughed again. That's when they realized that the conversation around the fire had trailed off and that a bunch of interns were staring at them.

Renee leaped in to save Cope any embarrassing questions. "I was talking about my aversion to furry spiders."

"Furry?" Bets shuddered. "I don't know why, but they seem worse than regular spiders. But it's weird, I don't have a problem with daddy longlegs. You know the spider I mean? When I was a kid we had a lot of them running around our front porch and I played with them."

"Ewww," said Denise and Maddie.

"I know. Weird. They never bothered me at all, though, and they're perfectly harmless." She flashed a grin. "When I was a kid, insects didn't bother me as much. Something happened between then and now."

"Adulthood," Maddie suggested, to a chorus of laughter. A pixieish-looking young woman with tousled dark hair, she had a smile nearly as wide as her face.

Just as the interns began to gather up the dinner dishes for disposal, Gray Cloud joined them. All of a sudden he was there, like a ghost that had just popped out of nowhere. Renee noted how everyone froze, startled, and she had to admit she was a little startled herself. The man could move like an invisible wraith through these woods.

"Hello, everyone," he said. "I brought the map for Claudia to look at."

The crew finished tossing trash and food bits into a large garbage bag for transport to the dump tomorrow. Food couldn't be left lying around because of the animals. This load was locked inside a camper shell.

While the chores were being finished, Gray Cloud, Claudia and Renee gathered around a plastic folding table. Cope soon joined them.

"It's mostly a topographic map," Gray Cloud said as he spread the roll out and tacked the corners down with some rocks Cope handed him. "You'll probably see immediately the changes the opening cleft made last year. Even diverted the stream below somewhat." He traced it with his fingers.

"Who did this map?" Claudia asked. "Somebody bring a lantern?"

The ambient light around the campsite was nowhere near good enough to observe details. Renee leaned in, and as the fluorescent camp lantern was planted on the edge of the table by Carlos, she watched the blurry details sharpen. Claudia pulled some reading glasses from her pocket and perched them on the end of her nose.

"US Geological Survey," Claudia said, finding the

mark at the bottom of the map. "But this isn't the whole thing."

Gray Cloud shook his head. "You don't need the whole thing, so I only brought the part you'd be interested in."

Claudia nodded. Renee felt a surge of amazement when she looked at the topography and absorbed how much had changed. "That cleft made a big dent."

"So it did," Claudia answered. "How old is this map?"

"Ten years. It was done after the interest in the wolf pack mushroomed. The tribe agreed to allow it because we wanted to have a reference to make sure outsiders weren't tearing the mountain up." He drew his finger along the area where they were digging. "That's you. But the cleft goes a lot farther up." Again, he traced with his finger. "Maybe another half mile. When you have time, you might want to check it out, but I didn't see anything obvious." He smiled. "Difference between you and me, Renee. I don't know what to look for unless it jumps out at me."

Cope appeared to have a knack for reading terrain maps, as did Claudia. A geologist and a soldier. Of course, Renee thought, putting her chin in her hand to listen.

"That rock dropped quite a bit when it opened up," Cope remarked. "That wall appears to be about thirty feet high now, but on the map that entire area slopes down from fifty feet toward the stream. How much fell into the cleft and how much height did we really lose?"

Gray Cloud smiled. "That's for you to find out. My guess is there's about fifteen feet or so of broken rock at the bottom between the two faces. I couldn't begin to imagine what might be buried down there."

"Enough to keep me working until retirement," Renee said. "More than enough. Big stuff first, though."

Gray Cloud nodded. "The kind of fossils people might want to steal."

"Some of it is in plain sight," she agreed. "Fantastic fossils. But hard to remove from the matrix. Nobody's going to whisk it away overnight."

"That's a relief," drawled Cope a tad sarcastically. Renee darted a look at him and decided she was going to have to ask him what was going on when they could get a moment alone.

Gray Cloud left the topographic map with them and disappeared into the night.

Then, astonishingly, the entire group that had wanted to camp out here to save travel time took a fast decision to head into town for a few hours, maybe stop at the bar or something.

Renee didn't object, but she wondered how many of them had any idea how little amusement they were likely to find.

"Just come back sober," she warned, not caring if she sounded like a mother hen. "No drinking and driving. DUI will be the end of your work here."

A chorus of promises followed them toward the cars. All she could do was wonder what bee had gotten into their bonnets.

Chapter 5

"That's weird," Cope said when silence filled the woods after the last car drove away. He liked the silence, though. It concealed nothing from his senses. Only the sigh of the wind in the trees and the crackle and pop of the fire at their feet disturbed the night.

"You mean them wanting to go to town? I know. One of *them* suggested camping out here."

"I guess camping is more boring than they thought."

Renee laughed quietly. "Maybe so." She turned a little in her folding chair. "What did you mean a little while ago that it's a relief that no one is going to steal a fossil overnight?"

"I was being sarcastic," he admitted. Leaning forward, he put some small pieces of wood on the fire. He wanted the heat. Sometimes just making the soles of his boots hot could warm his blood enough to reach the rest of him.

"Why?" she asked bluntly.

How much of this did he want to stir up? He really had nothing at all to go on. Nothing, except some instincts born in a war far away. They weren't at war, so he should ignore them. Maybe. But he couldn't. "I'm not sure," he admitted eventually. "Not sure at all. Just a feeling."

"A feeling that something bad could happen?"

He shook his head a little and wondered at what point since leaving the military he'd lost his ability to just shut his mouth. "I don't know. I can't shake this feeling of uneasiness. Blame it on my past experience, because there's sure nothing else to blame it on."

Very true, he thought, picking up a long stick to poke at the fire. A shower of sparks rose upward a few feet, then died. Not a damn thing about any of this should be making him feel this way…except for the sense he'd had a few times that they were being watched. Well, it was only some damn fossils. If they were being watched it was by a strangely reticent curiosity seeker. If anyone wanted to know what was going on, all they had to do was ask. Hardly a national secret.

He watched Renee in the dancing firelight. She appeared lost in thought, but the flames added mystery to her face, highlighting some features and then others. Until that moment, he had thought of her as an engaging extrovert, but now in some subtle way his impression shifted. He'd bet the woman was more complex than she initially seemed.

Then he realized she was worried. She hadn't dismissed the feelings she'd gotten from the shadows in the forest, even though Gray Cloud had assured her his men would keep an eye out.

"Renee?" He hardly knew what he was going to say.

She turned her head, the firelight now highlighting only one side of her face. "Don't dismiss your feeling about this place," she said slowly. "I've been spending a lot of time wondering if this sense I get means Gray Cloud and my cousin are right. What if this mountain is sensate? What if *it's* watching us."

"Then we'd probably appear like transitory ants," he said, trying to be light.

She didn't smile. "I'm all about science, Cope. Right now I'm not feeling very scientific. Something's out there. It's interested in us. Is it human? Probably. But then why the hell doesn't it just come sit by the fire?"

Good question, he thought. Exactly the one he'd been asking himself.

But then he heard Renee draw a sharp breath. He followed her gaze and nearly caught his own breath. A gray wolf with eyes that reflected the dancing firelight stood at the edge of the clearing, motionless, staring. It almost looked like a creature out of myth, so still it might have been a statue.

No sound. No growl. No bared teeth. Simply a measuring stare that reflected red in the firelight.

"Beautiful," he heard Renee whisper.

He couldn't have agreed more. Perfection. Almost hallucinatory.

But then the wolf turned and, as it did, perfection vanished. It was still shedding its winter coat, looking scruffy along its sides as it vanished into the night woods.

"Wow," he said.

"Magnificent," she answered softly. "It's been such

a struggle to protect them. The tribe and Gray Cloud have been working hard at it, and my cousin Mercy has been doing what she can, but the ranchers want them gone." She felt a soft smile on her face. "That was magical. I feel blessed."

"Me, too." But that wolf was not what was making him uneasy. If he'd wondered before, he didn't now. It was almost as if he'd made an appearance to let them know he wasn't the problem.

"My hands are getting cold," she remarked and leaned toward the fire. "I guess I need to dig out my gloves for the evening." She stuffed her hands into her pockets, pulling out dark knit.

He'd have offered to warm them for her, but he didn't think they had that kind of friendship yet. Although he'd have liked to do it for her. "Renee?"

"Hmm?"

"I don't think that wolf would have come this close if someone else were out there. So you can relax."

She smiled as she tugged her gloves on. "That's nice to know. Thanks."

But his thoughts had already begun to run back into the rut that had been troubling him since his first sense that they were being watched. "Is there anything at all besides fossils someone could be interested in here?"

She looked over her shoulder at him. "Still feeling it, huh? I keep expecting some ogre to march out of those trees, and he won't have gray and white fur."

"I told you, yes. But in my case..."

"Quit blaming it on Afghanistan," she said. "I can't blame it on anything. It's fleeting. It comes and goes. But I'm damned if I can understand why anyone should be interested."

"The fossils have to be worth something."

"Sure," she agreed. "But first you have to release them. Right now I've got plenty of photos that would uphold the tribe's claim to them. Try to sell that on the black market."

He shook his head, feeling a frown settle into the corners of his mouth. "You wouldn't believe what I've seen disappear into the underground trade in antiquities. Don't say those fossils couldn't be sold."

"Maybe. But for enough to make it worth someone's while? I haven't seen anything like that yet. I know we're only getting started but that egg that so fascinates me? It's a museum piece, and not the kind of thing that would bring a small fortune. It's not *obvious*, if you get my drift. You wouldn't place it on a shelf in your private underground collection and show to a few good friends. It would be out of context, and without the context…" She shrugged. "It's of purely academic interest. Especially to me."

Then she leaned back, rubbing her hands together, and gave him an almost impish smile. "I hope I'm not being too optimistic here."

He laughed. "I get your point. It's a dinosaur egg. Rare enough, I'm sure. But a long way from a whole skeleton of something identifiable. You'd probably make more money collecting meteorites."

"See? I went into the wrong field."

He rubbed his chin for a few minutes, erasing the chill. Ever since he'd been grazed by a bullet underneath his chin, the area below his lower lip needed occasional help in staying warm. This night was turning unexpectedly frigid, he thought. "Maybe your team would be better off staying in town, Renee. I'd bet we're going to fall below freezing tonight."

"You might be right." She flashed another smile. "You will note that I wasn't the one who suggested camping out here. It's still early enough in the spring to turn really cold. Of course, it can do that in the summer, too, I hear."

"July Fourth snowfall. No joke. Mercy must have mentioned it to you."

"Actually no. July Fourth. Really?"

"Really. I'm told this area doesn't get a whole lot of snow, but it can get some big blizzards some years, and some completely random weather. As for temperatures…" He shrugged. "Variable. Most of the time it's what local folks would call normal for the time of year, but then it goes and shocks everyone."

"I think weather everywhere is becoming random," she answered. "Well, not random so much. Just more extreme." She paused. "I wish there was some way to tell the team to stay in town if they want. Cells aren't working out here, but it feels like the temperature is truly plunging. I have questions about whether my sleeping bag is good enough, and I have no idea at all about theirs."

"Easy enough," he said. "I can hop into my truck and drive until I get a signal. I could also check on just how cold it's going to get. But I'd have to leave you here because of the fire."

He didn't want to leave her alone. The irritation at the base of his skull might come and go, but his reaction to it was sticking like glue. Nor did he want to put out the fire. If he dumped water or sand on it, they'd have trouble getting it started in the morning.

She chewed her lip a moment. "They can come back if they want, or stay in town if they want. They're not soldiers under orders. They all know I don't need them before eight in the morning, so I'll leave the choice to them."

Best way to handle it, he thought. The interns *were* all adults, after all. If they realized how cold it was getting, they knew their way to the motel. If they came back here, they'd better be prepared to shiver.

He also took a little comfort in the idea that if someone was watching them, he'd be pretty uneasy tonight as well as cold. He'd spent a lot of nights like that, and the thought made him grin.

"There can't be any reason anyone other than another paleontologist would be interested in this site," she said a few minutes later, sounding thoughtful.

So she wasn't able to shake the feeling that something bad might be afoot out there somewhere. If he hadn't been a soldier for so long, he might have found it easier to dismiss the matter entirely. But when you felt eyes on you…

He leaned in toward the fire, warming his own hands. "Unless that cleft has revealed a huge vein of gold ore, I don't see the point. And that has me wondering if I might be losing my mind. Again, it could be a touch of PTSD."

He sensed, rather than saw, her look at him. "Scratch that idea, Cope. You keep coming back to it but I've been feeling it, too. Denise felt it the first time we came up here. I'm wondering if we shouldn't just ignore it. Gray Cloud is going to have his nephews check around from time to time, and considering the lengths required to get permission to dig on sacred ground,

I'm quite sure they wouldn't be happy with someone else lurking around out there. But there's absolutely no reason to lurk!"

He nodded, holding his palms to the flames and feeling the heat seep into cold skin. "None," he agreed, without adding, *that we know of*. Always the qualifier.

With time, the fire began to die down. Shadows seeped closer to the camp from their dark caverns in the forest. To the east, the finest sliver of moon began to rise, ice in the sky.

"You know," Renee said quietly, as if she were afraid of being overheard, "sometimes I so absolutely *get* why Gray Cloud's people think this mountain is sacred. Like right now. I could be sitting almost anywhere in the darkness, but I know I'm not. I can *feel* this mountain. Like a sound just beneath the audible. Oh, I don't know. I'm just being unusually fanciful."

"I don't think so," Cope said. "As you say, there's the belief that the very stones are alive. Why shouldn't we be able to feel it if we hold still and be quiet long enough?"

She turned to him. "Are you a mystic?"

"I don't think so. It's just that this isn't the first mountain I've been on that made me feel it might be living force. Mount Shasta was the first."

Why the hell was he wandering down this trail with her? To convince her he was as mad as a hatter so she wouldn't be interested in him? Because he was sure interested in her, and he didn't know if his walls were secure enough to withstand her.

"Mount Shasta," she repeated. "That's a volcano, right?"

"On the Pacific rim, the Ring of Fire. In Northern California. Beautiful mountain."

"You've been to some interesting places," she remarked a few moments later.

"And you haven't?"

He loved her light, quiet laugh. "A few," she admitted. "I'm not widely traveled, though. I think my biggest adventure was a cruise I took with a college friend. She found some last-minute tickets for a seven-day Caribbean cruise. Seeing Mayan ruins enticed me the way little else could have."

He was watching her face, enjoying the play of firelight and expressions that combined to create an aura of mystery about her. "Why do I think the trip had some problems?"

"Not exactly problems," she said. "Me."

"You? What could you have possibly done?"

"Realized that the very, very cheap stateroom we had was in the bow of the ship and well below the waterline. I think that was the strongest encounter I've ever had with claustrophobia."

"Ouch." While he didn't suffer from any phobias himself, as far as he knew, he'd known others who had. They could be overwhelming. "Did that ruin the entire trip for you?"

She shook her head slightly and laughed again. "Not the entire trip, by no means." Rising up a little, she curled her legs beneath her before settling again. He wouldn't have believed that possible in the small camp chair, but she did it, heavy boots and all. "I wasn't exactly thrilled, but I dealt with it. Most of the time we were above deck anyway. High up. There was this nifty little lounge at the very top, so on the occasion when the weather got bad we had a nice place to hang out. The rest of the time at sea I was all for fun in the sun."

Her gaze grew distant and he suspected she was remembering the trip. He waited until she spoke again.

"Weird experience," she remarked. "We hit some bad weather before we reached the Florida Keys. The captain announced we'd have to skip our stop at Key West because it was too windy to enter the harbor. Well, we'd noticed the growing wind, which is why we went up to this lounge at the very tippy top of the boat. Anyway, we're sitting there gabbing when I looked out the panoramic windows at the front. It was unreal, Cope. It looked like the sea had tilted to a forty-five-degree angle. Kid you not. But I didn't feel a thing."

"I've seen that," he acknowledged.

"Then you probably know the weird feeling it gives you. You know the sea shouldn't be tipped but the room you're sitting in doesn't feel tipped. It wasn't like we were sliding across the floor or anything."

"Probably because it happened so slowly."

"Maybe." She turned to him, smiling. "I was trying to get a fix on just what I was seeing and why, when the captain announced that we were listing to port because of the wind, not to worry, they were moving ballast to level us out but it would take time. Then he said it would be wise for all of us to get to our staterooms as the seas were growing rougher."

She shook her head a little. "I think most people already had, because we started heading down and didn't run into anyone. But what I most noticed was that once we left the lounge, we had to seriously cling to the railings along the corridors to keep our footing.

Like everything changed suddenly." She paused. "Of course, by then we were beginning to feel the waves."

"I guess so." He had absolutely no problem imagining everything she described. "Would you ever take another cruise?"

She surprised him by laughing aloud and spreading her arms as if to embrace the world. "Definitely. That storm was some of the most fun I had on that cruise. Twenty-two-foot waves, the TV swinging on its gimbal with every rock of the ship, losing the satellite connection every few minutes... Oh, it was cool."

She was delightful, he thought. Totally a delight. "You didn't get seasick?"

"Only a bit and it went away fast. I had more trouble with seasickness going ashore on the tenders."

She fell into thought, and he contented himself with watching her, while his other senses remained alert to the woods around them. When she pulled up her jacket hood, leaving him with an obstructed view, he forced himself to full attention again.

She was right about sensing the mountain. It was a massive presence, palpable if you paid attention. Maybe he was just sensing its gravity, upthrusting from the familiar pull of the ground beneath them. Warping space and time, given how huge it was. Subtly, not that much, but maybe enough to be felt by those who paid attention.

He spoke after a bit. "Will Claudia do a complete analysis of the samples she took? I know you're hoping she can find out why this fossil bed is so magnificent, but what about other things?"

She turned, her hood slipping backward. "Like ore, you mean?"

"Thinking about why anyone might be interested in this area if it's not about the fossils, yeah, I guess that's what I'm driving at."

Renee nodded. "I'm sure she will. Claudia's thorough. Impeccable. That's why I was so glad to get her on my team."

After a bit, he stood to stretch his legs and walk the perimeter again, peering into the dark shadows beneath the trees, shadows that in some places were giving way to the frigid light of the rising sliver of moon.

Maybe he was making too much of the sensation of being watched. Maybe he was encouraging Renee to do so as well. While he had not the least doubt that the fossils she was so eager to unearth were worth a lot of money in some places, actually getting them out of the ground would take time. It wasn't like some kind of diamond heist where someone could slip in and out.

Nor would there be any real reason to interfere with Renee and her team that he could see. "Renee?"

"Yes?"

He halted and faced her across the fire. "Do a lot of people in your field know about this site?"

"Have I staked a claim, do you mean?"

"Something like that."

"Yeah, I let it be known in enough places what I'm looking at out here. I didn't exactly hire a town crier, but people know. Why?"

"Just wondering about claim jumpers."

"It wouldn't be the first time. But we'd have to abandon this site for that to work."

"Okay." Abandon the site? In other words, scare her off? Well, that might provide a motive for someone.

"Don't you guys have some sort of collegial relationship so you can all work together?"

"Most of the time," she answered. "There are always exceptions, but we pretty much get along. Say I needed someone's particular expertise. He or she would lend it willingly for a mention in the papers we'll be writing. So it's not something I usually worry about."

He reached her side and squatted. "But this time is different?"

"This site may be different. So many fossils together…it's a big deal, Cope. Maybe. If I'm right about what's here."

He nodded, raising one knee and resting his forearm on it. "I think getting past Gray Cloud might prove to be difficult for anyone who wants to shove in here."

"Probably so. And I feel like I'm blowing up a little thing all out of proportion. Gray Cloud's nephews will check in from time to time. That's more security than I've had at most sites."

"So let it go?" he asked. Although right now his mind was skipping past the things they'd discussed to something a little more chilling. What if not everyone in Gray Cloud's tribe supported this dig? What if a group felt this was a desecration?

"I'd like to."

He understood that. And more power to her if she managed it. He vowed there and then to keep his mouth shut unless something definite happened. She really didn't need to borrow his paranoia. He had plenty to share, but he didn't want to give it to her.

A short while later she decided to turn in and try out her sleeping bag. He sat up, watching the fire, seeing dancing images in the flames.

All was not well on this mountain. And the problem might lie with the very people who had invited Renee.

Hundreds of miles away, Caron Broadus sat at his desk in the executive suite of Broadus Oil. From the large triple-paned windows, he had a distant view of the Bakken oil fields, of the natural gas flares burning from the tops, lighting the night with the promise of power. Now the oil companies needed to tap those flares because natural gas was worth more than the crude coming out of the ground.

Broadus didn't care. He'd pulled what he wanted out of the hundreds of square miles of drilling and was thinking about moving on. He saw a different kind of "peak oil" on its way, and it was time to diversify.

Electronics and solar power had garnered his attention. He had engineers and accountants working on the financial prospects of both areas. He could, however, corner an important market in the world of electronics with just one mineral, one rare earth that was truly rare. He'd found it.

The only problem was that the land was owned by Native Americans and there was now a major fossil find on the land. It struck him as totally wrong that some ancient bones could get in his way. The earth was full of bounty needed for human life and progress. Nothing should stand in the way, and certainly not the bones of something that had died sixty-five million years ago.

Tribes he could handle. They could always be handled. But museum pieces?

There were some people who needed to be scared off, and others who needed to be legally pushed off.

That's what he had lawyers for, as well as some muscle. A combination of both should do the trick.

But for now he still hadn't firmly made up his mind. Turning a paper clip absently between his fingers, he stared out at the fire-punctuated night, waiting. His ducks were already being lined up whichever way he chose to go.

But he still needed the results of the tests on the ground involved. Rare earths weren't rare—about like copper for the most part. But there was one that was rare indeed, and essential to a lot of electronics. Earlier testing had given him hints that it was there, but he needed to know for certain.

Because he was going to stir up a hornet's nest no matter how quiet he tried to be about this. One way or another, some folks were going to be furious. Like that Gray Cloud character.

Guardian of the Mountain? God, these people needed to step into the modern century. Too bad if he was going to have to shove them into it. It was high time.

And he did have some allies within the tribe, sensible men and women who could see the advantages to having some money to share around and improve their lot. The fossils wouldn't do that for them. No way. They might just get that sacred mountain trampled by curiosity seekers.

Unlike him. He usually tried to put things back the way he'd found them. As much as he could, anyway. The tailings ponds? Time would manage them. Time managed most things.

Which was why he was a patient man. He'd get rid

of those paleontologists and clear his path once everything was ready.

Not that hard, after all. If his luck held, no one would die.

He preferred clean victories, but he'd take them any way they came.

Chapter 6

Ten days later work on the site was in full swing. Each day brought more discoveries, whether from the rubble down below by the creek, or above from the wall and crumbled rock on which they stood.

When lunchtime came, Renee sat on a rock facing the egg she was still gently easing free, her mind already writing abstracts for the various papers that could come out of these discoveries. Work had consumed her once again, everything else forgotten. She figured she wasn't very good company unless someone wanted to talk shop, but that's the way she'd always been. She unwrapped her peanut butter sandwich from the waxed paper and took a bite, still amazed by the incredible egg, as amazed as she had been the first time she saw it. A baby dinosaur was emerging bit by bit, arrested at a significant point in its development by whatever catastrophe had buried all these bones. Around it more eggs were emerging, and the very first signs of an adult or juvenile of the presumed species.

She just wished the report on Claudia's samples would come soon, with answers to the mystery of what tragic fate had befallen all these animals.

Denise dropped down beside her with her own lunch. Glancing at her, Renee laughed.

"What's so funny?"

"You're covered with dust. I guess I must be, too. I only rinsed my hands at the water jug."

Denise grinned. "As long as I'm not covered with enough dirt to plant with corn, I'll be fine."

The nights were still chilly, so the day ended with a quick, fully-clothed dip in the icy stream below and a race down the hill to the fire. Somehow Cope always arrived first and quickly got a good blaze going. They shivered together and laughed as they dried out, quite rapidly because the mountain air was nearly bone dry, and waited for the coffee and tea to warm them up again.

On the weekend, they broke up into two teams, one for Saturday and one for Sunday, and hit the showers at the truck stop just outside Conard City. God, what a luxury that was. All the hot water you could ask for.

But right now she was covered head to toe in light gray dust. A rinse of her hands and a swipe at her mouth had been her only concession to hygiene.

"Do you feel ladylike?" she asked Denise.

That brought a full-throated laugh from the woman. "Really? My family tried. They couldn't stop me from climbing trees and joining the hockey team."

It was Renee's turn to laugh. "I was a bookworm.

They always pushed me to go outside and play. When I couldn't escape it, I spent my time digging and scraping away at the side of a hill."

"So you never quit."

"I can't even remember when I started."

Cope joined them, sitting on the rocky surface near Renee while wiping his face with a damp rag. "I've been dirty countless times," he remarked, "but I still hate grit. This is gritty. Did Maddie bring you up that rib and vertebra we found below? I wasn't sure if she just put it aside for later discussion."

Renee's interest quickened. "No, she didn't bring it up. Did you have an impression?"

"Only that the fossilization kept them together. There must be what was once soft tissue in there. But I'm no expert, so I could be all wet."

"I need to get down and look at it." Renee eyed her sandwich, missing only two bites, the egg in the wall that so fascinated her, and the possibility of something interesting below. Her appetite was waning, so that left an either/or choice. But the egg... The whole thing that had set her on this quest. The emerging signs of other eggs and a juvenile or adult saurian.

"Eat," said Cope, almost as if he read her mind. "I'll pry the bones from Maddie or have her bring them up for you to look at."

"Thanks." Renee offered him a smile. "I just hope she marked the location."

"Maddie's meticulous," he answered.

With a sense of shock, Renee felt an unexpected spear of jealousy. Were Cope and Maddie developing a "thing"?

Then she scolded herself and bit into her sandwich

as if it were cement rather than peanut butter. None of her business. She had no claim on Cope. Anyway, she was so wrapped up in her work she didn't leave much room for anything else.

Except once or twice she had almost thought…

She brushed the notion away before it could fully form. She must have misinterpreted the occasional glint in his eye, or the way he sometimes just watched her. Why would anyone want a career-obsessed and often filthy paleontologist anyway?

Just then came a sound no one ever wanted to hear: the sound of falling rock and a cry. The cracking and tumbling continued for a little longer, then Renee, Cope and Denise all leaped to their feet. In this canyon it was impossible to tell exactly where the sounds had come from as they echoed.

Then from below Maddie called out, "We're gonna need some help down here."

Renee scrambled for the path, Cope just ahead of her. She glanced to the side and saw that part of the "tooth" had collapsed again, pouring rock on the team below. Damn it, why hadn't she kept an eye on it, knowing it could collapse again?

She practically slid on her bottom all the way down, trying to keep up with Cope, who was taking the rugged path as if he were a mountain goat. Even as fear pushed her, bringing her to the brink with thoughts of one of her team being seriously injured, she couldn't move any faster without risking her own neck. Cope seemed oblivious to the danger.

Catastrophe met her. Part of the "tooth" rock above had crashed down and Larry was partially buried in it.

At least his eyes were open and he was talking. Grimacing with pain, too.

The below-team had already started to lift rocks off him, and Cope joined them swiftly, telling them to be careful not to move Larry at all. As soon as she reached them, Renee bent to the task with everyone else.

"Sheesh, Larry," she said, trying to sound light-hearted.

"I know," he answered. "I told you I was always in the wrong place at the wrong time." He paused to pant a couple of breaths. "Of course, I may have just unleashed a bigger find than yours."

She had to laugh for his sake, but she was seriously worried. Cope organized them to get the weight off his chest first so he could breathe better, a good thing considering he was looking awfully pale.

Finally they had Larry uncovered to the waist. Cope bent over him. "Deep breaths?"

Larry provided them without coughing, which was amazing considering how much dust filled the air after the rockslide.

"Your lungs are fine, anyway. Where do you hurt?"

"Mostly my leg. I think other parts will get sore later. These damn rocks are a hard bed."

Cope nodded. "Just hold still and let us do the work, okay?"

"I never argue with that," Larry said gamely.

"That's my man."

For the first time, Renee was getting a true look at the former Marine. He seemed to know exactly what to do, and he was tossing out orders to everyone. While more rocks were lifted, he sent a couple of the team members to find wood that might make a good splint and two longer poles in case they needed a stretcher. He was thinking of everything.

Renee was grateful. She was still dealing with the shock of seeing Larry under those rocks, and while her brain would have kicked into gear before long, she doubted it would have been as swiftly or as intelligently. It was clear this was not the first such situation he'd dealt with.

Just as they were about to clear Larry's legs, the next horrifying sound reached them: rock was falling above on the upper level. The sound was loud, no little patter of pebbles. As the rumble rose over them, Renee was aware that everyone looked upward and no one moved a muscle. Frozen, they awaited fate, their only protection the hard hats on their heads.

No one even attempted to run. Time seemed to stretch endlessly as the rumble continued. Cope moved, forcing everyone down, ordering them to cover their necks.

At last the rumbling faded away until silence filled the forest again. Only the gurgling stream could be heard, and the occasional *pop* of another falling rock.

This had always been a possibility, but a remote one. Now the worst was happening. Renee absorbed it as she scanned her group and found that no one else appeared to be in trouble. Then her other main concern leaped to the forefront: the entire find might be buried again.

"Nobody's up there?" Cope asked almost as soon as the slide stopped.

Renee did a quick nose count, glad of a useful task. "No."

"Then once I get Larry stabilized I'll go up and see whether we can get out of this damn place."

Another thing she hadn't thought of. She was beginning to feel like a true dolt. Nature's violence had opened this cleft. Why had she so blithely assumed it wouldn't close it? Especially since part of the "tooth" had broken off during the winter. This had been predictable, and she should have been better prepared for it. At the very least she should have splurged on a satellite phone so they could call for help.

She'd endangered them all with her narrow focus on the fossils and hoping to prove a pet theory. She looked from dusty face to dusty face and realized that she'd failed them. Their safety should have been her biggest concern. Yeah, they'd volunteered, but they hadn't volunteered to get injured or possibly killed by a rockslide. And Larry. If they couldn't get him out of here, his death would be on her head.

She looked up again at the mountain above, and wondered how she could have been so blind. So careless.

Cope had apparently put it behind him for now. He once again squatted by Larry's injured leg and told them to get him those saplings.

From the way Larry was acting, Cope felt fairly safe betting his injuries weren't life-threatening. But a safe bet or not, he couldn't judge just how much of Larry's cheer owed to shock. None of this had probably come home to him yet. The sounds of the rock falling from above had wakened them all yet again to their precarious position on this mountain. He wondered how many would stick around if they got out of this without too much more trouble.

Maddie and Carlos returned with some saplings that

could be used either as splints or as stretcher poles. "Good job," he told them as he hunkered over Larry's legs. They were uncovered now and he began to feel their length with his fingertips, watching Larry's face for signs of pain while he felt for anything that didn't seem right.

At last he elicited a yowl from Larry, who quickly apologized for screaming.

"No apologies," Cope said. "You just told me one of the things I need to know. I'm guessing a simple fracture to the tibia. I don't feel anything out of place." He finished running his hands over the young man's legs, then palpated his abdomen. Soft. No hardness. That meant no rapid internal bleeding. Yet.

"I think you were lucky," he said encouragingly.

"Sure. Lucky to be under a rockfall. Man, your priorities are skewed."

Cope flashed a grin in response and some of the others managed laughs. No one was seeing any real humor in this, however. The strain was audible as they tried to respond to Larry's attempt to be light.

He pulled out the knife that he always wore in a leather case on his belt—a habit left over from his past—and began to shave the saplings into pieces suitable for a splint.

"We're still going to need to carry him down," Cope remarked. "I'm going to need jackets or shirts or something to sling for a stretcher. I don't want to chance making anything worse."

"So it's not bad enough yet?" Larry asked. But he no longer sounded quite as cheerful. His close call was beginning to hit him.

"Bad enough," Cope answered, "but I think you'd

rather be wearing a walking cast tomorrow than be in a hospital bed in traction."

"He's got a point," Larry muttered.

Renee had busied herself using her jacket and Denise's to string between the two much longer saplings. As Cope positioned the shorter pieces around Larry's lower leg, Carlos offered up his shirt, ripping it into long strips.

"Someone's been taking first aid," Cope remarked. "Thanks." He began tightening the strips around the splint, making sure it wouldn't move too much.

"Okay, I'm headed up to see how we can best get Larry out of here. If I'm going to need to leave to call for help, I'll shout down so you won't wonder. Somebody give him some water, please?"

Then he hurried up the path, feeling as if he'd stepped back in time to a different country and another continent.

As worried as he was about getting Larry out of here before hypothermia could complicate matters, he was growing equally worried about Renee. He didn't like the expressions that had flitted over her face once the second slide faded away. She was blaming herself, taking too much responsibility.

Well, he could hardly blame her for that. It was one of his own failings. Didn't matter that he wasn't in control. Nope. It was all *his* fault. Renee apparently owned the same tendency. Except that rocks had moved without her help, and without her ability to stop them. What was she supposed to do?

The argument about whether the mountain was sentient was moot anyway. Aware or not, it was a mountain and behaved like a mountain, and he'd yet to meet one that never moved at all. People had a tendency to view them as eternally unchanging, but anyone who'd clambered around on some of them soon learned that they were never perfectly still, but were constantly reacting to every stimulus that reached them, from wind and rain to less obvious activities, such as the movements of the earth itself, or even, sometimes, a human footfall.

If groundwater levels halfway around the planet could react to an earthquake in Alaska, then why shouldn't a mountain, and probably to even smaller forces? Forces human senses couldn't detect. Sentient? Pointless to wonder. The inescapable reality was that the entire planet was alive and constantly changing. Leave it at that.

When he reached the top of the path, the view of the space at the bottom of the rock face was hardly encouraging. At least the egg that Renee was so fixated on remained undamaged, although there were a few cracks around it. But as he pushed up the last bit so that he stood on his feet and could survey the entire area, he felt a knot of anger settle in his stomach. Not for himself, but for Larry, for Renee. It was a damn mess up here now. The slide buried part of the base of the cliff. The work area they'd so carefully leveled out was now a tumbled mess again. Looking upward to the top of the cliff, he didn't like what he saw. It no longer looked stable. It looked as if it hadn't quit falling yet.

What the hell?

He didn't know a whole lot about geology, but his instincts were once again sounding alarms. Something was wrong. They needed to ask Claudia to evaluate this.

In the meantime, he needed to pick his way carefully

along here and see if they could get Larry through to the path downhill. If necessary he could take off and run for help, but he felt uneasy about leaving Larry behind. He might have internal injuries. He might succumb to shock and hypothermia. No, not even with most of the team present would he feel okay about leaving Larry behind. They had to get him out of here until they could call for a helicopter evacuation. Even if he got all the way down at top speed and put the pedal to the metal until he could get a cell signal, he doubted even one of the county's rescue copters would have enough clearance between all the trees to send down a Stokes basket.

Even as he weighed options, however, he was moving, seeking a way across the freshly fallen rock rubble. The project had just stepped back several weeks in time. Once Renee got past her worry for Larry, she wasn't going to be happy about this. Nor could he blame her. She was on a grant, which meant limited funds and limited time.

"Cope!"

The voice came from above and he craned his neck. Tall Bear, aka Tim, looked over the upper ledge down at him. "Everyone okay?"

"No, we've got an injured man below. I've got to get him down this mountain and call for help."

"Hang on. Shorty and I will come help. Gray Cloud can place a phone call, too, so I'll make sure we get the message to him. Just one to be evacuated?"

"So far. If no more rock falls."

Then Tall said something that chilled Cope. "This wasn't any accident. Stay there. We won't be long."

Cope chewed on that while he scanned the rockslide

and the way ahead. Taking a moment, he called down to Renee and the others, telling them to stay put, that Tall Bear was bringing help.

Then he squatted down and eyeballed the surface they'd have to cross. He had to make it safe so nobody would break an ankle. But almost as important was making sure they didn't grind some unique fossil into dust by trampling over it. Well, they wouldn't grind it into dust, but they could sure damage it.

Two birds, one task. Not the first time he'd had more than one thing to deal with at a time. Inching forward, he began to move loose rocks to the side, or wedge them in tightly where he could, always being careful not to unleash yet another, smaller slide from the hill of gravel and stones that lay ahead of him.

Forty degrees, he thought. Nature's natural balancing angle. The reason pyramids stood without falling. The rock had tumbled into its most stable configuration, and now he was going to move it and hope that he didn't make it shift again. No choice, because there was no other way to get Larry out of there. The only way up to the level where Tall Bear had been standing was by way of the other end of this rock face. Behind him lay rugged, nearly impenetrable woods.

Nor could they hope to move Larry downstream from below. He'd checked that out the second day they were here. The stream had carved a gorge with very steep sides. No way could they get Larry through there. One man with climbing gear maybe.

So they were boxed in unless he could clear a path here. After what Tall Bear had said, he seriously doubted the man was going to offer to lower ropes over the edge and start pulling people up. Not if he believed the slide was unnatural. He'd be hyperalert, wondering what other weak points had been created, either by the rockfall or by whomever.

Cope knew *he* would.

He'd moved and wedged his way through about a foot of fallen rock before pausing to call down again.

"Is everyone okay?"

"Larry's getting cold," Renee called back up. "We need to do something soon."

"I'm going to be fine," he heard Larry call back. "I'm buried in everyone's jackets. They're in more danger than I am."

That Larry was incredible, he thought. And he probably *was* getting colder because he couldn't move, added jackets notwithstanding.

It wasn't a bitter day by any means, but it was no day for sunbathing, either.

"We could build a small fire," Renee called up. "If it's going to be a while."

"I don't know how long it'll be," Cope said frankly. "I'm trying to clear a path for us up here that won't cause another slide. Go ahead and start a fire. You *all* need to stay warm."

"Need some help up there?" he heard Claudia call.

"Actually, yeah. That would be great." He hoped he wasn't offending Renee, but Claudia was the geologist. He wanted more from her than help moving stones. He wanted an assessment. To him it seemed extremely odd that that bottom rocks had fallen before the ones on the upper rock face. He wanted to ask her about it without it becoming a group speculation.

"I'm on my way," Claudia called back.

Cope didn't answer. He just kept working. Before

long, time would become very important, because Larry was getting cold and might go into serious shock at any moment. So far the guy seemed to be staving it off, but he didn't like the fact that Renee had said he was getting cold. Larry would be the last person to recognize he was going into shock.

Forty degrees, he reminded himself, and edged forward.

Maddie and Renee sat on opposite sides of Larry, trying to keep him awake and engaged. Renee watched Claudia hike up the path to the upper level to join Cope and felt a twinge of envy. But of course, Claudia was an experienced geologist who would be able to survey the damage and perhaps explain it…or have some ideas about how to avoid a repeat.

She wondered about the fossils, about the egg that had been her goal for so long, but knew in the balance they mattered less than getting Larry out of here safely. Getting *all* of them out of here safely.

Carlos, Bets and Mason set about building a small fire upwind from Larry so the heat would reach him. Denise, apparently feeling basically useless at the moment, was sorting through the rocks that they had cleared off Larry, looking for interesting pieces. When she found one, she held it up for Larry. "Name it," she said.

Larry gave a weak laugh. "Are you kidding? There isn't enough to identify it. It comes from something big, though."

"Maybe a juvenile?" Denise suggested.

"Could be," Renee answered as Denise handed it to

her. "A big one. Hey, Larry, this would make a great paperweight for you."

"Get it engraved," Maddie suggested. "With today's date so he'll never forget."

"As if I could."

"Does anyone use paper anymore?" Carlos asked from where he was nursing the fire into life with the assistance of Bets and Mason, both of whom were visibly shivering now, beginning to feel the lack of their jackets.

"Clearly," Renee said drily, "you haven't worked enough with computers. All they've done is make it possible to generate even more paper."

Laughs greeted her, and even Larry brightened a bit more.

The day wasn't a cold one, but it wasn't balmy, either, and the gorge this river was running through drew a steady, swift breeze that was beginning to chill them all.

Denise spoke. "Think they can get a helicopter in here? Or lower a basket from one?"

Renee instinctively looked up, as they all did. "I doubt it," she heard Mason say. "Strong wind down here, and there's not a whole lot of room. Although I guess Larry wouldn't notice it now if he got banged against all the trees on the way up."

"Word," said Larry, then added, "not."

Renee finally felt the steady breeze beginning to carry warmth from the fire behind her. She glanced over her shoulder and saw that it wasn't exactly a small one, but to warm all the way over here, it couldn't be.

"Feel that?" she said cheerfully. "It's almost ready to toast Larry over the flames."

"Nah," said Carlos. "He's broken. We need a perfect offering to the mountain."

For some reason that made a chill run down Renee's spine, a chill that had nothing to do with the breeze or the day's cool temperature. An offering for the mountain?

The others were off and running with various rituals they'd read about in their studies, and she could see they were keeping Larry's attention, so she let them continue. Feeling next to useless, she wrapped her arms around herself, trying to block as little heat as possible from getting to Larry. As her team grew warmer, they talked more freely, and she was glad to hear Larry joining in.

She looked up at the rocky cascade left by the landslide and hoped no more of those stones would move. If they did, they'd fall right on Larry. Chewing her lip, she tried to remember all her first aid training and figure out if they could safely move him to a place farther from all those loose stones. At this point, however, there was no way to know if moving him a few feet to the side would make him safer, and pulling him straight back would put his head in the stream.

Dang, she thought, looking upward again. Where were the rescuers? The help Cope had promised?

She knew she was being unreasonable. Since there was also a slide up above it was probably hard to move yet. How much stone would he and Claudia have to get out of the way without triggering another slide?

As for Tall Bear, she was sure he'd run as fast as he could for help, but she had absolutely no idea how long it would take him to get somewhere useful and then to bring people back.

Patience, she told herself. *Keep your attention on Larry.* At least the area was starting to warm up. The air that blew toward them no longer felt as if it were blowing off a snowfield. Important. They could all take care of themselves, but Larry couldn't even move.

Conversation continued to rattle around various rituals, and folks were getting warm enough now to drink from the water jug.

Larry finally complained, "I'm getting hot under all these jackets. Anyone want theirs back?"

"As long as you're not trying to be tough," Renee answered. "Promise you'll tell me if you start to feel cold."

"Promise," Larry said. "Man, I feel useless right now."

Denise held out the fossil she'd found. "You can hang on to this for me."

He made a face at her.

The fire *was* doing its job, however. Everyone took their jackets back, but no one zipped up.

"We should have had this going all morning," Bets remarked. "Dang, I thought I was going to freeze my fingers off running water through that sieve and looking for stuff."

Larry laughed quietly. "Imagine panning for gold?"

"Is gold worth it?" Bets retorted.

It was clear to Renee that the initial fear caused by the rockslides had worn off. Everyone was getting back to normal, including Larry. She just hoped they weren't being overly optimistic.

Then Cope's welcome voice called down. "We've cleared a path. Tall and Short are coming down with me and we'll get Larry up here. Claudia's checking the rock faces for us."

With a rattle of pebbles on the path, rescue began to arrive, first Tall, then his brother Short. Cope followed.

Cope immediately knelt beside Larry, checking him out. "You're looking pretty good for a guy who just battled a mountain."

"I'm okay," Larry said. "I was a little woozy when it first happened, but I'm fine now."

"You may get woozy again. It's not going to be a smooth trip up that path or across the ledge above. If the splint isn't sturdy enough, you may feel it."

Larry nodded, but he skipped saying he could take it, which somehow surprised Renee. She was used to the bravado of young men.

In short order, Cope and Tall checked out the impromptu stretcher and once again tested the splint tied to Larry's lower leg.

They exchanged looks and nodded. Without another word, Short bent and lifted the poles at the head of the stretcher. "Strong but a little bouncy," he remarked. "Hey, kid?"

"Yeah?"

"I'm going to carry you up headfirst, okay? Given how steep that path is, I don't think you'd want your head down."

Larry managed a feeble laugh. "You're right."

"You will, however, have a view of my denim-clad butt."

That pulled a real laugh out of Larry, and Short smiled back. "Hey, some might like it."

Then he set the stretcher down and lifted it once again so he was carrying it behind him. Tall took the bottom.

"Lead the way," he said to Cope. "Eyes on, as they say."

"After you douse that fire, everyone else come behind us," Cope told the team. "Be careful, especially when we get above. Single file. Claudia and I had to be cautious about how we stacked the fallen rocks up there. Got it?"

Then he astonished Renee, reaching out and taking her hand as he pulled her to her feet. "You come with me. We need your eyes to let us know before we crush something priceless under our boots, okay?"

"This isn't the time..." she started to say. Fossils were of much less importance than Larry and getting her team out of here without another injury.

"This is the time to watch out for everything," he said sternly. "Nobody thinks that rockfall was natural, so don't give away the store."

What a thought! Someone was trying to push them off this site? She'd been upset about Larry, but if it wasn't accidental... Rage began to stir in the pit of her stomach. What here could possibly be worth risking a life over? Yeah, the find could wind up rewriting parts of Cretaceous history, but to kill over it? To even *risk* killing over it?

"Let's go," Cope said, tugging her hand gently. "Eyes on, my friend. We've got an intern to save and a site to protect. Time for all hands on deck."

"Yeah," said Larry. "The site's gotta be protected. I'll be fine, but if someone's up to something ugly..." He didn't finish.

Cope spoke. "We'll talk about ugly later. First to get you out of here."

Renee nodded and followed closely behind Cope.

A glance over her shoulder told her Short and Tall were right behind. The fire was already smoking as Bets and Carlos doused it with river water.

Why did she feel as if she were leaving for good? Shaking her head, she began the trek.

Chapter 7

Carrying the stretcher slowed them down considerably. Everyone willingly spelled Short and Tall, who acted as if they could have carried Larry all day. But Cope stepped in at one point, relieving Tall, and Carlos insisted on giving Short a break.

Getting past the rockslide had proved to be the scariest part. Those rocks looked as if they could let go at any minute, and while Renee scanned the ground beneath her feet as Cope had wanted, she wasn't really focused on whether there was anything important in the loose stones. If there was, it would still be there in the morning.

She just wanted Larry safely in the hands of medical professionals. She doubted any of them, Cope included, could say with certainty that a broken leg was his only injury.

God, the horror of all that rock falling on him. She'd been so afraid as she raced down from the upper level that she was going to find Larry in dire straits, possibly even dying. To get off with what seemed like only a broken leg was nothing short of a miracle.

For the first time she wondered if pursuing this site might be a big mistake. Yes, the fossils were exciting, perhaps even revelatory, but as she'd thought earlier, they certainly weren't worth a life.

And why was everyone being so quiet about the slide? Most of her team, when they could catch their breath, talked lightly about other things, but she didn't fail to notice that Claudia and Cope were grimly silent, and Tall and Short about the same.

Something unnatural had happened and she supposed she just ought to be damn grateful that when the upper level slid it hadn't caused more rock to fall down below and onto Larry.

The rest could wait. It would *have* to wait. Right now, all that mattered was Larry.

Before they cleared the last trees before their campsite, the sound of a helicopter became unmistakable. The tops of trees tossed in rotor wash as they marched closer. Apparently medical help was waiting.

So, she discovered, were the Conard County sheriff and a couple of his deputies. No one could say much because of the noise made by the chopper, so they all hung around while Larry was checked out by the EMTs, then carefully transferred to a Stokes basket and strapped safely in.

Before the chopper departed, one of the EMTs took a moment to tell Renee, "He seems to be doing pretty good. By the time you get to town, he'll probably be ready for a visitor or two."

Then they were gone, powering up into the sky and away.

Which left the dig team, Tall and Short, and the three members of Conard County law enforcement.

Renee had recognized Gage Dalton on sight. Last year when Gray Cloud had shown her the fossil site, she'd taken the time to meet with Dalton. A man who bore burn scars on one side of his face, limped painfully and had a rough voice, he'd apparently been the victim of a bomb years ago. Beyond that, Renee hadn't tried to pry. She'd also met his wife, the county librarian known to everyone as "Miss Emma" for some reason. Emma had been thrilled beyond words at the fossil find on Thunder Mountain, and Renee had been delighted to have someone to share her enthusiasm with.

So there was Gage, and two deputies identified by brass nameplates on their khaki uniforms: Marcus and Sanchez. Once the world had quieted down a bit, Gage put a hand on his hip and looked at Renee. "Gray Cloud said it was deliberate."

She caught her breath and looked immediately at Claudia. Remaining silent, Tall and Short had folded their arms and barely nodded. Cope was the first to speak. "I'm taking Tall's word for it. I haven't been up there to look, but Claudia, who's a great geologist, agrees. The rockslide had a little help."

"Well, doesn't that beat all," Gage remarked. "Why would anyone want to shut you folks down? Fossil hunting on tribal land doesn't seem like it would get in anyone's way."

"Unless there's something else up there we don't

know about," Claudia remarked. "I found quartz, usually a sign of gold, but I doubt there's enough gold up there to make it worth digging out. You'd have better luck panning the stream."

Gage nodded. "We had gold mining around here about a hundred and twenty years ago. It played out fast, nobody could find enough to make it worth their while, and most of them moved on."

Claudia spoke again. "There are also rare earths. Essential to electronics, but honestly, most of them are as common as copper. While copper is worth money and people might fight against mining it because of the pollution, they're not going to kill over it." She shrugged. "Unless I find something that stands out—and I've got some people working on it even now—I can't give you a reason anyone would want to violate sacred lands to stop a fossil dig."

Short spoke. "Violating sacred land doesn't disturb most people if they want something."

"True," Gage muttered. "Well, I guess I need to take a look. They might have left some evidence behind."

Tall held up a hand. "It's a hike, Sheriff. You might want to spare your leg."

Dalton scowled. "To hell with the leg. Marcus, bring your K9. We're going for a hike."

"I'll ride shotgun," Claudia said. "I'm a geologist."

Dalton nodded.

Renee was torn. She wanted to climb that mountain and be there for whatever they found. She also wanted to be with Larry to make sure he was all right. And regardless of which she chose, she couldn't leave the site unprotected. Not after this.

Mason stepped up. "You need to stay here, Renee. The site needs someone to keep an eye on it."

"I agree," said Cope. "I'll stay with you. We need to provide protection."

The others decided to run into town to keep Larry company, and Renee made a decision. "Don't come back tonight. I want all of you somewhere safe until we figure out what is going on here."

"But how can we keep in touch?" Bets asked. "You'll be worrying about Larry and we'll be worrying about you and Cope, and nobody's cell phone works out here."

The sheriff spoke. "Cadell, you got an extra sat phone?"

The K9 officer nodded. "Always."

"Then let's leave it with Renee here. Now get Dasher ready, because we're going to sniff around really good."

Short spoke again. "Sheriff, I already carried one man down that mountain today. My shoulders would be very grateful if I didn't have to carry you as well. Not your fault you have a bum leg."

Dalton sighed, hitched his gun belt and gave in. "You're right. Emma would have my hide if she found I was out here gallivanting on a mountain. Okay, I'll stay here. Sanchez, you go with Marcus and his dog to sniff out any clues."

Renee's decision was made. "I'm climbing up there, too. I want to see what happened."

Now Cope put his hands on his hips. "I'm not going to stay behind when you're out on the mountain."

"Sheesh! Someone has to watch the fossils with Gage. After what happened to Larry, I don't think anyone is safe alone." But then it struck her that she was being a bit unreasonable. She closed her eyes and drew a deep breath.

"Okay," she said finally. "Cope, you and I will keep an eye on the site. Maybe we can find some clues in the rockslide. Claudia, are you still going with Tall and Short?"

"Damn straight," said Claudia. "You know I looked over that rock face when we arrived. No reason there should have been a slide. But I'm a geologist, so you can count on me to notice anything unnatural. Or to notice if I screwed up my evaluation."

Renee nodded. She didn't like this splitting up. Not at all, but she didn't see how it could be avoided.

"And I'll be right here," Gage said. "I can warn you if anyone comes and keep in touch with base about what you all find. Good enough? And let me know if you want any help. Sanchez?"

"Yo?"

"Take your sat phone up there with you. I love this county, but I hate the communications around here."

Tall smiled faintly. "You're beginning to sound like the old sheriff, Nate Tate."

Gage's grin was lopsided. "Yeah, next I'll be swearing the country's going to hell in a handbasket."

"Isn't it?" Marcus asked. He clucked. "Come on, Dasher. Let's go do our thing."

Dasher's entire demeanor changed; the Belgian Malinois with his brown body and dark snout immediately signaled his eagerness.

Renee watched Claudia take off with the two deputies, the two Native Americans and the dog. "I hate this," she muttered.

"Dividing forces?" Cope asked. "I couldn't agree

more. But we've got more than one prong here, so we have to."

She nodded and turned to Gage. "Can I make some coffee for you, Sheriff? I think I'd like to take a thermos up there with us, too."

"I've never yet refused a cup of coffee," Gage responded.

Renee set about quickly filling the big tin coffeepot with water and coffee grounds, then turned on the gas flame beneath it.

Gage was evidently feeling talkative. "I can't imagine any rhyme or reason for this. Nobody should be willing to kill over some fossils, I don't care how rare they are." He paused. "Of course, I reckon I've seen people kill over less, but it usually wasn't cold-blooded. And the two of you have no ideas at all?"

Renee shook her head as she joined the two men at the camp table. "I've seen claim jumping in my field, but it usually involves showing up the next digging season only to find out someone with more seniority and a bigger grant has taken over, and oh, would I like to join the team? But that happens almost never. Something like this?" She shook her head vehemently. "I kept it under wraps, didn't say much about my high expectations, and there are a lot of fossil beds in this state."

Gage nodded. "Isn't this where they found Sue, that big, complete T. rex?"

"On the Cheyenne River reservation," Renee said. "I don't know if you remember the heist, but the big boys moved in and wanted to take it away from the local museum and…well, after all the ownership questions were settled, I guess she was auctioned to Chicago for over eight million dollars."

"You sound like you don't like that," Cope remarked.

Renee sighed. "The people who found her were doing a reasonably good job of caring for her, she was bringing money into the local economy, and, well…" Another sigh. "I guess she's in a better place now, and at least Cheyenne River and the local town got something for her."

"What are you planning to do with these fossils?" Gage wanted to know.

"That'll be up to the local tribe. Their land. I just want the information."

"Altruistic?"

Renee smiled. "Reasonable. I don't need to own the bones to learn from them and I'm not planning to open up a mountainside museum. Plus, Gray Cloud promised me as much access to the finds as I want."

A short while later, she and Cope hiked upward with fresh backpacks filled with dried foods and medical supplies just in case. Over their shoulders they strapped the insulated bottles of coffee.

"I'm sorry about all this," Cope remarked. "You needed this crap like a major headache."

She grabbed a handhold and decided that looking up at his backside was far from the worst view she'd ever had. "Things happen. Rare is the dig that goes without complication. I've got a friend in Turkey, an archaeologist, and he's going nuts trying to get his work done in between periods of unrest and combat, and living with the constant fear that something really priceless will get destroyed. I'll take this any day, as long as no one gets seriously hurt."

"I can see that." He turned and offered her a hand over a particularly rough part of the trail. "I saw where the Taliban blew up those Buddha carvings in the mountains. A crime against human history. I guess it's been even worse in Iraq with all the theft from the national museum there."

"The stuff we're losing can never be replaced," she agreed as she caught her breath. That last little push had been hard. Instead of opening her coffee, she reached for the mouthpiece and sipped from her camel pack. Time to change the water, she decided. It wasn't exactly fresh.

She'd have loved to drink straight out of that icy stream, but she knew the recklessness of that. Years ago on a camping trip, she'd learned the hard way that if beavers could get there, the water was apt to carry giardia. She never wanted to experience that again.

At last they reached the top. "Now it's a gamble," Renee remarked. "Do we gamble that if we stay at this end we won't get rock dropped on us?"

"Let me think about it. I want a cup of coffee first. You?"

Even inside her gloves her hands had begun to feel chilly, so she welcomed the idea. As they sat on boulders with their hands cupped around mugs, she studied the mess. "Part of me feels lucky," she said. "It doesn't seem to have covered up the important parts of the rock face. At least as far as I know."

"Yeah." He blew a breath over his coffee and a puff of steam arose. "On the other hand…"

She shook her head at him. "Let's not get to the other hand. We're eventually going to have to find a way to move that debris out so no one gets hurt. That'll waste a lot of time. Then we'll know if anything important got covered."

A few minutes later, she rose and walked over to the edge of the slide.

"Be careful," Cope called. "It's pretty much in a state of natural balance right now. Move the wrong stone and that may all come down."

"Which might not be so bad," she remarked. "No one's down below." But she didn't touch anything, merely studying the rocks she could see. Given the size of the fossil bed she believed she was trying to uncover, there was probably lots of good stuff buried in there. Dang. Moving it piece by piece would be a pain.

Glancing over her shoulder at the egg that had started all this, she wasn't sure that it was the most important thing after all. If someone was trying to drive them out, surely they thought there was something of more importance here.

And why was it so damn cold today? It was mid-May, and even here in these northern latitudes there was such a thing as summer. Last autumn when Gray Cloud had shown her this, it had been quite toasty, although with the low humidity it had felt invigorating. Now she had a team wrapped up in jackets and trying not to freeze their fingers off if they needed to use the stream water.

But thinking about the weather was only a distraction and she knew it. She looked over at Cope, who sat on his boulder and stared at the rock face as if it might answer the questions of the universe.

"Cope?"

"Yeah?"

"Why would the lower rockfall happen first?"

"Well, it could if there was a slight earth movement and it was more on edge than the upper level."

She nodded and returned her attention to the rock-slide. Fortunate indeed that none of them had been standing there when these rocks came down. The fall below had been much smaller, but still enough to break Larry's leg. This one, even with hard hats, could have done some true damage to a human body.

"How are we going to get it out of here?" Another distraction, thinking about the work rather than worrying about Larry and whether someone wanted to stop the dig. Easier to avoid it all. Oddly enough, she'd never before thought of herself as a person who avoided tough subjects. A new self-understanding made her uneasy.

"We'll move it carefully, rock by rock, with no one below." Cope's answer sounded calm and reasoned.

"Sure." Of course. No other way. It wasn't as if they could bring in heavy equipment to dispose of it.

"It'll slow us down," Cope added.

"Yeah." All of a sudden she wasn't worried about that. Her eyes felt hot and started to burn, and she realized it was all finally penetrating. No tears, she thought, squeezing her eyes closed. She wasn't the weepy sort.

She drew a couple of shuddery breaths and felt the tightness in her throat ease as her eyes blinked away the tears that never quite started.

But she was beginning to wonder if these fossils were worth the risk to any life.

Someone had been watching them. She, Denise and Cope had all felt it. For what possible reason? This? To hurt someone? Why?

What was valuable enough for that, unless it was just some sick mind?

"Renee?"

"What?"

"Come sit with me."

So she made her way over to the boulder beside his and sat on its reasonably flat surface. "What good will this do?"

"What?"

"Sitting here and staring at a bunch of fallen rocks. I ought to be starting to move them out of the way."

"Not on your own," he said firmly. "We'll take care of them. But right now, I want an assessment of what happened above. A good assessment, because you wouldn't want any of your team in the way of another rockslide."

She caught her breath. She hadn't even considered there might be another one. "Maybe I should just shut this dig down, at least temporarily. I don't want to risk lives."

"And maybe that's exactly what someone is hoping for."

She twisted her head to look at him. "What are you thinking, Cope?"

"I'm wondering what's here that's more important than the fossils. No clue, so far."

From across the gorge, through binoculars, the man watched. He knew this mountain like the back of his hand, had walked nearly its every inch. Now he had to save it for the man who'd hired him.

It struck him as a little strange that someone would be so worried about the fossil hunters, but equally strange that he was supposed to stop them, make them give up, and preferably without killing anyone.

That wasn't likely to work and he knew it. So did

this Broadus, although the guy pretended to be above it all, purely in it for the greater good.

Well, Stockman, the guy watching through binoculars across the gorge, believed in the greater good, too. A different good than Broadus believed in evidently. Didn't matter. He'd pull it all together, and if someone died…well, dying on a sacred mountain wasn't the worst fate.

He heard sounds approaching from behind, and darted quickly into a hummock of moss and decayed tree, becoming nearly invisible. Nobody would be looking for him, so it would be good enough.

Before too long he saw the neighboring rancher, Loren Butler, wending his way on horseback between the trees. The deep layer of pine needles mostly quieted the hoofbeats, but not entirely. Butler didn't seem to be in a hurry, or even especially attentive. But he *was* heading directly for the gorge. Why? Stockman's hands tightened around his binoculars.

Butler rode with the ease of a man who'd spent a great deal of his time on horseback. He also rode like a man who trusted his mount. The reins were slack; his legs and feet didn't send any commands. Stockman knew a moment's envy. He'd once had a horse like that.

But what the hell was Butler doing out here? The man had a ranch to run, and Stockman knew just how time-consuming that job was. It sure didn't leave a whole lot of time for wandering in the woods.

Maybe he'd heard all the hoopla with the evacuation and helicopter. That helicopter was hard to miss when it flew in. A reconditioned Bell UH-1 left over from Vietnam, its rotors made silent approach laughable.

So yeah, Butler could have heard it. Maybe he was

just curious. But ambling along like that didn't suggest an overwhelming curiosity.

Maybe Stockman needed to keep an eye on Butler as well. Then Butler cut to the rising side of the mountain, revealing an intimate knowledge of the terrain. Not many people knew that it was possible to get over the river gorge a mile upstream.

Remaining hunkered down, Stockman waited.

Even over the sound of the rushing water, the approach of horse's hooves was unmistakable. Renee started to lean over the edge, but Cope pulled her back. "I trusted that yesterday, but not today."

He had a point. Instead they both stood and looked down into the gorge. It wasn't long before they saw Loren Butler on horseback, picking his way through the stream and then up the path that would bring him to them.

"Him again?" Renee said. "What's he doing?"

"I wager he'll tell us," Cope said, a tremor of humor in his voice.

She pretend-frowned at him. "This place is beginning to feel like Union Station."

He laughed, a pleasant sound that bounced off the rock face directly in front of them.

"Howdy," Loren Butler called when he and his mount reached the top of the path. They both stopped before the rockfall. Renee rose and went to greet him.

"I wondered what happed," Butler said. "I saw the medevac copter. I hope the injury wasn't bad."

"Broken leg," Cope said, joining her. "What brought you up here?"

It sounded like an innocent question, but Renee realized Cope was looking for information. Butler paused a moment, then swung down from his saddle, walked his horse back ten feet and tethered it to a tree. The wind was picking up again, and instinctively Renee looked upward to the treetops. She didn't like the way they were tossing. Yeah, they needed bad weather on top of everything else.

Butler wore cowboy boots, great for riding in the stirrups, not so good for crossing this rough ground, but he managed it. He apparently understood the danger of the slide, because his move across the path they had created was cautious.

When he reached Renee and Cope, he looked backward and said, "This shouldn't have happened."

"Why do you say that?" Renee asked.

He settled his gaze on her. "I've been living around these mountains my entire life. They're mostly granite, except for a few areas of sandstone, like where you want to dig those fossils out. Anyway, point being, if that wanted to slide naturally, it would have happened after freezing and thawing during the winter, not after two months of dry weather. Ask your geologist friend."

"You know Claudia?" That surprised Renee.

"I wouldn't say I know her. Ran into her in town the other day and we jawed a bit about your fossils. Nice gal. Anyway, back to important matters."

He frowned from beneath the brim of his cowboy hat and scanned the rock face once again. "Gray Cloud will tell you the mountain opened this up for you." He gave Renee a piercing look. "And I'll tell you someone else is trying to close it down."

Renee drew a sharp breath. "Do you know who?"

Butler shook his head. "I'm just guessing because I

don't think that slide should have happened. But Claudia will know. Anyways, I saw the medevac fly in and I got to worrying about you folks. I tried to mind my own business, but that didn't work so well." His smile crinkled the corners of his eyes. "Around here we take care of each other or look the other way, depending. This time looking the other way didn't feel right."

"We were lucky," Cope said frankly. "Only one injury, what appears to be a simple leg fracture as far as I know."

Butler nodded.

"Pull up a rock," Renee suggested, drawing a laugh from both Cope and Butler. "We were sitting here staring at the mess we need to clean up and waiting for word from above."

"Above?" Butler found himself another boulder and looked up to the top of the cliff. "Who went up?"

Renee hesitated. Why should he care?

"Never mind. I hope it's the rock lady and a cop or two. Attempted murder burns in my craw."

Attempted murder. The words, spoken so matter-of-factly, sent a fresh chill coursing down Renee's spine. She hadn't allowed those words to cross her mind. Sure, she suspected someone had tried to shut down the site with the rockfalls, but it *hadn't* crossed her mind that they might have wanted to actually kill anyone. Suddenly, her jacket and gloves failed to warm her, and she fumbled when she tried to pour herself some coffee from her thermos. Without a word, Cope took the cup and jug from her and poured for her.

She seized it in both hands and brought it quickly to her mouth. Hot. Good. Murder?

"Coffee?" Cope offered Butler.

"No, thanks. I've got to be heading back before the shadows get much longer. But you all take care, hear? And if I run across any strangers nosing in these parts, I'll let you know."

Renee spoke. "It might not be a stranger." Gads, now her lips felt numb.

"Well, if it's somebody raised around here, I'm going to be mighty disappointed." He shrugged. "Guess it wouldn't be the first time for that, either."

Before he left, however, he sat staring at the rock face. "Never been much into dinosaurs, at least since I got older than six or seven, but I have to admit this has got me interested. Maybe even a little excited. You thinking about building a museum here if you find lots of good stuff?"

"That will be up to the tribe," Renee answered. "Their land, their find."

"So it should be. I got a little worked up when the whole world decided that fossil on the Northern Cheyenne reservation had to be moved. Wasn't like they weren't taking care of it." He looked straight at Renee. "Don't you let them do it again. Wyoming's fossils belong in Wyoming, and this branch of Cheyenne have full title. Damn sight more than they got for their gold."

Then he was off, picking his way across the rockfall and mounting again. With a fingertip to the brim of his hat, he bade them farewell and began riding away up the mountain.

"I think I like him," Cope remarked.

"Me, too." Then she faced him. "What do you think he was trying to find out?"

Cope paused, a study in thought. "How paranoid do you want me to be?"

"I thought so. If he was interested in what the chopper was doing here, he'd have come to the area of the base camp, wouldn't he?"

Now Cope took a minute before responding. She could almost see the wheels spinning behind his bright blue eyes. "That depends," he said finally. "He might have already been riding over on his property, in the mountains there. Or maybe he wanted to see if he stumbled on something on his way here. Or maybe..."

She waved her hand. "Okay, Cope. I get it. Mindreading is a waste of time."

"Well, we can speculate until the sun goes down, and we won't know anything for certain." He rose, absently dusting the back of his jeans, and looked back over the gorge.

He froze.

"Cope?" Renee felt her own heart quickening. "What's wrong?"

"Nothing. I thought I saw a glint of something across the gorge, but it could be anything and it's gone."

Just then the radio crackled but Renee didn't know exactly how to operate it, so she handed it to Cope. He squatted beside her and showed her the all-important button. "Cope here. What's up?"

They heard Short's voice. "We're headed back down to the camp. Join us there."

Renee started to stand, but then hesitated. "Maybe I should stay here. To keep an eye on things."

"Over my dead body," came the stern response. "Besides, if anyone wants to start another landslide, you won't be able to stop it and you could get killed. Nor will there be anyone up there to prevent them from doing it. Let's go."

She wanted to scowl at him but stifled the urge. She might not like it, but he was right.

On the way back down, her thoughts started drifting. There was Bears Ears National Monument, recently protected, and even more recently opened up to drilling. Some of her colleagues were having fits because there was a rich fossil bed there that included the full skeletons of some Triassic-era crocodilians. The loss of such a site would be immeasurable. They'd already had one theft of half a skull, and complete skulls such as they had at Bears Ears were rarer than gold. What if someone came in here and chiseled out half her egg, the part that was easy to reach? The remains might become nearly worthless.

Somehow she had to get to the root of this. Put a stop to it. Protect all the scientific knowledge that was awaiting a careful exposure.

Damn!

Then Cope startled her. "You have the prettiest frown. But then you're pretty regardless."

Her immediate response was to disagree. "I'm covered in dust!"

"Part of the appeal. Now tell me I'm out of line, boss. Oh, wait, you're the boss so you can't make a pass at me. I'm just a volunteer…"

If it was his intention, he succeeded. She released a laugh and felt the tension lift a bit. "Which way does sexual harassment go?"

That provided an interesting discussion as they descended to camp.

* * *

Stockman watched them leave and decided to call Broadus that night. Clearly he hadn't scared them off and might need to go further. Just how much further, he didn't know. Broadus had been clear that nobody better die, because it was Native American land and the Feds would be all over it.

Even Stockman didn't need anyone to explain why they didn't want the Feds involved. Those guys were worse than burrs. Once they made up their minds something was going on, they wouldn't let go until they'd found the dust in every nook and cranny anywhere. And worse, if you ever opened your yap to them and then didn't repeat yourself exactly, they could get you on lying to them.

Hell, who wouldn't lie to a Fed? Everyone wanted to cover their butts. So you had to be a clam. Stockman wasn't all that good at being a clam. He could manage it for just so long.

So no, no Feds. Tribal lands, major crime and, apparently from what Broadus said, that added up to FBI.

Part of Stockman wished he had known that before he agreed to this job. Stirring up a little trouble was one thing. Getting into it with serious law enforcement was another.

He muttered a few cusswords to himself, taking pleasure in the fact that since only trees and small animals would hear him, no one could get annoyed.

Life had come to a sorry state when a man couldn't utter four-letter words without receiving frowns of disapproval. Dang, those were *useful* words.

"Limited vocabulary," his mother the English

teacher used to sniff. "You need to be more creative with your language."

Creative how? He'd never figured out that one.

Chapter 8

They had quite a convocation around the campfire that night. Renee had advised the students who followed Larry into town to stay until they knew more about what had happened. Nobody argued with her.

That left the sheriff; the two deputies, Sanchez and Marcus; Claudia, who was beginning to bite her lip; and Cope and Renee.

It was enough. Cope took over making boxes of black beans and rice for dinner, while Sanchez made a huge amount of coffee in the large camp pot.

Everyone was quiet, and Renee had the distinct feeling that no one wanted to address what had happened today. As if speaking about it would make it more real. But it was already real. Larry was in the hospital. Word was he'd be released in the morning, but Renee doubted he'd be able to hobble his way up to the work site. One down.

She gnawed her lip as everyone took recycled paper plates and filled them with beans and rice. Coffee immediately followed and soon they were all gathered around. Still silent.

"We know it was no accident," she said finally, finding her voice. "We've been pretty sure of that since the slide earlier today. The question is, did we find out anything useful, and is this the game of *And then there were none*?"

"Whoa," Dalton said.

"Yeah," Cope added. "No way to be sure that anyone was *supposed* to be hurt."

Her hand tightened on the cheap tin fork she held. "Maybe not. But you're sure it was no accident."

"No," Claudia said quietly. "Someone worked hard to find a crevice and loosen that stone. Whether they expected such a large fall, or there to be one down below, I don't know."

Renee drilled her with a look. "How could the lower slide be an accident if it happened first?"

Claudia gave her a look that spoke volumes of sympathy, even as she took a professional tone. "Renee, that lower slide was probably not even intended. You know part of that lip tumbled sometime over the winter. It may have just been a bit insecure. So some banging around above might have shaken it loose enough to finish the job."

Renee shook her head, not denying it but still not certain she could accept the accident theory.

"Vibrations," Claudia said. "We've talked about how an earthquake affects the entire planet. People aren't truly appreciative of how those vibrations pass through rock. Someone chipping away above sent vibrations spreading out. They didn't need to be big vibrations. My opinion is that they reached a weakened spot on the lower lip. It was set up, accidentally, before we even got there this morning. Maybe sooner. We were driving some pegs into that rock face, too. More vibrations. Even with the chipping around that someone did above, all of that could have happened at any time, including when we weren't even there. Like the middle of the night."

At last Renee released her breath and let her shoulders relax. "But it was deliberate."

"Oh, no mistaking that," Claudia answered. "Someone wants to shut down this dig."

"The question," said Cope, "becomes why."

"I agree," said the sheriff, speaking at last. "The Bear brothers are keeping watch tonight, but I'm not sure the message hasn't already been sent. My men are going to start nosing around for anything unusual in the area, but without a clue as to why this should be happening…" He shrugged. "I make no promises."

"How well do you know Loren Butler?" Renee asked him.

"Pretty well. Why? Has he done something?"

"He showed up today, said he'd noticed the helicopter. He also came by the first day we started digging."

Gage shook his head. "I've known that man for thirty years. He doesn't strike me as the sort to get involved in something like this. Most who know him consider him to be forthright and as honest as the day is long."

"That was my impression, especially today," Renee admitted. "But we haven't seen anyone else around."

"Nobody has. Doesn't mean he's not there somewhere."

Cope, who'd been listening and saying little, finally entered the conversation. "All we have to go on is that it's very likely someone doesn't want this dig to continue. That leaves a whole range of suspects."

Renee met those blue eyes of his, now reflecting some of the red from the firelight, sort of like the wolf had the other night. "Meaning?"

"Well, it could be a tribal member who doesn't want to see sacred land torn up. It could be someone who doesn't want to see this part of the mountain become a point of interest for tourists. Not that I think a whole lot of people would go out of their way to get here. I'm just spitballing. I suppose there could be a lot of other reasons."

"Mining," said Claudia.

Renee's head whipped around. "Did you find something?"

"Nothing yet that would make an all-out war with the tribe attractive. I'm still waiting for all the data, though. It's entirely possible the unscrupulous would want this land for those reasons."

Cope spoke. "Isn't tribal land protected from that? Unless the tribe wants the mining?"

"Look around you," Renee said. "I told you about Bears Ears."

"But that was a national park," Claudia reminded her. "Easier to take away the protections. Still…" She frowned. "Anyway, we don't know what this is about. Mining seems like a stretch right now, but that could change."

Shortly after they cleaned up, Deputy Marcus took

the bag of trash and put it in the back end of his SUV. "Less to attract bears," he remarked as he slammed the tailgate shut. "You want, I can stay tonight with the Dasher."

"Thanks so much," Renee said, "but Cope and I will be fine. I think the action is over for today, especially with Short and Tall walking the area up in the mountains."

"I agree," said Cope. "Plus, I've been in worse situations."

Renee urged everyone else to head into town for the night. "I'll worry a lot less, okay?"

They exchanged good-nights and Renee watched the taillights fade into the extremely lightless Wyoming night. It was time for the quarter moon, but it hadn't risen yet. Darkness closed around them like a thick, muffling blanket. There must be clouds above, because the usual diamond scattering of stars didn't show.

She felt a warm hand take hers and she looked toward Cope. There were still enough embers from the nearby fire to highlight his face, making him seem mysterious. Without a word, he drew her close and wrapped her snugly in his arms.

"We'll get through this," he said, his breath warm against her ear. "Whatever we're up against, he's a novice. Everyone's giving him too much credit. He *accidentally* hurt Larry. Which brought the attention of the police. I'm sure he didn't want that. No, you were supposed to scatter and run because the ground is unstable. Except you're not stupid and you're not a rabbit. So we'll find him and deal with him."

His embrace was so comforting. His words and

voice were soothing. She just wished she were capable of believing in them.

But she wasn't. Whoever was behind this wasn't going to walk away simply because she and her team kept digging.

"He'll try something worse."

"Maybe. We'll see. But this time we'll be prepared."

"How?"

"I'll show you in the morning. In the meantime, I suggest we let Short and Tall do their thing up there, and we get some rest down here. Tomorrow could wind up being a very long day."

The sound of a wolf's howl pierced the night. Beautiful, forlorn and solitary. A warning or a promise?

"They don't seem to be far away tonight."

"Let me build up the fire a bit. Come on. It'll push the dark things back."

As simply as that she found them sitting side by side before dancing flames while he held her hand. And it felt so darn natural.

For a little while, Cope didn't speak. He loved the quiet of the night woods, the sound of wind sighing in the tree tops. There were plenty of animals busy out there, following their nocturnal lives, but they were quiet about it, even more quiet than the animals in the daytime. During that time many animals were large enough to ignore the hawks that might fly over, or even each other if they avoided a direct confrontation. At night many of the animals were smaller, and they didn't want to attract the attention of an owl or some other predator for whom they'd make a nice snack.

The dividing line between night and day created whole different worlds.

"It was a tough day," he remarked after a while. "Long, exhausting. Mainly because of fear." Her fingers felt so small within his grasp. Yet she was a powerful woman. Of that he had no doubt.

"Do you get afraid?" she asked.

"Hell, yeah. Do I look like a robot?"

At least that pulled a small laugh from her. He squeezed her hand, then eased his grip. He was willing to bet that a day like today had never been a part of her plan. He'd seen her excitement more than once over the last year about these fossils. Now today she'd been faced with an injured intern and a clear attempt by persons unknown to interfere with her discoveries.

What should have been simple and endlessly fascinating may have become seriously dangerous. Sticky. Now she'd have to make all kinds of mental and emotional adjustments, and he wondered how long that would take and the kind of changes she'd make.

Right now she was sitting in the dark next to a man she didn't know very well, all alone basically, dealing with today's events and trying to piece things together. A far cry from the evenings the team had spent around the campfire chatting, telling stories, looking forward to the next day.

Was she even able to look forward now? He suspected it would take a helluva lot more to make her abandon the site, but how much more? And what if someone wanted to push it to that limit?

Was she sitting there wondering if people would die? Possibly feeling selfish?

Damn, he didn't know of any way to get inside her

head. His years of experience in the Marines had been a whole different ball of wax. Zipped up, tight-lipped, rarely did anyone spill their guts. Not that he thought Renee needed to spill her guts, but he didn't even have a can opener in his tool kit to get her to spill just a little of what she was thinking.

Maybe it was none of his business, but the simple fact was that he cared. Worse, it was beginning to feel like more than a casual caring. And that was probably the furthest thing from *her* mind right now.

Besides, he'd dated often enough to know he didn't seem to have anything a woman truly wanted. The minute things began to get heavy, the minute bits of his past eased their way out, they seemed all too happy to move on. He was no beast, but he certainly had some uncivilized parts to him.

He stifled a sigh and forced his attention back to the really important matters. "Got a plan?"

That made her laugh again, but it was no cheerful sound. "Plan for what? I can't prevent another rockslide, so I can't protect my team. Maybe I should just send everyone home and work on this on my own."

He hesitated. "We may be able to do something about the rockslides."

She turned to look at him, her expression almost painfully hopeful. "How?"

"I asked Gage to talk to our road engineer, Blaine Harrigan. I'm sure he's dealt with situations like this when they cut a new road."

"Oh, that would be great!"

"I'm not making any promises. There might be reasons he can't do anything about this, from cost to equipment. But I thought it made sense to put my finger in the wind. If nothing else, Blaine might have some ideas."

She nodded, but some of the distress slipped off her face, letting it smooth a bit. "Even if he just has some ideas. Cope, our time is so limited here. I don't want to let this go another winter. Everything that opened up might close again." She hesitated. "Then, of course, we have to clear everything with the tribe. Sacred ground is serious stuff."

Almost as if summoned by their conversation, Gray Cloud emerged from the night and into the reddish firelight. "Sacred ground is serious indeed," he answered her, "and someone messed with it."

"Pull up a chair and join us," Renee suggested. "I think we've still got some hot coffee." Indeed the pot was sitting on a rock by the fire.

"No, thanks." He pulled over a chair, though, and sat facing them across the fire. "The Bears told me what they found up there. Someone was jimmying along a crack."

"So it seems," Cope answered.

"He'd better get his tail down off that mountain then," Gray Cloud said without a hint of humor. Dead serious.

Renee squirmed a little, Cope noticed, but didn't say anything. Then Gray Cloud smiled.

"You don't believe me, Renee. That's fine. I hope you never have reason to."

He waved an arm upward. "This mountain is older than mankind, older than types of animals it shelters right now. That's why you want to dig out those fossils."

"True," she agreed.

Cope watched, waiting. He knew more was coming.

It had to be. Gray Cloud wasn't much of a talker, but when he spoke he had more than a few words to say.

"Mountains are some of the oldest dwellers on this planet," he continued. "These particular mountains are younger than many, but their ages are still staggering. Among the first was Thunder Mountain."

Renee leaned forward. "How do you know that?"

"The mountain speaks to those who listen." He said it the same way someone might have said the sky was blue. "Whether you listen or not, Thunder Mountain is aware. Whether you believe in it or not, the mountain can defend itself. Treat it with respect. Someone has failed to do that. For some reason the mountain opened a cleft full of treasures for those who appreciate those treasures. Someone has tried to interfere."

Renee nodded slowly. Cope had felt during his time in Afghanistan that at least some of those mountains had been alive and aware. He'd put it down to being weary to the bone, but the locals had been of a different opinion. He was certain that Renee's scientific background rebelled against these ideas as much as his did, but at this point in his life he was prepared to keep an open mind about a whole lot, including this mountain.

Renee stirred and he realized she was still holding on to his hand, as if she didn't care that anyone saw. What did that mean, if anything?

"Why is it called Thunder Mountain?"

Gray Cloud smiled. "Because sometimes it speaks, Renee. Not very often, and few of us have a memory of it even though we have stories handed down. But there was a time *I* can remember. A perfectly cloudless day and without warning, the mountain spoke. Thunder rolled down its sides, deafening. Then the sound was gone and we wondered about it. We're still wondering, but it happened. After that the wolves appeared, so maybe the mountain was welcoming them. Make of it what you will. I'm not trying to convert you to my way of thinking, but I've heard the mountain speak in many ways, most of them not that loud."

"I think I'd be petrified if thunder rolled down that mountain on a cloudless day."

Gray Cloud laughed. "You don't need to be frightened. You're welcome here. But whoever started that slide…he may be in trouble. As for you talking about needing our permission to stop the slides from occurring again? We probably won't have a problem with that. History is buried in those rocks, a story we want to learn. Within reason, we'll help make the site safe for you."

Stockman made his way to the truck stop on the edge of Conard City and bought one of the burner phones on sale there. He doubted it was needed but the action made him feel like a superspy, a bolster to his self-confidence he was needing right now.

Now if he called Broadus, no one would be able to trace it. Good, yeah? Especially since he didn't want anything to point his way if someone got hurt.

But he also didn't understand exactly how a landslide was supposed to scare anyone off. It was the mountains, for Pete's sake.

"Just make 'em edgy," Broadus had said. "That'll slow 'em down and that's what I want right now."

Okay. Right now. Did that mean he'd want Stockman to kill someone later? Because Stockman wasn't a killer. Not by choice. Any deaths in his past had been purely accidental. Like today. He'd never expected the rocks to slide on the lower level and hit that kid. No, he'd expected a clean fall that would make everyone nervous.

But then the kid had been hurt. And the cops had shown up. Over a landslide? But he heard them talking, bits and pieces anyway, and learned they didn't think the slide was accidental.

So now what? The woman had sent her team into town but she was still camped below the fossil site with that guy, some college professor. The retired soldier turned teacher didn't strike Stockman as much of a threat. For that matter, neither did the boss lady. Digging up bones was hardly preparation for serious trouble.

And Stockman suspected that at some point he was going to be asked to make serious trouble, to really throw a monkey wrench in the works of this dig.

What was it with that Butler guy, too? Second time he'd shown up, but this time he'd hung around awhile and talked. Somebody else Stockman needed to worry about?

Screw it. He ordered a huge platter of fried ham, scrambled eggs and home fries, savoring every mouthful. He could eat breakfast any time of day.

After he paid his bill, he stepped outside, filled his lungs with the diesel fumes of the rumbling, resting trucks in the parking lot, then headed back to the mountain.

Nobody could have been more surprised than he was when he returned and found Gray Cloud sitting at a campfire with the other two. Hell, that was one guy Stockman had hoped not to have to deal with. Gray

Cloud gave him the creeps. The man seemed to see right into you.

Gads. Stockman hung back in the deep shadows, hoping he was invisible to that man's eyes. Hunkering down, he waited for everything to quiet down so maybe he could work some more mischief at the dig. Frustrate them. Make them walk away, at least for a while.

He hadn't expected it to be a difficult assignment. Maybe he was wrong.

The only thing lacking from the group around the fire, Renee thought, was her cousin Mercy. They'd been following separate paths for years, but they'd made a point of keeping in touch and getting together whenever their trails crossed.

Tonight would have been a great night for such a crossing. The wind in the trees stiffened suddenly and she looked up. "Are we getting a storm?" she asked Gray Cloud.

"Maybe. It feels like it."

"I didn't think there was anything in the forecast." Instinctively she looked back to the path up the mountain. She should have found ways to string a few tarps up there. A heavy rain could cause new instabilities they'd have to deal with.

"It isn't always in the forecast," Gray Cloud replied.

"No," Cope agreed. "Big mountains like this can create their own local weather that won't show up in a forecast. Not enough data points."

"Or," said Gray Cloud, smiling faintly, "they will it to be."

Cope laughed. "I'm not going to argue," he said, spreading a hand. "All I hope is that if our miscreant is still out there that he gets soaked to the bone. That's never comfortable on a mountain night. And we can just move beneath a canopy." He indicated one of them that had been set up to shelter beneath.

"Speaking of canopies," Renee said. "I was wondering if we should put some tarps up at the site. A heavy rain can make the ground slippery and unstable again. Of course, it's too late to do it tonight. And they probably wouldn't have withstood the rockslides anyway."

"We're asking the county engineer to come out and look at the situation," Cope reminded her. "If anyone knows how to stabilize the rock, he will."

"Good man, Blaine Harrigan," Gray Cloud remarked. "He's worked with us several times to protect our heritage from the addition of roads that might be convenient for someone else but useless to us. Invasive. I'll be glad to hear what he proposes." Then he eyed Renee again. "Is Claudia in town with the others?"

"Yes, I thought it best not to expose my team unnecessarily." Renee hesitated. "Did you need something from her?"

"Talk," said Gray Cloud. "That one may not hear the mountains, but the rocks speak to her."

Renee nodded. "They certainly do. We're still waiting for her test results to come in, to see if there's a reason someone would want to shut this dig down. It seems strange, with the tribe's permission. It's not like this land belongs to anyone else."

"There are many who would not agree with you. And some among the tribe may not be pleased by the notoriety this could bring our way." He laughed quietly. "Personally, I think we're so far out of the way that only fossil hounds will want to come look. I'm not expecting to be putting up hot dog stands and neon lights."

Cope had to laugh with him.

"And no cigar-store Indians," Renee remarked a bit tartly.

"Ah, you've been to the Black Hills."

"A travesty."

"The people tried to get the land back."

"Instead," said Cope, "all they got was some money they've refused to take. There seems to be a disconnect somewhere between the dollar value of land and the sacred value."

"A distinction that can be very hard to explain," Gray Cloud agreed. "Regardless, the land was lost. This land isn't lost, and we intend to make sure it isn't. The history Renee will pull from the rocks will be fascinating, but not a threat to anyone. As far as we know."

Renee voiced a point. "Claudia didn't seem to think there was much here worth wanting except the fossils. So maybe this will all pass away."

Cope looked a bit quizzically at her. "And when has life ever been that easy?"

Stockman watched Gray Cloud get up, say goodnight and leave. In the other direction, thank goodness. He decided to wait awhile and see if these two got up to anything, and wished he could hear what they said, but he decided that getting closer would be unwise. Ten minutes. Then he'd leave and find a place to call the boss.

Rising, Gray Cloud laughed, reminding Renee once again of what Mercy had found so attractive in him.

At first, Mercy had said, he'd been a pretty much taciturn monolith, worried about his mountain and the new wolf pack she was studying. But he'd proved to have other sides as well, among them the man who could laugh and, except when it came to his mountain, was able to take things lightly. Renee supposed there were plenty of other things Gray Cloud didn't take lightly as an elder of his people, but Mercy hadn't mentioned them and Renee hadn't run into them.

The mountain, though...that was a touchy spot.

She realized almost abruptly that she was still holding Cope's hand. All this time! What must he think of her? But he'd made no effort to tug away so she guessed he wasn't annoyed in any way. Still, they had a professional relationship, and she had seriously breached it.

"Sorry," she said, starting to pull her hand away. His fingers tightened.

"No need," he said. "I'm enjoying this. You know, thinking back I can remember plenty of times I sat with my unit around a small fire when we felt safe enough to light one, but I swear I'm quite sure I never held a lovely woman's hand when I did it."

He brought a smile instantly to her face, and even though muscles complained a bit because they were growing cold, it felt good to smile. She sought safer ground. "I can see why my cousin is head over heels with Gray Cloud."

"Easy to see. Are you getting a little cold? I can put more wood on the fire unless you want to crawl into your sleeping bag."

The day should have left her exhausted. Apart from the slide and Larry's injury, it had been endlessly stressful. She didn't think she'd ever really relaxed a muscle from the time of the first rockfall.

But instead of feeling weary to the bone, it was as if Cope's touch fed energy to her. "A little more wood would be nice. I don't feel at all ready to sleep."

"Good enough."

Of course, that meant he had to release her hand, and she felt the absence of his touch immediately. *Get your head straight*, she told herself. *Stop acting like a kid with a schoolgirl crush.* Cope was just being nice to her, taking care of her. He seemed like the care-taker sort.

He gathered some dried wood from a stack her team had been steadily building over the last couple of weeks. It didn't take much to get the friendly blaze leaping again and shedding warmth in every direc-tion. Renee instinctively held out her hands toward the flames as Cope sat beside her again.

"I have a challenge," he said.

"What's that?"

"Let's talk about anything except the crazy things that have been happening around here. We can jaw it to death, but I don't think we'll get any closer to an-swers without more info."

"It's true," she agreed. "I hope Claudia gets the rest of her results back, soon, but even that may not give us answers. So what should we talk about?"

"A sky that has more stars than you can count." He reached out and claimed her hand again in a gentle grip. "I was amazed once by a friend. She'd lived her entire life in the metropolis we call the East Coast, and she didn't even know you could see the Milky Way from everywhere on Earth because she'd never seen it. I took her on a nice long drive to a place that didn't have much light pollution and she was totally wowed. That sky we have up there? Not everyone gets to enjoy it."

"That's such a shame. I've seen photos of the earth from space and you can see those sprawling places that are simply whited out from lights, but I never thought about not being able to really see the sky."

"Most people probably don't even miss it," he said a bit drily. "How could they? But there are places in the desert where the sky seems close enough to touch, and you can understand why our ancestors found it so easy to believe the gods came from above. Then, if you can lie still on your back long enough, you can actually see the stars wheeling overhead as the earth turns. I call it heaven's clock."

Her head tipped back against the bar of the chair as she stared upward at nature's marvel. "You can tell time by it?"

"I can tell the passage of time. I often have as long as I could see enough sky. If you have a general idea of your latitude you can count the hours between dusk and dawn, which can be really useful."

She imagined it could, especially if you were a soldier.

"Anyway, I didn't mean to get geeky about the night sky. It's just so awesome."

She couldn't argue that. And what was more, sharing it with him made it even better. "I think too many of us fail to look up, and I count myself among them. Always busy, always preoccupied, missing the most beautiful things just because we don't look for them."

"Life kinda keeps us busy." He shifted a little in his

chair, and the movement caused his hand to rub lightly against hers. "I used to dream of a vacation on a beach somewhere on an isolated island. Nothing but the gentle whisper of waves and the endless sky above."

"Used to? Why don't you still dream about it?"

"Dreams are nice but they need to be practical. I could get to a beach some summer, I'm sure, but it wouldn't be on a deserted island. Too dang pricey."

"Same here." She felt him shift to look at her.

"No desert islands for you?"

She stared up at the stars, reminiscing. "You'll laugh."

"Promise I won't."

"I wanted to travel to the stars."

She felt him sit up a little straighter. "Be an astronaut?"

"Heck, no," she admitted. "I wanted to travel farther than the International Space Station or a shuttle flight. I want to lift off and keep going and maybe find another inhabited world."

He gave a low whistle. "That's kind of amazing."

"Also ridiculous, but we're talking about dreams here. When I was in high school, I'd lie on my back in the grass staring up at the stars like we are right now. Except there weren't as many of them visible where I was, but a lot anyway. And while I'd lie there, I could almost feel myself starting to fall upward into the stars. And somewhere out there, I was absolutely sure, was another girl just like me, staring up at her own nighttime sky and wondering about the same things. Even after all this time I can remember the image of her I always had. For some reason she was standing at the waterline on a huge beach with an endless ocean in front of her."

"I like it. That's cool."

She laughed a little. "Of course, you're talking to a woman who when she was a kid could *not* be persuaded that Lake Michigan wasn't the ocean."

"I've seen that lake. It'd be hard to persuade anyone it isn't an ocean."

"Maybe. Anyway, my great-grandfather captained an ore freighter on the Great Lakes. Maybe that was what gave me my hankering to travel long-distance."

"Another solar system seems like a much longer trip than taking a shuttle ride."

"Or sailing the Great Lakes," she admitted on a laugh. "I always loved the sea, though, so sometimes I wonder how I wound up so far away from it."

"That can be fixed. When you shut down the dig for the winter, you can head south to the Gulf Coast."

"Nah, I'll be back in the classroom and lab."

"Christmas then. A nice long cruise."

"What a lovely idea," she remarked. "I wonder how long it would take me to go stir-crazy."

He chuckled. "You probably wouldn't. First of all, most cruise liners are big enough to get lost on. Secondly, they actually let you get off and walk dry land every other day or so. Usually on junkets or what they call shore excursions."

"I'm not the junket type," she admitted. "I tend to want to wander on my own, take my own time. If I'm lucky I'll have a few friends with me who feel the same way."

He hesitated, then said, "Well, there might be some places you'd visit where you wouldn't want to wander on your own. Not every country likes us, and not every one is peaceful."

"True." She turned a little on her side so she could see him better. "I guess I've lived a sheltered life."

When she'd turned in her chair, she'd released his hand. He took the opportunity to throw a few more sticks on the fire. Embers danced upward until they vanished in the darkness.

"Depends on what you mean by sheltered."

She tipped her head a bit. "You were a Marine, right? You went to war. You've seen and done things that make me feel naive."

"Hold on there," he said quietly. The crackle from the fire was a contrasting sound of cheer. "War is never a good experience. Be glad you're naive."

"I guess that came out wrong." Stirring, she sat up and stretched, then regretted it as the chilly air found its way inside her clothing. "Dang, is it ever going to warm up?"

"At night not so much. You want warmer we should camp in the valley."

"Too far away. I'm just being a wimp. And I'm sorry if I seemed to be making light of your experiences. I wasn't."

"I didn't think you were."

"Good. I'd never make light of that. I meant only that I feel…parochial. Where have I been? What have I done?"

"Well, you're here in the wilds of Wyoming making what you believe will be a history-changing find if it bears out. That's pretty spectacular. You don't have to go to Belize and discover a new Mayan temple."

"Lots of those to find," she remarked.

"Still. Is it true a lot of them are being left buried to preserve them?"

She nodded, pulling her jacket closer around her. "It's true. They've been protected for centuries under accumulated dirt and even growing trees. Exposing them to the air isn't really good for that limestone. It deteriorates. And then there are the paintings. Much better to save them for future generations with better techniques and equipment. Of course, it seems a lot of them haven't been found yet. Satellite imagery is picking them out, but then people can't find a way to get to some of them."

"I like that. People lived there once and now we can't find a way to reach them. A giant puzzle."

"The whole thing's a puzzle. A huge civilization with major cities and all of it abandoned. The Maya remain, but not the occupied cities. Lots of theories for that."

She sat up, realizing she was beginning to shiver. "I guess I need to hit the sack. I may not feel sleepy, but my body is beginning to tell me it's done."

"Go crawl in and get warm. I'll stay up for a while and tend the fire."

"You could just put it out."

"Nah. I like it." He flashed a grin. "It keeps the wild animals at bay, too. I wouldn't mind conversing with a wolf, but I have a different opinion of bears, especially grizzlies."

"I don't think there are many grizzlies around here." She rose, stuffing her hands into her pockets. "Although Gray Cloud would be likely to invite them and protect them."

"Hah!"

His laugh still rang among the trees as she disappeared into her tent.

That guy clearly intended to sit watch tonight with that fire for company. Well, at this point that wasn't much of a problem for Stockman. He'd been told not to do anything too soon after the rockfall, and he was frankly glad of that.

Did Broadus have any idea how creepy it had been to stand at the top of that cliff and work those rocks loose? Had he even thought that it would take almost nothing to make a landslide begin, but what if it hadn't gone according to plan?

What if everything had bollixed up? What if Stockman had fallen with the rocks? He could be dead right now, but he supposed that wouldn't make any difference to Broadus. Hell no, it'd probably give him the result he wanted without making it seem like an attack on the paleontologists.

Stockman began to wonder just how much he mattered to Broadus. A thousand dollars? An excuse not to make the second half of the payment? Or less?

Killing Stockman sure would get Broadus what he wanted without drawing suspicion to the site.

Cussing under his breath, Stockman headed back through the trees to the truck he'd parked a couple of miles away. Something wasn't right, he told himself for the umpteenth time.

Don't kill anybody. Just delay the work.

Huh?

That didn't sound like much of a plan at all. He was

not supposed to know what his betters were up to. He was supposed to be the dumb muscle.

But how dumb could you be to set up that rockslide so that it came down without killing someone? Huh? Sure, that kid had a broken leg, but Stockman had had a few of those himself. In a day or two the kid would be running around here again in a walking cast and a single crutch for balance. So yeah, no dummy could have accomplished that delicate a job.

He reached his truck, beat his battered cowboy hat on his leg to remove any loose pine needles, then slid into the driver's seat, slamming the door with great satisfaction as he locked out everything. Broadus wouldn't be able to get him tonight because he'd changed cell phones again. If a damn cell could even reach here. He had no desire at all to open the new phone to see if it found a signal.

Broadus was crazy, and he'd allowed himself to be talked into being crazy along with him. Always a good thing, right? No. Almost never. And the amount of the promised money shouldn't have allowed him to be deluded, either. For the love of man, hadn't he learned anything in his forty-odd years?

Then there was this guy he was supposed to meet, someone who didn't want this dig, either. Bunch of damn bones seemed to be getting an awful lot of interest.

Stockman turned on the ignition and began to slowly roll away from the mountain. Damn mountain gave him the creeps, too. He could hardly wait to get away from here, and he didn't think it had to do with the stories running around. There weren't a whole lot of them, but the people who lived in these parts seemed to share the idea with the Native Americans that that mountain was alive.

Damned if it didn't feel like it sometimes. Sometimes he wanted to bang his head on the steering wheel, just for being such a damn fool. Never should have taken this job. Never should have messed with that damn mountain, alive or dead. Shouldn't have agreed to run some bone hunters off, or at least scare them away for a while.

What was the freaking point? The fossils were there and they weren't going anywhere. They were on tribal land, which might as well have been surrounded by a neon "do not touch" sign. They weren't about to let anyone do anything with that land unless they wanted them to.

Sure, you could take the land away or mine it if you got your papers in order. He didn't quite understand how that worked, but he'd seen it done other places. But why would anyone want that heap of rock and fossils enough to risk trouble over it? Enough to pay a guy just to slow them down?

The more he thought about it, the more uneasy he got. Stockman didn't like working jobs where he didn't know what was going on. Slow down the dig, keep them from pulling out any good fossils, don't hurt anyone… He didn't quite buy that bit about not hurting anyone. In his experience, people who got in the way often wound up dead.

Don't hurt anyone. What the hell kind of plan was that? Why not just blow up the whole dig? That'd send them running for sure. And then there'd be no fossils.

Honestly, no matter how hard he thought about it, he couldn't imagine why those fossils were so important.

So it had to be something else. Trouble was, he couldn't imagine what else. Gold had played out here years ago. He knew because he'd asked around. Occasionally some greenhorns would show up and pan the rivers and creeks. The jeweler in town said one guy had turned up just enough gold flakes from panning to make a slender band for his girlfriend's engagement ring. A summer of work for that?

He knew some guys who hunted for other kinds of gemstones in the mountains, but not around here. And even when they found a rich deposit, they barely made enough to live on.

Not a great way to make a living.

Of course, his current method wasn't yielding very good results, either. Stockman had always figured that he was destined to live on the water and smoke fine cigars while pretty women brought him drinks. Not exactly original, and he figured he'd die from the boredom, but *this*?

Then he reminded himself he'd accomplished the first step in his mission. A few more steps and the bone folks would decide to take the rest of the summer off and he, Stockman, could leave that godforsaken mountain and move on to something that suited him better.

He couldn't exactly figure out how he'd gotten involved in this in the first place, except a friend of a friend who worked for Broadus had suggested it would be easy money.

He sighed and gave up his internal squabble for one night. He'd completed the first step. He reached into his pocket, pulled out a cigarillo and stopped long enough to light it. The cigarillo would do. So would the next few days before he had to act again. Lull them.

Then when another surprise happened they'd be even more shocked.

Yeah. Stupid job or not, he was good at everything he did. And maybe he'd never deliberately killed before, but he wasn't against it if he needed to do it. He'd like it to be that Gray Cloud, but he'd settle for that self-important guy who thought he was guarding something at the fire.

One guy. Useless. Stockman was far better than that.

Chapter 9

The morning dawned slowly, or at least it seemed so to Renee. When she opened her eyes inside her tent, she wasn't sure it was morning at all. Yet she could smell the rich aroma of freshly perking coffee.

Gads, Cope must already be up and at 'em. Of course, the thing about camping, which she'd learned years ago, was that your biological clock quickly tuned to the sun. It didn't take long before you were rising early and falling asleep early. And the thing was, if you weren't living by the clock, you didn't even notice.

She quickly changed into some clean clothes. One thing she definitely did not like about camping was having to dress in the morning in chilly, damp clothes. Maybe she should roll them up and put them at the bottom of her sleeping bag the way her dad had suggested so long ago. Who out here would care if she looked like she'd slept in them, not just above them?

A soft little giggle escaped her. Once her boots were tied, she eased out to greet the day.

The sun hadn't yet risen above the eastern horizon but was busy announcing its pending arrival with streamers of gold and pink. The air smelled so fresh, of pine needles and aging loam, not to mention the fire and the coffee.

"Morning," Cope said, appearing from the direction of his tent. He'd changed, too, into a bright blue flannel Western shirt and jeans that weren't already covered with tons of dust and dirt. "Coffee's almost ready. I waited to start making breakfast until you got up."

"Thanks. I'll help."

In the pale dawn light, barely brighter than night, or so it seemed, he looked almost archetypal. Dressed for the woods, a geologist's hammer and pick attached to his belt, wide shoulders and narrow hips...

Renee sighed at herself. Could she think of any better way than that to unbalance the team and create tensions? Nope. Getting involved with Cope was bound to put sensitivities on high alert and maybe make some think there was favoritism. No, it was best to put that on the back burner. The very backmost burner. Like out of her mind entirely.

But dang, he looked good.

He built up the fire, poured them coffee and asked, "You in a hurry to eat?"

"Nope. Coffee before all else."

He laughed. "A woman after my heart. Hey, I was brushing my teeth a little earlier and I remembered a funny experience. A package of cheap toothbrushes arrived at the forward operating base, along with minuscule tubes of toothpaste. But what was so funny was everybody was happy to get a chance at some personal hygiene until they tried those brushes. Have you ever had to pick toothbrush bristles out from between your teeth?"

She gaped. "Seriously?"

"I kid you not. And there was a distinct lack of floss to help with the issue. One guy was threatening to burn them out of his mouth. We dissuaded him." He shrugged. "I don't think he really would have, but I can understand his frustration."

"What an awful thing to do to you guys. Could you do anything about it?"

"We complained and then made a bonfire with them. One wag sent a photo of the fire to HQ." He smiled as he remembered. "Took a couple of months but we got better toothbrushes after that. Sometimes the lowest bidder is just a con job."

"More like war profiteering, from the sound of it."

His smile widened. "Hey, that's a time-honored tradition."

Renee shook her head, smiling faintly, and sipped her coffee. Man, the first cup on a chilly morning outdoors was better than ambrosia. She closed her eyes, savoring the taste and aroma. Then, much as she wanted to enjoy the peaceful sunrise, she spoke. "Do you think that landslide was intended to kill?"

"Hard to know intentions." He leaned forward, grabbed the coffeepot and freshened both their cups. "It *could* have killed, although it's interesting that it happened at an end of that ravine where almost no one was working. Plus, it had to have been set up during the night or someone would have heard our perpetrator chipping at rock."

"You're right. No way to tell. It's just making me uneasy." In fact, now that the shock of it had passed, she felt a million butterflies in her stomach. What if something worse happened? What if one of her team got seriously hurt? She wouldn't blame them at all for abandoning ship. And weren't Tall and Short supposed to be on the lookout? Although in fairness, she supposed even they had to sleep sometimes, and they couldn't be everywhere at once.

"How well do you know Gray Cloud?" Cope asked her.

She swiveled her head and looked at him sharply, the butterflies dancing more rapidly. "Are you suggesting something?"

"Absolutely not. Just casual conversation. We've met a few times. Nice guy. But your cousin is married to him, so I just wondered. He seems like an impenetrable box of secrets sometimes."

She had to smile at that. "That's what Mercy said, too, at first. I guess they got past that. I've talked with him several times over the years. We get together like family. Maybe because we are." She shook her head, realizing her command of words hadn't quite awakened with her, then laughed. "I'm sure there were easier ways to say that."

His blue eyes twinkled, and his face reddened along with the sky as the sun poked over the horizon to the east. "It's early. I need at least three cups of coffee to function."

The shiver that passed through her as his eyes met hers had nothing at all to do with the temperature. "Anyway," she said, trying to change the direction of her thoughts, "I always liked him. He doesn't open up quickly, but once he decides he likes you? No better man. Mercy feels very lucky. And I agree with her. He's truly honorable in a way that I often think died in the last century."

"I don't think it went completely out the window, but words like *honor* and *duty* aren't heard very often anymore. Not in ordinary conversation."

She eyed him. "But in the military?"

"Drilled into us."

She nodded and leaned back a little, cradling her coffee and keeping her eyes on the day's dawning. It was amazing how fast light washed the world when even the smallest bit of sun poked up. So honor and duty were drilled into him? She liked that. Her own family had been strong on those principles, and it sometimes troubled her that so many people seemed to think they were archaic words.

"What are you going to do?" he asked without warning.

Back to the problem at hand. No talk of starry skies or dawning days. Business. And he was right. "I'm not sure. I don't want anyone else to get hurt, but at the same time, I'm not giving up that site. Priceless fossils are in there. New knowledge. Walking away would be a crime. If someone wants me out of there, I'll pass along the location of the site and others will come after me."

"Which is what makes this even weirder. Someone used a pry bar on a crack in the rock to loosen it. That rock could have fallen at any time, as we discussed, including the middle of the night. That basically announces no intent to kill. Frighten you away? Maybe. But why?"

"If it made sense, we'd know what to do about it."
Renee started to sip her coffee and realized it had gone
cold. She tossed the liquid away onto the bare ground.
As she started to reach for the coffeepot, Cope beat
her to it. He refilled her cup and she cradled it in both
hands.

"You ready for breakfast?" he asked.

She shook her head. Those damn butterflies wouldn't
leave her alone and her nerves were stretching like fine
wire. No intent to kill, but clearly an intent to disrupt.
If someone seriously wanted her and her team out of
there, the situation could get truly dangerous. How long
could she stay here without causing the disruption to
turn into something worse? Like seriously injuring or
killing someone. She needed to give her team a chance
to just leave. They shouldn't be risking their necks. That
hadn't been part of the job description.

But she thought again of the fossils up there, the
promise of that egg to tell a previously unknown story.
She could send her entire team away, but she would
stay and keep digging.

Certainty settled over her, calming her nerves. She
stood up. "They'll have to kill me to get me out of
here."

She felt Cope's gaze on her but ignored it and went
to start breakfast. This morning she'd give her entire
team a chance to quit with a high grade. They didn't
need to stick their necks out because they were afraid
of a bad grade.

A few seconds later, Cope joined her at the cook
table where she was trying to turn powdered eggs into
something edible.

"Wish we had bacon," he remarked. "I'm also thinking a bakery run might be smart in the evenings. Some croissants, some Danish…"

"Oh stop," she said. "Gads, Cope, I'm looking at powdered eggs and milk that's been irradiated so it won't spoil and you're talking about Danish?"

"Because of certain past experiences, I'm not averse to eating well when I'm camping." He winked at her. "Besides, you know we'll need the calories. The work isn't exactly a desk job."

God, he made her laugh so easily, and she did now. "It doesn't take much to talk me out of powdered eggs."

"Okay, so every night someone will be the designated bakery person."

Her smile faded. "If we have anyone left."

"I think you're going to be surprised."

She so hoped he was right. She hadn't chosen her interns based on physical courage, but rather based on their general knowledge of the subject and their willingness to work hard and get dirty.

Soon they had the "pretend" scrambled eggs ready—well, that's how Renee thought of them—and Cope was proving yet again that he could make toast over an open fire. With strawberry jam, at least that would be delicious.

When they sat to eat, paper plates on their laps, Cope took her breath away. He said, "Apropos of nothing, you are one beautiful woman, Renee Dubois."

She sat frozen, a piece of toast halfway to her mouth, and felt her heart skip several beats. Oh, man, did it feel good to hear that from him, but she didn't exactly know how to respond. She lived her life inside her head, often dirty with dust and dirt, and had never made room for a guy, at least not since high school. She was definitely a single-track kind of person.

She turned her head slowly, swallowing hard, wondering if her heart were going to beat its way out of her breast.

He was smiling. "You don't have to respond. I just needed to say it. You're beautiful, especially in this morning light."

Her voice cracked a little as she found it and tried it out. "Uh, especially when I'm cleaned up?"

He laughed and just shook his head. "Covered with the dust and dirt of the ages as well, but I'm through making you uncomfortable. I just felt a strong need to let you know. I like looking at you, so if you catch me, don't wonder why. Now you'll know."

She quickly glanced down at her plate. He liked looking at her? Maybe it was time for some truth. "I like looking at you, too," she replied, her voice cracking again as if her vocal cords were covered in rust.

Even though she didn't meet his eyes, she could hear the smile in his voice when he answered. "Well, I like the sound of that. Look all you want."

He seemed to think that settled everything and went back to eating. She tried, but now the jam-slathered toast wanted to stick in her mouth. Giving up, she put her plate to one side and reached for more coffee.

"The ants are going to find that toast faster than you'll believe."

She knew he was right and picked up her plate to balance on her lap while she wet her mouth with coffee almost hot enough to burn.

The sun had climbed fully over the eastern horizon, and the day now blazed with light. Hopefully some of the team would show up soon. Working days here were short because when the sun went behind Thunder Mountain, it was still bright but the light was so flat it could be difficult to make out smaller variations in texture and lines. Risky. That was the time of day she reserved for washing their finds and getting ready to bring them down the mountain.

But the egg remained. She wanted to clear out enough of the limestone around it to ensure she didn't destroy something else valuable in the process of freeing the egg.

Patience was usually her forte. Her job would drive her nuts if she were impatient. But right now... Darn, she wanted to get to work. Instead she busied herself trying to get her breakfast down. "I guess I should go to town to find out how Larry's doing," she remarked. "We haven't heard anything since last night."

"At which time they said he had a simple fracture and would be on a walking cast today. I'm sure he's fine. The team is probably enjoying a six-course breakfast at Maude's or the truck stop rather than coming back here for dried eggs."

She had to laugh at that description. "Well, I would."

"There you go."

But almost as soon as he spoke, a familiar gray SUV drove toward them.

"Claudia," Renee said.

"Looks like it."

Holding her plate in one hand and her cup in the other, she stood, no longer able to tamp down her impatience. Claudia might have some information that could shed light on this whole mess before it got any deeper. If there was reason to believe this wasn't just some kind of harassment, that this could be dangerous to life she'd have to… Oh man, she didn't want to think about that. She'd stay here and work the site by herself.

Claudia pulled up to the mostly grassy spot that had become their parking lot, and climbed out of her vehicle holding a big white paper bag.

"I hope you two have an appetite for Danish."

Cope and Renee looked at each other and burst out laughing.

"What did I do?" Claudia asked as she approached.

"Echoed what we were thinking earlier," Cope said. "I think you'll find plenty of takers for the Danish."

"I may give my eggs to the ants," Renee added.

"Yeah, camp food can become real boring because of the freshness issue," Claudia agreed as she pulled out some new paper plates from the plastic-wrapped stack and passed them around. "I hope that coffee's fresh."

"Fresh enough," Cope answered.

A short time later, they were enjoying the Danish and drinking coffee. Claudia reported on Larry.

"He's doing fine," she said. "And enjoying all the attention. Well, who wouldn't? The girls on the team are all over him with TLC. He should be released early this afternoon but they told him not to come back out here for a few weeks. They're starting with some kind of pressure cast, so his mountain-goat days are over for a little while."

"I am so relieved he's all right," Renee said emphatically. "That was such an awful thing to happen to him.

And I'm thinking about telling the others they can bail if they want. Danger wasn't part of the job description."

"Right now I don't think they're even considering the danger aspect," Claudia said frankly. "In fact, I'd judge that Larry in a hospital bed holds more attraction than the fossils."

Despite all her worries, Renee was amused. "You're probably right."

"I know I'm right," Claudia said as she wiped the frosting from one corner of her mouth. "Boy, that bakery is good. I need to make regular stops there."

Cope looked at Renee. "Does she read minds?"

"I'm beginning to wonder."

Claudia winked, then her mouth made an O. "I just remembered, I checked my email last night. Hate to tell you, there's something in this area that could definitely be valuable if mined."

Renee's stomach flipped. "What?"

"I told you there were some rare earths, needed for electronics but so easy to find they wouldn't be worth making trouble over them. However, there *is* one that's extremely rare, but let me get on my geology horse and give you some background."

Renee wiped her fingers on her napkin and leaned forward, hoping to hear some clues.

"Rare earths are mostly common. There are seventeen of them, fifteen lanthanides and two others that have similar properties." She paused. "You probably don't want to know all that. Anyway, the point is these rare earths are scattered everywhere, but typically not in veins that make them economically feasible for mining, however much we need them. There are a few that are more common than copper, but again, it depends on how tangled they are with each other whether it's worth the effort."

Renee nodded.

Claudia sipped more coffee. "Okay, there's one in particular that *is* truly rare. It's called promethium and it's radioactive. It's also extremely useful in making nuclear batteries, among other things. And apparently when that gorge opened up, it revealed a rich deposit. Now I don't know how far it goes. You might be able to take it all out of the ground with a shovel. Or…somebody could know something I don't yet."

Renee's first thought was safety. "Is it radioactive enough to be dangerous?"

"In the open air? I seriously doubt it. I don't think it would threaten anyone. I have a Geiger counter I'll use to check it out for you so you don't have to worry."

"Thank you."

"Keep in mind there's radioactivity all over these mountains. You get down five or six feet and you're digging into uranium and radon. The thing is, it isn't concentrated unless we concentrate it. Or unless we're in a closed mine shaft. But out in the air, no problem. As for mining this promethium…" She shook her head. "I'm sure the tribe won't allow it. So let's get going with the dig."

Renee looked at Cope and saw him frowning. Apparently he had some qualms, too. He spoke. "If you found a rich deposit, how likely is it that it isn't everywhere around here?"

She looked up just as she had bitten into her second Danish. "It doesn't matter," she said firmly. "You can't mine a mountainside without buying the property, getting the environmental clearances and otherwise cross-

ing enough *t*'s that'll take more time than you're going
to need to excavate."

"You sound awfully confident."

"No," she admitted. "Hopeful." She took another
bite of Danish. "I'm just a geologist, like you're a paleontologist. What do we know about most of this crap?
But I've studied enough to know you can't rip the side
off a mountain unless you own the mineral rights or
the property." She sighed. "Tell that to the Havasupai
in Arizona."

"Meaning?"

"Uranium mining poisoned their water and then
started giving them cancer. Navajos wanted the uranium trucks to stop coming through their reservation
because they noted an increase in cancer along those
routes. Yeah, nobody's safe."

On that unpleasant thought, they finished eating
without another word.

The team still hadn't shown up by the time Renee
wanted to get going. After burning paper plates, Cope
banked the fire safely and they headed toward the
mountain path.

He insisted on climbing first with the two women
behind him. While he didn't say so out loud, he was
concerned that someone could have set up booby traps
on the path. It wouldn't have made much noise during
the night to string some trip wires that could bring
rock crashing down on them, or to move rocks into
unstable positions.

He'd spent years learning to look out for such things
and he planned to put every one of his skills to work before letting Renee start digging again. Her idea of dig-

ging was so gentle that her patience left him in awe, but she might have been working to unearth delicate gems.

She certainly wasn't prepared to play the kinds of games she was encountering here.

He was also more concerned than he wanted to admit aloud. The rockslide was weird, all right, but basically pointless. Any way he looked at it, he couldn't imagine that it had been intended to cause serious harm. Maybe it had been a warning. Maybe it had been meant to slow Renee down.

But he was worried as he led the way up the path that it was the opening salvo in something that could get much worse. Since the rockslide had been no accident, that left only the conclusion that there would be more threatening activity, since he could imagine no other reason for it than to clear this area of the paleontology dig.

No one had booby-trapped the path, however. At the top, he and the women stood a few minutes, catching their breath and shaking out limbs that had worked awfully hard during the last stage.

He was getting out of shape, he realized with a bit of self-disgust. All those years of staying at the peak of physical fitness, and give him a year behind a desk and he was turning to rubber? Apparently running around the campus track wasn't going to be enough. *Weight room, here I come.*

Renee turned slowly, scanning the area, especially toward the important rock face. "Everything looks the same. I'm just wondering how we'll get rid of that rockfall."

"Leave it," Cope said. "Claudia can tell you that if we start moving any of those rocks we could set off another slide. Unless it buried something essential to what you're trying to do, I'd leave it until the summer's work is over. Then maybe we can get some people up to remove it carefully."

Claudia nodded. "I know you, Renee. You might have the patience of a saint, but those rocks are going to annoy you. Don't let them without good reason."

Renee nodded as if she weren't very happy. "Needs must," she said finally. She started to walk toward the work area when Cope held out an arm.

"Be very quiet," he said, "and let me go first. If I hear anything start to shift, I'm outta there, but we don't all want to be in the line of fire."

"Good point," Claudia agreed.

Renee nodded. Cope realized that this whole mess was starting to hit her in a dozen ways. It was easing past yesterday's shock and upsetting her, making her angry, making her wonder if she'd be able to continue her voyage of discovery, if someone else might get hurt...

At that moment, not one of those questions could be answered. He wished he had something to offer that would lift up her spirits, but the simple problem was, nobody knew any answers about why this had happened. Until they did, there were no cheery words other than that nobody was supposed to get killed. And that was a reasoned guess.

Cope walked very slowly along the ledge, his ears straining for warning sounds, his eyes checking the space right ahead of him for trip wires, triggers or rocks that looked too carefully balanced. How many times had he done exactly this in Afghanistan?

Shaking away the memories, he focused on the present. It was slow going, and he could only imagine how the women behind him must be feeling, but he wasn't about to take any unnecessary risks with them. Except for the *crunch* of his booted feet on smaller rocks, he didn't hear any sound to alarm him. No shifting rocks above; in fact, no sounds but the early morning forest and the gentle rippling of running water. A world at peace.

At last he felt secure in motioning the women to join him at the rock face. "We're okay for now anyway. Insanity."

Renee nodded. "It just makes no sense. Driving us away isn't going to make this mountain any easier to mine for anything."

She sat down in front of her egg and began to gently apply a dental pick to its perimeter. *Easy does it.* Claudia sat beside her, looking at her tablet.

Having done all he could do up here for the moment, Cope went down below to examine the mess there. Considering how much rock they'd moved to free Larry, he bet he could move some more safely. Carefully, but safely. Renee would probably like the space down here open again.

He set to, using muscles that enjoyed a good workout.

An hour later the rest of the team showed up, ready to get to going. They chattered nonstop about what had happened yesterday and how Larry was doing.

"He's going to have to go home," Maddie told Renee. "He's fine but the doc said there's no way he should be walking on rough ground for at least a few weeks. He wants to know if he can come back when they release him."

Renee sat back, egg momentarily forgotten. "He wants to come *back*? After yesterday?"

"Yup," Maddie said, flashing her patented pixie grin. "You didn't think any of us were going to bail, did you?"

"Maybe the guy with the broken leg," Renee answered.

Maddie shook her head. "It was scary, but this is an important job. Besides, we think someone just wanted to give us a fright. We don't scare easily."

Renee guessed not. Torn between a sense of responsibility that made her feel she ought to be sending these young folks home, and an overwhelming desire to expose the mystery of these fossils for the world to study, Renee gave up the argument. If she tried to send any of them away, she was certain she'd hear that they were adults capable of making their own decisions.

Why add insult to injury?

As the day wound down and the light flattened, Renee took photos of the partially revealed egg, while the others took photos of their discoveries at the river's edge, and Denise took a picture of the rock face with its new geometry. Everyone seemed to be in high spirits as if the rockslide had never happened and Larry's injury was merely an accident that could have happened a million ways. Renee wondered if they were all in denial or just trying to maintain a facade for the others.

Eventually cases were filled with fossil pieces, none exceptionally big. The big ones would come later, after they'd been completely freed.

But then there was the egg. Renee sat cross-legged

in front of it and didn't want to move. It was more exposed now, easy to damage if someone wanted to. A shudder passed through her as she considered that possibility.

"Coming?" Cope asked.

She slowly shook her head. "I think I'll sleep up here tonight."

The others were already heading down the trail and didn't hear her.

Cope immediately squatted beside her. "Talk to me."

She pointed to the egg. "See how much has been revealed? I don't want to leave it. It would be so easy for someone to come by and simply snap it off with a crowbar or something."

"Like was used in the rockslide."

"Exactly." Here was a nearly intact dinosaur egg containing a perfectly formed fetus. A very rare find. Irreplaceable. That egg was important enough to have gotten her the grant for this expedition. If she had to sleep right in front of it, she couldn't risk anything happening to it.

After a minute, Cope spoke. "It's not going to be a very comfortable bed."

She shrugged. "Some things matter more than comfort."

His blue eyes crinkled at the corners as he smiled. "I agree. Okay, I'll run down and get your sleeping bag and maybe some foam to ease the roughness of the rocks. And something for you to eat. We kind of skipped lunch today."

"Only because Claudia brought all those pastries!"

His laugh followed him down the trail and left her smiling in his wake.

The egg drew her attention again. Reaching out with her gloved hand, she ran her fingertips over it, feeling its every contour along with an amazing awareness of how far back in time it carried her. Her hand was making a connection with a lost world from approximately sixty-five million years ago. Whether an ancient building or a fossil, she always felt that connection to the past, that awareness of how much had lived on this planet before she came along.

Fanciful, maybe, but it moved her and kept her going. Mysteries faced her, and sometimes they had answers. And sometimes they would remain forever mysteries.

Leaning back on her hands, ignoring the sharp pressure of some of the rocks, she studied the entire wall. Here and there more secrets poked out like a promise of treasure to come. The excitement washed over her again, the same excitement she had felt the first time Gray Cloud had shown her this cleft.

A wonderful gift, maybe accidental, maybe from the mountain as Gray Cloud believed. But whatever its source, it burgeoned with stories of life long lost, and a cataclysm that had ended it. What's more, it might even help prove her pet theory that the saurians had lived in family groups.

She had trouble understanding why that would trouble anyone. Why wouldn't they care for their young?

Years ago she'd been walking across the floor of her garage when she spied what looked like a small, slender piece of string. Before she could take another step, a slightly larger anole lizard had darted out of a bush, grabbed the little string in its mouth and carried it off to the bush. Curious, she'd begun researching and had discovered the anole hadn't been snatching up lunch but had been protecting its baby from the big human feet. Why wouldn't dinosaurs, some of the earliest reptiles, have the same instincts?

Dreams, such dreams, filled her waking thoughts and even some of her nights as she imagined the stories that might be found within those rocks.

It was also beginning to occur to her that if she didn't get some rib-sticking food into her soon, she was likely to spend the night being a comatose guard. Even those canned baked beans that everyone had curled their lips at yesterday were sounding excellent.

Ahh. She let a long sigh escape her and put her head on her knees. It was all going to be all right. Gray Cloud was aware of yesterday's hanky-panky and by now he probably had more than the Bear brothers keeping an eye on things.

She had the distinct feeling, a very strong feeling, that Gray Cloud wanted the information in the rock strata to be unearthed. He was curious, of course, but he'd also mentioned several times that they would reveal more of the history around here.

Whether one faced up to it or not, the Native Americans had been left with very little by the storming of settlers across their lands. Oral tradition had been all that remained, and plenty of schools had been ruthless about expunging such tales.

Of course the fossils she was looking for reached back further in time than the first humans who had lived on this continent, but she could still easily relate to wanting to know.

There was a whole picture here of times lost, a picture that could help provide some context for those who wanted it.

And if some guys wanted to mine promethium, or whatever it was, they just needed to stand in line.

Reaching out her gloved hand again, she traced the outline of the egg and felt that ineffable connection across time.

Then she heard a strange sound. Like a flute, but so far away it couldn't be from around here. One of the Bear brothers?

She leaned sideways against the rock wall, curled protectively around the egg, and listened. Beautiful. Haunting. The longer she listened to it, the more she felt it was otherworldly. If it hadn't been so beautiful, she might have been frightened. It was nearing night, after all, and there was no reason that anyone should be making music on this mountain.

Closing her eyes, listening, she thought about whether Thunder Mountain might be alive after all, if it might be making this enchanting music. Her rational mind said no. Her emotional mind nearly wanted to believe it.

Then as suddenly as it had begun, it stopped, and heavy booted feet reached the ledge. She looked toward the ruckus and saw Cope with the two Bear brothers.

"Did you hear that?" he demanded.

For an instant she was taken aback. "The flute? It was lovely."

Three men exchanged looks. Burdens were dropped and the two Bears took off into the woods in different directions.

Cope knelt beside her. "Are you all right?"

"Why wouldn't I be?" Now she was feeling totally confused.

Cope hesitated. "Gray Cloud will answer that when he gets here. It seems there are some things we don't know about Thunder Mountain."

Chapter 10

Cope pulled up the large bundles the rest of the way. One was Renee's sleeping bag and camp pillow. The other was Cope's. He wasn't going to leave her here all night alone.

Then he unpacked plastic containers offering sandwiches made with cold cuts, and some carrot sticks. "The gang brought some food out with them. Eat. They're going to spend tonight in town at my suggestion."

She felt a chill creeping along her bones, and it wasn't from the deepening evening. "Cope, what happened? What's wrong?"

"I'll let Gray Cloud explain it."

She resented having to wait, but she was growing seriously tired. Biting into a ham sandwich, she hoped food would give her more energy.

"Don't look like that," Cope said.

"Like what?"

"Like your dream is about to go down the drain."

"Maybe it is." And as quickly as that she felt like crying. The feeling shocked her. She ordinarily kept her emotions well in check. A professional woman had to do that. It was hard enough getting to the top ranks in any field without letting emotions of any kind show. Men were allowed anger, but not women. If she got angry she was labeled a bitch. She knew it too well.

Cope surprised her by wrapping his arm around her shoulders and drawing her close. "We won't let it happen, Renee. We won't."

"You can't promise that." Her voice hitched and she hated the sound of weakness. Pulling away, she sat up and resumed eating a sandwich that now tasted about as good as sawdust. She couldn't afford to lean on anyone. She knew that. Everything she did had to be her own effort and better than everyone else. How else could she keep ahead when she was starting from behind?

Focus on the job. Put everything else away.

Cope didn't say anything. She'd pulled away from him as if he smelled bad or something—and nothing could be further from the truth—but he didn't seem in the least offended. Thank God. Right now she didn't need one more thing to deal with.

Someone had hurt Larry. That weighed heavily on her. Her determination to get at these fossils might be endangering others. Was she obsessed? Maybe so. She'd been so career-focused for so long that maybe she was only half-human now.

"What's the thing with the flute?" she asked when she trusted her voice.

"I don't know. I just know the three of them reacted to it as if it were important. I assume that'll be part of what Gray Cloud tells us when he gets here."

"I thought it was beautiful. It made me want to relax and maybe sleep." She darted a look his way and caught his smile.

"It *was* nice."

"Then why did everyone get so activated? Although I was starting to wonder if the mountain was making the music."

He shook his head. "We'll have to wait for Gray Cloud. He has the answers, not me."

She sighed and leaned her head against rock. "All I need is a magic mountain. You don't have to stay up here with me tonight, you know. I'm not afraid to be alone."

"I'm sure you're not," he said easily. "I'm equally sure that between a priceless egg and what happened to Larry, I'm not going to leave you here alone. Don't bother arguing. I'll just move farther along the ledge."

The image might have made her laugh, the idea of them planting separate camps on this ledge, if she hadn't suddenly started to feel so blue.

"Finish that sandwich. There's a treat that you might like."

"What's that?"

"Corn chips and guacamole."

She sat up a little straighter. "Really? Where did that come from?"

"You'd have to ask Maddie. She said something about a guy named Tino who used to be DEA but now works a few days a week in Melinda's bakery..." He paused. "I'm sure it's a fascinating story. But I didn't get all the details. Which makes me feel kind of dumb because I'm living here now and I should know this stuff. I need to get out more."

She felt her spirits lifting a little. "So I'm not the only one with a case of nose-to-grindstone?"

"Clearly not." He reached for a second sandwich and stared out into the darkening cavern of night, across the ravine toward the trees on the other side of the river. "I'll be honest, Renee. While I've been luckier than many, I'm still having some readjustment issues from the war. Nothing like PTSD, but occasional moments where I fall into a memory. Or get uneasy about nothing in particular. Even a rare outburst of anger that's hard to explain. So for now I limit my socializing. I thought this expedition, out in the woods with a small group of people, might help me. Plus, I'm fascinated."

"I'm glad you're here." That was the truth. She was *really* glad he was here. Something about him seemed to have a calming effect on the hijinks she would have expected from some of her interns, given their ages. Of course, that might not last, but if looking at the big former soldier encouraged them to act more like adults, she wouldn't complain.

Of course, in fairness to all her interns, they were here out of a serious interest in paleontology. Man, why else would they come to the middle of nowhere for a summer?

"Anyway, I'm not ruthlessly using you," he continued. "From the moment Gray Cloud told me about what had been revealed when this cleft opened up, I was on board. I could hardly wait for you guys to get here."

"I could hardly wait to get here myself."

"You must have broken land speed records to get a grant so fast."

She looked at him and could see, even in the failing light, the dance of humor in his eyes. Some of the tightness of worry that had been binding her chest let go. She figured Cope must have dealt with threats she could scarcely imagine. Good hands to trust, this man's.

Then she answered his indirect question about the grants. "There was a danger that the find could be lost if the mountain moved again, plus weather is always a threat to exposed fossils. I think my proposal got shoved to the top of some priority lists." She finished her sandwich and put the wrapper back in the now-empty plastic container. She regarded it thoughtfully. "It's amazing. We can't do anything these days without pollutants." She waved the container at him.

He answered. "Don't get me going on that. I'll keep you up all night. It sounds like the dark ages, but I remember my grandmother washing and reusing plastic bread bags, aluminum foil was off-limits and everything was wrapped in waxed paper. Although I'm not sure the waxing made the paper much better, pollution-wise. And then of course, she never had a scrap of cloth that she didn't use as a rag until finally it fell apart in the washer. I don't believe she ever bought a paper towel."

"Times have sure changed."

"While no one was paying attention, I guess."

"Yeah. Convenience is everything."

He took the container from her and stuffed it in the bag beside him, only to pull out another container and a bag of tortilla chips. "Now, a very odd dessert to a ham sandwich."

"I could eat guacamole all day. I should probably learn to make it but getting the avocados to the right ripeness defeats me."

He nodded, giving her another smile. "I have a friend with a method he says never fails. I'll email him and let you know."

Dipping chips with him into the generous tub of guacamole seemed pleasantly intimate, and finally Renee felt some of her tension releasing.

"I can't possibly stay wound up for the next three months," she said. "I have to find my peaceful place."

"You've got one?"

"I used to live in it," she said wryly. "Delusion, I guess."

That drew a laugh from him. "Peace seems like a rare part of life."

"I think most of mine came from keeping my head down and my eyes on the floor."

"Really?" Though it couldn't have been comfortable, he twisted around on the gravel so he could look straight at her. "You don't strike me as the type."

"You'd be surprised. Even in academia, a woman needs to be careful."

He sighed, actually sighed, and just shook his head. "I've seen it," he replied after a minute, his tone clipped. "In the military. The last place I'd honestly expect to see it because we have rules and regulations, and when you're in a foxhole, who the hell cares who is guarding your back? Well, apparently some people just can't get over it."

"I've heard."

"I imagine you have. Some of the headlines have been downright ugly. I'd have expected better at this level because you'd be dealing a lot with more mature men."

"Is there such an animal?"

Far from being offended, he grinned at her. "I'm working on it."

Man, she liked him. He was so honest and so unassuming, and his lack of a fragile ego made him comfortable to be with. Heaven knew, she'd worked with plenty of egos since embarking on her graduate program. It was odd, perhaps, that highly intelligent men could feel threatened by a smart woman or need endless praise to feel good. She sometimes thought of them as having artistic temperaments. Maybe that wasn't fair to artists, though. How would she know?

Then there were the outsize egos. The ones who couldn't see past their own brilliance to any idea offered by another person. She didn't know which was tougher to deal with.

"Penny?" said Cope. "Or is it more expensive these days?"

She smiled his way. "Just meandering. Nothing of import."

He held up the guacamole. "More?"

"Thanks, but I'm stuffed."

"Then I'm going to put this food far enough away that if a bear wants it, it won't need to bother us. We can just sit here and watch the party."

"I love your sense of humor."

"Constructed in response to tough situations, although I must say if a bear does actually show up, I won't be telling jokes."

She leaned her head back against the rock, watching with a smile as he carried plastic containers back toward the far end of the ledge away from them. He returned carrying a sleeping bag under each arm with a roll of foam pads perched on his shoulders.

No question that he was a man used to carrying items over rough terrain. He had it down to a science.

"I don't know how much good these foam pads will be on the gravel," he said as he dumped his load a few feet away from her. You use both of them, because I don't need one."

"That's not fair to you!"

He just shook his head. "Dear Dr. Dubois, if you'd slept on some of the ground I've slept on, you'd know I'm impervious. Don't argue. I'll probably be more awake than asleep anyway."

Now she felt bad. Was she being unreasonable refusing to leave the egg unattended tonight? There was no reason to believe anyone would try to damage it, at least not this soon after the rockslide. Whoever had made that mess must have been aware the cops had crawled all over the place.

Obsessive. Maybe she ought to talk to someone about that.

Cope insisted on tucking one of the pieces of foam behind her back as she leaned against the rock. It actually made her more comfortable. "That feels a whole lot better, Cope. Thanks."

"I thought it might. Suffering in the name of science has its limits, don't you think?" He opened her sleeping bag and spread it over her like a blanket. "It's getting chilly."

More than chilly, actually. Her fingers were beginning to stiffen. "When is Gray Cloud supposed to come back? You said he had some stuff to tell us about the mountain. And did he explain that flute?"

He tucked his rolled sleeping bag behind him and propped himself on one elbow. "The flute seemed to galvanize him in some way. That's when we started hurrying up the path. The Bears heard it, too, and got kind of antsy, but Gray Cloud seemed surprised that I heard it at all. Then you heard it." He tilted his head a little as if pondering. "I don't know where it came from, but I think you and I weren't supposed to hear it. That's the feeling they gave me."

"Well, that makes me feel better. A secret signal? Something going on that we're not supposed to know about? Something that shouldn't have happened and has them worried?" Her questions were growing by the minute now.

Cope gave a quiet, short laugh. "Nothing like a mystery to get the mind running at top speed. I have as many questions as you, but Gray Cloud doesn't move or speak until he's ready. Surely your cousin told you that."

Mercy certainly had. "I'll be honest," she said, lowering her voice in case anyone might be approaching. "I've sometimes thought that being married to that man could be taxing. He can shut down like a sealed chest. But Mercy seems awfully happy with him. Different strokes and all that."

"Gray Cloud carries a lot of responsibility," Cope told her. "From what little I've learned, he's the personification of what we might think of when we say tribal elder. Font of knowledge. Caring for all. Playing Solomon when necessary. Setting an example."

"And guarding this damn mountain."

"And guarding the mountain," he agreed. "Protecting the sacred land for his people. Considering how much has been stripped from Native Americans despite the treaties we signed, I imagine he's fended off more than one attack on their rights."

"Probably. Mercy doesn't say much about it. Seems like she took a vow of silence about tribal matters. Which I can understand, if she did." She paused. "It's a different world, though, Cope. From what I've learned from my studies, there are so many sacred teachings, so much essential oral history, so much that is private. When ethnologists go to live among a people for several years, thinking they'll be allowed into all the secrets of the society, I think they're fooling themselves at least a little. Worst case, they simply don't understand, coming themselves from a totally different culture."

"You might be right. One thing for sure, we haven't left them much but their secrets."

"I like the way you think."

He pushed himself a little higher on his elbow. "I've been lucky in one way. I got to see some other cultures up close and personal. Mind-opening, if you let it be."

She slid down a bit against the foam padding and raised her knees, forming a warm tent beneath the sleeping bag.

Then she heard the crunch of booted feet on the ascending path. Craning her neck, she saw Gray Cloud emerging from the deepening darkness.

"Howdy," he said as he approached. "Are you planning to stay up here tonight, Renee?"

"Yes. The egg. I'm obsessed."

Gray Cloud squatted in front of her and Cope, smiling faintly. "Good reason to be obsessed. If you want I can place a guard on it, but tonight..." He let the words trail off. Then he fixed her with an intent stare. "You heard the flute?"

"It was beautiful. What was it?"

Instead he looked at Cope. "And you, too?"

"Yeah, what got you guys all wound up?"

"It's simple. Hearing a flute on Thunder Mountain is reserved for certain people. You're not among those people. Therefore, a person was playing a flute up there somewhere, and no one should be."

Cope levered himself into an upright sitting position. Renee leaned forward.

"What are you saying?" Cope asked.

"It's mystical," Gray Cloud said quietly. "When one of us comes up here to complete a vision quest, we know we have finished because we hear the flute. It is how we know that our vision is complete and correct. I have myself heard the flute twice. But that's not what happened this evening. Neither of you should have heard the flute. That means it wasn't spiritual, it was man-made."

He paused. "And while I'm reluctant to say it, since the music was so accurate, it must have been played by one of my people."

Renee's heart started to gallop. "What? But why?" For the first time she wished he'd told her it was indeed just supernatural, that the mountain occasionally made music. She could have lived with that more easily than the idea that someone had deliberately gone up there to play what she suspected was a sacred melody. That seemed somehow sinister. A magic mountain would be easier to accept, which seemed ridiculous after yesterday, but there it was. Her scientific self was beginning to lose ground to a more primitive state of mind.

She didn't like the feeling.

"I don't know why," Gray Cloud answered. "I'd hate to think one of my people would treat the sacred in such a profane way, but in the end, we're just people like everyone else, and our motives aren't always the best."

Shifting, he straightened enough to give his knees something of a break, then settled cross-legged on the gravel facing them. With his hands, he picked up two stones and tossed them back and forth.

"It is said the flute can be a warning," he remarked a few minutes later. "A warning to those who can hear that the mountain is about to shrug. Like it did when it opened this cleft. I heard the flute before this happened. Because of it, I was on the lookout for a change when I found this place."

Renee's skin prickled a little. "Do you think…?"

Gray Cloud shook his head. "I'm more inclined to think that an individual would *like* to create that impression. The mountain opened this ravine. No reason to suppose it wants to close it or shrug you folks off here. That landslide was manmade, which speaks for itself. If the mountain wanted this dig stopped, you wouldn't even be able to find these fossils again. They'd disappear into deeper rock as if they'd never been."

Renee glanced at Cope, uncertain what to make of this. She gathered that Gray Cloud was sharing something very sacred to him, but she was having a hard time with it anyway. Cope, however, listened intently. Apparently, his mind had been opened quite a bit.

Gray Cloud dropped the rocks. They hit with a quiet

click. Above, a wind started to blow, filling the night with the sound of swaying treetops, sometimes a loud whisper, other times accompanied by a cracking sound as limbs bent a bit too far. Looking upward, Renee saw that the stars had disappeared, which somehow made it all feel creepier, as if she'd slid into another dimension.

"The weather tonight won't be bad," Gray Cloud said as if he noticed her upward look. "Colder, but not bad. No rain, no snow." Then he looked at Renee. "Maybe two, three years ago, someone wanted to buy our lands on this mountain. There was talk of a resort, but I never believed it. I don't know if you're aware, but there've been a lot of efforts over the years to build a resort in the mountains south of here, just on the other side of the national forest land. It's never panned out." He smiled faintly. "It seems like the mountains have opinions there, too."

Nervous or not, she had to smile in answer.

"Anyway," Gray Cloud continued, "in this case I didn't put much stock in the story, the tribe turned down the offer, and the man left. I thought that was the end of it. Maybe it wasn't. Claudia mentioned some precious mineral up here."

"Promethium," Renee answered. "She didn't seem to think the area was good for mining it."

"A full survey hasn't been conducted," Cope reminded her. "There could be a vein big enough to make tearing up this mountain worthwhile. Even if someone's after a rare earth, this could only be a part of it, don't you think? I don't know exactly how big the tribal lands on the mountain are, but if you have a big enough vein, maybe…" He stopped, then shook his head. "I need to remind myself I'm a history professor, not a geologist. Claudia's the one to ask about all this."

"And all of this might have nothing to do with these so-called rare earths," Gray Cloud said. "That landslide indicates only one thing—someone wants your team out of here, Renee. Maybe they're after the fossils. Maybe the fossils will get in their way somehow. That's all we can safely guess."

He drew a long breath and closed his eyes, seeming to fill himself with something. "We'll find out. The mountain will keep you safe tonight."

Great, thought Renee, then felt shame. She knew how dear these beliefs were to her cousin's husband. She didn't want to disparage them. But trust the mountain to keep her safe?

She didn't think she was quite ready for that.

Later that night, as the cold seemed to creep down the mountain, bringing with it a stiff breeze, Renee shivered inside her sleeping bag. Okay, she was a fool. If she'd stayed below, the tent would have protected her from the wind at least. There could have been a fire if they needed the extra warmth. Or she could have climbed into her car and headed for town.

Instead she was preoccupied, chained, obsessed with that damn egg. She definitely needed her head examined.

A hand gripped her shoulder. "If this weren't stony ground, we'd all be shaking," she heard Cope say quietly. "You can't sleep like this."

"It is what it is."

"Ah, cut it out," he retorted almost sternly. "You ever heard of bundling? I'm going to zip these two bags together so we can share heat. It'd be good for everyone if you're awake tomorrow."

She didn't argue. She was shivering strongly enough that she wondered if she'd be able to stand when he zipped the bag open. But he was good at this, somehow, and no sooner was she unzipped, he'd zipped his own bag to hers, all without asking her to move more than a few inches. He tucked their pillows in close together, managed to tighten the bags around them, and the next thing she knew, she was wrapped in his arms.

"Hate to tell you this," he murmured in her ear as they spooned, "but it would be a lot warmer in here if we weren't wearing all this cold-weather gear."

"What are you suggesting?" she asked, her teeth chattering.

"Not a damn thing. Just stating facts. We're dressed for the arctic, and all this clothing is trying to hold our body heat in."

She heard a zipper, then felt the unmistakable cloud of warmth reach her cheek. "Jacket undone," he said. "That should help."

"I should do mine," she admitted. Because she knew he was right.

"Are your fingers working well enough?"

Before she could answer, she felt his hand reaching for her zipper. "Allow me, madam. You'd look awfully odd frozen next to your egg in the morning."

He was keeping it light, but the feelings flowing through her were anything but. As warmth inside the bags increased, she grew steadily more aware of him, of his proximity, of his large hand resting against her midriff. Heaven. And if it weren't so darn cold, she might be thinking of turning toward him and…

Her brain stuttered right there. Sex? She was neither good nor experienced in that arena. Good thing she was too cold, because she might make a fool of herself.

His head was close to hers, and she could feel his warm breath trailing across her cheek. Squeezing her eyes shut, she began to wish she were another person in another place with this man where she could cast aside all her hang-ups and just be a woman. Just a woman.

She had the feeling he might actually make her glad of her gender for the first time since childhood. Might make her feel strong and powerful, not weak and out of place.

With him holding her, it was hard to ignore the drumbeat of desire growing in her blood, the way her breath constricted almost as if she were afraid a small movement might cause him to remove his arm.

Focus on the dig, she told herself, a mantra she repeated over and over again. *Focus on the dig*.

But her body seemed to have other things in mind.

Cope felt Renee gradually relaxing and hoped she would soon fall asleep. The woman had been driving him nuts since he'd first set eyes on her, and holding her like this was akin to torture.

Although he had to admit that torture would at least keep him awake. He wasn't planning to close his eyes tonight. And it had the advantage of being sweet torture.

Since he had little enough to do at the moment except listen and remain alert, and he didn't want to think about Renee for fear he'd quit listening, stop paying attention and pursue lovemaking with her, he turned his thoughts around.

Instead of Renee, he considered his position, a good one. The ease with which he could slide out of the sleeping bag. Very easy since he hadn't zipped his side more than partway.

And why the hell was he once again in this position? He'd had enough, hence abandoning his military career and turning to teaching. Now here he was, sentinel on a rock, listening for an enemy he knew nothing about and didn't know would even come.

Dark memories wanted to swim through the dark night, inkier than black, like shades. He often counted his dead, but tonight would not be a good night for that. He had a woman to protect. Oh yeah, and an egg, too.

She'd mentioned that she might be a little obsessed, and he guessed it was possible, but she might well be sitting on the find of the century. Of course she didn't want anything to happen to it.

He didn't have to be a paleontologist to recognize how much could be learned from that damn egg. Or to appreciate it. A window into saurian reproduction. Possibly a view into how they lived. She said she thought they lived in family groups. At least this kind, whatever it was.

In his mind, anyway, it created quite a different image of that era than the usual dog-eat-dog, solo predators and solo grazers. From what she had said, he guessed they hadn't really found enough fossils to draw hard and fast conclusions about much. It was probably a continually changing field of study.

He seemed to remember a discussion back when about whether these animals were truly cold-blooded. Or something. His memory was fuzzy at best because the subject hadn't held his interest at that time. Back then, he'd left dinosaurs in his childhood.

Now he was smack-dab in the middle of a truly exciting exploration, and he wasn't bored with dinosaurs now.

If Renee was obsessed with that egg, he was getting there himself. And if the hints of various fossils poking out of that rock face were a good indicator, this might be a find of the decade. Or maybe century.

Their body heat had turned the shelter of the sleeping bags into a warm cocoon. The night was so dark he couldn't see a damn thing except from the corners of his eyes. Survival, to be able to detect motion with peripheral vision in the dark.

Anybody who came up here was going to need a flashlight or night-vision goggles. Given all the gravel, he doubted anyone could approach without making plenty of noise.

So they were safe.

Except he didn't feel like it. He half wished the wolf would return, because then he could tell himself they were being watched by an animal.

Damn, it was getting cold. Stockman, sitting about ten feet up in a pine tree, shivered in the darkness, his night-vision goggles pushed back on his head. Did he really have to stay out here watching two people sleep?

But the boss was starting to put the pressure on. He didn't want them dead, but he wanted them gone.

That was beginning to sound to Stockman like a sideways order. Broadus wanted them dead. That was what he was really saying.

So why didn't the jackass just come out and say it?

Stockman was not the brightest bulb, but he could read between most lines, and what he was reading here was that Broadus wanted people dead, but he didn't want to say it. Maybe because then he could deny it to himself, assure himself that Stockman had gone over the top.

Mind games. Stockman hated them. Worse, those mind games had him sitting in a tree on the side of this godforsaken mountain in cold weather that would have pleased a polar bear, watching two people sleep.

That sure made sense.

Then that flute earlier. What the hell had that been? It had sure galvanized them like a fire had been lit under them. Damn spooky mountain.

Broadus had said that someone else up here wanted these diggers gone, too. So maybe that was who played the flute. Sure, playing the flute was really likely to scare anyone away.

He was angry about the way the rockslide had worked out, too. If that one guy hadn't been injured, he doubted anyone would have looked closely enough to know it was no accident. There'd have been no cops.

Now, whatever he did, he had to be extra careful because the cops were alerted.

His head jerked back, banging the tree trunk. There it was again, that weird flute. It sounded as if it had gotten closer to him. Nah, that was just the darkness. Anyway, what did he have to fear from someone running around with a flute? Musical battery?

His own wit amused him, but only briefly. Here he was, sitting out here freezing so he could watch two people sleep. And try to come up with a way to scare them off. He really didn't want to kill them, but he supposed he might have to kill at least a few.

The thought soured his stomach. He hated having to do that.

Then some pebbles rattled. He could see nothing so he pulled on the night-vision goggles…and he could still see nothing.

Probably a deer, he told himself.

Until one of those small rocks came flying out of the darkness and hit the side of his head.

He looked around quickly. He should have been able to see anything with a smidgeon of warmth to it. All he saw was an owl. It stared back at him, then hooted.

Okay, he could take a hint. Shimmying down the tree, Stockman headed downhill at an angle to get to his truck. A couple of miles. Not too bad with these goggles.

A half hour later, the ground gave way beneath his feet and he found himself standing in a hole waist-deep. Probably dug and forgotten by some long-ago hunter, Stockman thought.

But the thought was not reassuring. It felt like this damn mountain was trying to get rid of him.

Which of course it was not. Mountains were just heaps of rock.

After pulling himself out of the hole with some difficulty, he continued walking, alert for anything alive. The woods tonight were devoid of life except for that owl. How weird was that?

Without realizing it, he quickened his pace as much as he dared.

He was beginning to feel hunted.

Chapter 11

In the morning, Renee stirred as the cold began to reach her. Cope was gone, she realized, and sat up to look around. He was a few feet away, nursing a small fire into life. Warmth.

God, she felt like she might never get warm again. The light of the rising sun was barely reaching them, casting a pinkish glow overhead. Making the trees look as if they had changed color overnight.

As cold snaked around her neck, she realized her jacket was still unzipped. Quickly, she remedied that, but kept the sleeping bag around her legs.

"Good morning," Cope said. "Sorry to be so early. I tried not to wake you."

"I got cold," she answered honestly. "And you don't have anything to apologize for. I'm the idiot who wanted to spend the night out here."

"I don't think you were being an idiot."

"You're just being nice."

His expression changed, and she almost shivered. She saw then the man who had gone to war and fought. The man who was capable of things she couldn't even imagine. There was steel in that look, steel and something darker. Then the expression eased away, but not entirely. "Don't call yourself an idiot."

That sounded like an order. Maybe it was. She just plain didn't know how to react. God, it was like finding a snake with two heads. This man had a whole side he'd never shown her.

"Anyway, it's a good thing we stayed up here. I heard the flute again."

"My God," she said. "It was so cold last night, I can't imagine anyone running around just to do that."

"Me neither, but there have been a lot of things I couldn't imagine that came to pass." He now had a decent flame licking upward and fueled it with just a few more dry pieces of wood. "This isn't going to be a big fire. I don't want to do a lot of damage to what's under it. I tried to clear the space." He shrugged, then smiled at her. "But, lady, I ain't no paleontologist. Right now I could be roasting dino's knuckles."

"We need the heat, and I'm sure you cleared everything away that you could. If you got dino's knuckles, they won't be the first fossils blackened by a little soot. Worse things have happened, like soot on walls of ancient Egyptian tombs, covering the paintings."

"Now that's a crime." Seemingly satisfied, he worked his way over to her. "I have some coffee in my pocket and I brought a small pan up here with me.

If you don't mind ignoring the grounds, I can make us some coffee."

"That sounds like heaven, grounds and all," she admitted. "I think my teeth are decent strainers."

That caused him to grin.

He'd lugged a gallon jug of water up with everything else last night, and he used that to make the coffee. Soon the delicious aroma was wafting among the scents of pine needles and loam.

"This place is close to perfection," she remarked as he offered her a tin cup full of steaming brew. "It's so peaceful, and watching the sunlight slowly paint the treetops and then dive into the lower places... How much more beauty could a person ask for?"

"Not much," he agreed as he sat beside her. "Is the warmth from the fire reaching you?"

"It's starting to. The coffee's doing a better job." Holding it in both cold hands helped warm her. Then she remembered something he'd said almost as if in passing. "You heard the flute again?"

"Yes, I did. In the wee hours, maybe an hour or so before the sun came up."

"Who in the world would be running around in the dead of night?"

He just shook his head. But of course, what could he say to that?

"Sorry," she said. "We went all over this ground last night when Gray Cloud was here. I must sound like a broken record, asking questions we don't have answers to."

"No broken record," he said easily. "You think those same questions aren't running around inside my head? All you're doing is saying what I'm thinking."

"Still, it has to be tiresome." Gingerly she moved, wondering how stiff she would be from the cold. Cope had kept her warm last night or she doubted she would have slept at all. But now that she was awake, the cold was penetrating her bones, and she wondered what had ever made her think it would be warm at this time of year.

"Some spring," she remarked. "All we need are some snowflakes."

"It feels that way, doesn't it? When I got here I was warned that it could get seriously cold at almost any time of year. I was regaled with stories of snow in July."

"Make you wanna turn tail?"

He laughed. "I'm still here. Besides, the mountains in Afghanistan weren't exactly warm all the time. And more than once I saw snow in the summer. The higher elevations lend themselves to it."

He rose and went to the nearby fire to get more coffee. "Dump out the cold stuff," he said. "I've got plenty here for a few more cups, grounds included."

The refreshed hot cup felt good in her hands. "The team won't be up here for a while. Not if they feel this cold. I can't blame them, either."

"Maybe they'll even bring pastries for you."

"That could get to be an expensive habit," she answered with a smile, even though her cheeks felt almost too frozen to move. "You know, I'm beginning to feel naive."

"Really? How so?" He sat beside her again.

"All I ever had to deal with before was interpersonal politics. This goes beyond anything I ever imagined except in a movie or novel. Someone actually tried to hurt us or stop us. And they chose a very dangerous way to do it. I don't care that it was at the far end and probably not intended to hurt anyone. The fact is, they did it and couldn't guarantee no one would be injured or killed. I mean, no one can knock down a part of a cliff and control the results unless they're a practiced road crew. Now we've got a mad flute player running around in the woods who probably wants to scare us off by making us think there are ghosts out there, or the mountain is yammering at us..." She trailed off. She was getting perilously close to losing it, and she definitely didn't want that.

Despite the comfort and warmth of Cope holding her throughout the night, she guessed that something, probably nerves, had prevented her from a deep sleep. She sipped more coffee and carefully turned so she could once again see her egg. Was it worth all this? A career-making find, perhaps, but someone had been injured and if it was an attempt to shut down the dig, how many more attempts might there be? How many more might get hurt?

"Renee?"

She turned her head a bit to look at Cope. "Yeah?"

"I know I'm a subordinate here, but would it be out of line to hug you? Because I really want to, and you look like you could use it."

She'd never had a nicer invitation. Polite. Crossing no lines. And who cared about lines, anyway? She ought to and seemingly he did. Military background? She had no idea; she was more used to just being pulled in for a hug whether she wanted it or not. And little of that happened now that she'd pretty much become a work-driven ice queen.

But she was not all ice. Inside was a woman who

had some long-unmet needs. She was also a woman who right now needed very much not to be alone. Unusual fears plagued her, the primary among them that one of her team might get hurt while she remained obsessed by the egg.

She still held the coffee, but as she looked into his amazing blue eyes she seemed to answer his question, because he took the cup from her and pulled her into a hug that seemed to surround her, envelop her, even protect her.

With that simple gesture, he drew the last bit of tension from her, leaving her soft inside in a way she had never felt before. As if everything about her were becoming runny and warm, like chocolate in the sun.

She wouldn't have believed a hug could do this to her, but she was in no mood to fight it. She reveled in it, loving the softness that was such a stranger as it moved in and took over.

She melted into his embrace and as if he could feel it, he tightened his arms a bit and pulled her closer until her head rested firmly on his shoulder and his breath brushed her hair gently.

The warmth that filled her now had nothing to do with sleeping bags, and certainly not with the chilly morning. No, it was all generated deep inside her, a yearning for something more, something deeper, something fulfilling.

She didn't care if it was a stupid, ridiculous urge. She just let it fill her and take over. Nothing would happen. She was safe here on this ledge where at any moment they'd hear the others approaching. Safe from what? Her own urges and needs?

Probably. Because right now she felt as if roots of

some kind were growing around her, roots that wanted to twine around Cope and hold on to him. Nor could she care at that moment that he might not want to be wrapped in a vine. Her heart was busy wrapping him anyway.

The whole experience was fresh and new to her, and she felt as if her eyes were being opened for the first time. Wonder of a whole new kind filled her. A wonder far deeper than that damn egg she was prepared to protect with her life. Deeper than any academic excitement.

A woman was being born into her full womanhood, she thought hazily, then gave up thinking. She wished this could go on forever.

Cope would have been happy to go on holding her. He felt as if she'd given him a precious gift, businesslike as she usually was. But the sun was getting higher, and all too soon he heard the approach of some of the team.

Trying not to be abrupt, he brushed a kiss on Renee's forehead and said, "The team is coming."

She looked up at him, her eyes softly hazy, then they snapped into focus. "Oh. Oh!"

She sat up at once and began trying to finger-comb her hair for some reason. He kept his smile to himself. Those hazy eyes had told him a lot. Someday they were going to have to find some time alone together and see where this went.

But not this morning. He stood and was tending the fire when the first fresh faces arrived at the ledge.

"We come bearing gifts," Maddie said. "Pastries

and a coffeepot that just needs to be warmed a bit on that fire."

"Pastries," Renee exclaimed. "Who's been reading my mind? Any news on Larry?"

"He's being released this morning," Maddie said as she put the coffeepot next to the fire on the stones. "And he is very upset that they've told him he can't come back up here."

"I imagine," Renee answered. She knew how she'd feel. Upset wouldn't begin to cover it.

"However," Denise filled in, "he's figured out a way to get out here. He says he's going to be our camp cook."

"Like he can move around enough," muttered Maddie.

"Oh, come on," said Denise. "Anything he can do will help even if it's burning paper plates on the fire. Would *you* want to be left out?"

Then she turned her sharp gaze on Renee and Cope. "What have you two been up to?"

Renee answered. "Guarding an egg. I guess I'm obsessed."

"I would be, too," Maddie responded. "Is there any way we can release it sooner and get it on its way to a safe piece of foam in a lab?"

"I'm worried about destroying evidence around it," Renee admitted. "But I'm wondering what's the priority here. Getting this egg out of here safely…you know, that seems destructive, like thieves going in and taking out valuable stuff without context."

Maddie sat down. "I hear you. But that egg is probably the most important piece at risk right now. If we're careful, maybe we can get it out of there without damaging too much."

"That goes against everything I believe about proper excavation," Renee admitted.

"Coffee's hot," Cope said. "Give me your cup, Renee?"

She passed it to him, muttering, "I don't know."

Cope managed to pivot on his heels until he faced her directly. "Look, here's reality. If one more thing happens—and frankly that flute is still bothering me—we're going to have to clear out before someone gets killed. So the question is, do we take the egg with us?"

That silenced everyone for the moment. Renee sipped the coffee, glad to find it free of grounds, and closed her eyes, trying to think things through. Part of her wanted to stand her ground, to not give an inch. The other part thought of Larry and her other students and how much she didn't want anyone else to get hurt.

At last she spoke. "This site is too important to abandon. But I don't want anyone else getting hurt or maybe killed. Ideally, we pull the egg as carefully as possible and as quickly as we can. Anyone worried about getting hurt—I've said this before—can be sure that if they choose to leave they'll get an A for the summer."

"So we get as many as possible to work on the egg?" Denise asked.

"*Possible* is the operative word. It may be a large egg, but more than three people working on it at a time would be impossible. Maybe we should shift teams in and out one at a time so not everyone is exposed to trouble at the same time."

"Excellent idea," Cope said before anyone could

answer. "We don't know whether the rockslide was intended to hurt anyone, but since it didn't succeed in getting us out of here, worse methods could be tried. I want everyone to understand that, as I'm sure Renee does."

Renee flung the sleeping bag open so she could unfold until she stood upright. Most of her body lodged a protest about having slept in the cold on a hard surface, but she ignored it. The kinks would shake out.

"Okay," she said. "You guys take over here. I need to get down the mountain to change clothes, then I'll be right back. Assuming you don't want to run right now."

Maddie flashed her patented grin. "I don't run. Besides, this is more exciting than a regular dig."

Denise rolled her eyes, making Maddie laugh. "I could do without the added excitement. I'm more into the discovery thing than the death-defying stuff."

"We left some of the others waking up over breakfast and discussing whether to go into town to see Larry, but I think Larry was discharged."

"I'll look into it when I get down there," Renee said. "Thanks for sticking with me, guys."

Maddie stuck out her tongue. "Like I'm going to be deprived of having my name at the bottom of the list when we announce the discovery of the century? No 'et alia' for me."

The laughter felt so good. The night's shadows receded from Renee's mind and the brighter light of day began to reach her soul. Such good people. She'd tried to be wise in her selections for the team, but now she felt she'd also been lucky.

She headed down the trail with Cope as Denise and

Maddie got to work with dental tools, breaking away small bits of limestone with care. "It's amazing," she remarked, "to realize this was all once under water."

"I think my mind has been blown enough," he said humorously. "Invisible flute players in the dark, dinosaur eggs that make beach balls look small. Gads, imagine if you were a chicken and had to lay that thing."

A giggle escaped her. "Relax. This would have been one big chicken."

"You hoping to find one of those, too?"

"Several of them, actually. That's probably more luck than I can hope for, but if we could find even small bits of fossil from the parent species, and could prove they were from different adults..."

"You get closer to proving the family unit hypothesis."

"Yup. A few years ago, someone postulated that T. rexes were too big to actually hunt for themselves, so juveniles hunted for them. If true, that's family and requires a lot of organization. It's still up in the air, though. More proof needed. Maybe I'll get some."

"I thought reptiles were solitary, that they just spawned and moved on."

"Then you haven't see an alligator carry her young on her head until they're able to strike out on their own."

"I guess I haven't," he murmured, then surprised her by taking her hand. "I enjoyed holding you last night."

She caught her breath at the unexpected turn. Her heart leaped with a surprising amount of happiness. "I enjoyed it, too."

He squeezed her hand. "Then let's make a date for after we get this place clear of interlopers, claim jumpers, or whatever they are."

"And ghosts that play the flute in the middle of the night."

He broke step, stopping them, and looked down at her. "You think it was a ghost?"

"Or a lunatic. Although at this point I'm starting to wonder if Gray Cloud isn't right about this mountain. God help us if he is, and it doesn't want us digging."

He caught her chin with his fingertip and turned her face to his. "You're overtired. This doesn't sound like you. But whatever. If the mountain's alive, it practically rolled out a red carpet for you, as if it wanted to spit out its secrets. Somebody else has a problem with that, and Gray Cloud or no Gray Cloud, it ain't that mountain."

She knew he was right. But it was as if the injury to Larry, and all the suspicions floating around, and her inability to really dive into her work and forget everything else were wearing on her. Like last night when she'd almost shed tears.

No, she wasn't like herself, but she was beginning to wonder who she really was. The career-driven loner was steadily getting replaced by a career woman who desperately wanted to be able to share some of the burdens.

Not like her at all. Not at all. But when she felt Cope's hand wrapped warmly around hers, she didn't think it was totally bad not to be herself. Maybe it was even an improvement.

But soon they were approaching the camp and he let go of her hand. Mustn't start talk. Things were getting rough enough for her team without any rivalries.

They found Carlos, Bets and Mason gathered around a warm fire, half-buried in their sleeping bags, which had been opened for use as blankets. All three were trying to eat pastries and some eggs that looked almost gray. Oops, somebody had screwed up the dried eggs. At least they had the big pot of coffee.

"It's cold," Mason said frankly. "We oughta have snow. How's it all going up there?"

"Going," Renee replied as honestly as she could. "I don't think this weather is usual..."

"Also not unusual," Cope interrupted. "Stiffen up, gang. There's not much bikini weather in these parts."

Renee looked at him, not sure whether to be angry that he'd stepped in or to just laugh at what he'd said.

"Easy for you," Mason muttered. "That whole Marine thing. Ruck up, suck up, press on. My brother said that a lot. It's one of the reasons I didn't follow him into the Corps."

That drew laughter from Bets and Carlos. "Probably just as well," Carlos said. "I don't think the Marines much like whining."

Mason waved a dismissive hand at him. "I just need more coffee. When my fingers and toes thaw I'll be ready to go."

"Look," said Bets suddenly, pointing north.

Toward them rode a cowboy, limned brightly in the still-rising sun. He was buried in a shearling jacket and his chaps were probably warmer than jeans.

He came up close, touching his finger to the brim of his hat. "Howdy. I'm Jake Madison, chief of police in Conard City, which means I'm out of my jurisdiction. However, I'm also a rancher, and secrets don't keep well around here. Somebody tried to bury you in a rockfall?"

"Someone made the rock fall, all right," Renee said, "but we don't think it was intended to cause serious harm. Unfortunately, one of my interns got a broken leg."

Jake pushed his hat back a little. "Serious enough." He rested both hands on the pommel of his saddle and leaned forward a bit.

"Coffee?" Renee asked, suddenly remembering her manners.

"Love some," he answered, then took the cup from her with a gloved hand. "I don't like that kind of messing around," he remarked. "If they want you out of here, use the law, talk to the tribe, but don't try to hurt anyone."

"There doesn't seem to be much anyone can do," Renee answered. "It was obvious the rock was loosened with some kind of pry bar, but no bar, no fingerprints, no footprints…" She paused. "And no good reason as far as we can tell. Some rare earth metal, but even our geologist isn't sure there's enough to bother mining."

"If there's one thing I've learned, some folks don't need much of an excuse to want to make someone else miserable. You folks have a sat phone, right?"

"Yes," Renee answered.

Jake reached his hand inside his jacket and pulled out a card, passing it to her. "You guys want any help for any reason, I can get here faster than the sheriff because I'm closer. And Gage won't mind if I step on his toes a bit." With one motion he drained his coffee and passed the empty cup back. "Don't hesitate to call if anything worries you. I don't like the feeling that somebody's screwing around out here, and worse that he's doing it on sacred ground."

He tipped his hat, turned his mount and headed back the way he'd come.

"Nice guy," said Renee.

"Yeah, he is," Cope agreed.

Well, hell, thought Stockman. More people were getting involved in this than a church barbecue. Now the chief of police? Not that he could put handcuffs on anyone out here, but that didn't make him much less of a problem.

Last night Broadus had been annoyed with him, wanting him to do something more spectacular. "Make the place haunted!"

Haunted. Judging by that flute last night, the mountain was already haunted. So what was he supposed to do? Bring a sound system out here to play weird sounds at night? As if he could conceal it. Besides, these people didn't even sleep up on the mountain. No help. Stupid idea.

Then, out of the blue, he remembered his old cat, Thumbelina. Whenever his larger tom bothered her, she could let out a scream that made his skin crawl and his adrenaline hit the roof. Hadn't he seen some recordings of that scream on the internet? So maybe a small tape player? Maybe he wouldn't need huge speakers or an amplifier. All he needed to do was make someone's skin crawl enough they never wanted to go back.

Thumbelina's cry had instantly evoked images of an eviscerated animal, although she'd never, not once, been hurt. Nope. She was just terrified.

Maybe that would work.

Those Bear brothers prowling around weren't making his life any easier, though. Keeping a step ahead of them was difficult, complicated by trying to hide his tracks anytime he got close to that ravine. So far, they hadn't seemed to get wind of him, but they'd probably walk right across him if he got too close to the dig again. That kind of dirty trick was definitely off the table now.

Of course, if he just killed somebody, they'd be scared off, all right. The cops would swarm over the place, the digging would cease, and Broadus would be essentially free to carry out his plans, whatever they were.

Stockman had a little Native American blood in him, from his grandfather, and yet he couldn't begin to imagine why anyone would want this piece of land. Sacred to the tribe, maybe, but beyond that and a few fossils, it seemed like a lousy piece of real estate.

What the hell did it matter, anyway? It was Broadus's problem. Stockman's assignment was to clear the area for a while. Spook noises might rattle them, but he doubted they'd be enough to keep that woman and her students away. Hell, the flute had sent him running last night, but the woman hadn't budged.

He kinda admired her for that. Of course, she probably didn't feel like she was being followed, the way he had.

Dang. He made sure the stones around him were arranged in a semicircle facing east. An alignment for a vision quest, his cover story if he happened to need one.

But he didn't need a cover story. He needed to find a way to run a bunch of people off this mountain. He sensed a growing impatience in Broadus, one that might dictate that someone had to die.

Stockman sighed when he thought about that. It sure wasn't to his taste, but he'd do what was necessary. He always had, no matter who was giving the orders. And man, he really needed the money.

Chapter 12

Two weeks passed and nothing more untoward happened. The egg was revealing itself beautifully, no more flutes had been heard in the night, and Renee had concluded that some mischief maker had set off the rockslide more as a joke than a threat. The rest of the team, except for Cope and Larry, who was stuck at their base camp, seemed to agree with her.

In fact, Renee thought as she finished up another day of working to remove the egg from its trap in time, denial was doing a great job for all of them.

"But really," she said to Cope that night as she prepared to bed down on a new air mattress in front of the egg, "why would someone go to all that trouble, then just vanish?"

"Maybe the Bear brothers are making them nervous," he answered.

She almost sighed, then looked at him straightly. "Am I being a fool?"

"No, you're being human. We all play the denial game. Done it a time or two myself."

She nodded. She supposed everyone did. "You know, I haven't seen Gray Cloud in over a week. Or Claudia. Did she say anything to you?"

"Only what she said to you, that she had some business."

"Well, it must have been important. I'd like to talk to Gray Cloud, though. Find out if the Bears have learned anything at all."

"My guess is not at all, but I thought I heard someone say that Gray Cloud has disappeared from the face of the earth. Good luck finding him for a conversation if he's doing a vision quest, or something equally important."

Standing, she reached for the brightest flashlight she had with her and turned it on, angling it against the rock face. She drew a long breath. "I didn't realize we'd come so far. Do you see it, Cope? Man, I hope Denise has this all recorded."

Awash in sudden awe, Renee looked at the remnants of a long-lost world beginning to emerge from the rock face. Here and there she could see what appeared to be a foot, or a snout or a tail, just parts but evocative nonetheless. Some of those feet were identifiable to certain species and she recognized them at once, even though they were only partially revealed. Other items still held their mystery, waiting to reveal it on another day.

This whole rock face was worthy of a museum. She wondered if someone would replicate it for display.

Because they sure couldn't take it out of here in one piece, especially since there was no telling how deeply the fossil bed reached.

"Oh look," she exclaimed, training her flashlight on one spot. "Do you see it?"

"What?" Cope stepped closer.

She moved in and touched it. "Skin. I think it's armored skin."

"Looks like pebbles to me."

Renee laughed. "It's too regular. These were armored plates, I'm sure of it." She ran the palm of her hand over it. "And this is why we have to protect this. My God, it's so rare to find preserved skin and scales."

She felt Cope's arm slip around her waist, let herself be drawn to his side and rested her head on his shoulder. "It's beautiful. Absolutely beautiful."

She didn't need to turn her head to know he wasn't talking about skin and armor plates. The sizzle between them that, for her at least, had never quite quieted, leaped to life as if someone had poured gasoline on the flames.

Every instinct warned her not to let this grow. Remain professional. But there was another need, deeper than instinct, that made her want to move toward him on an entirely different voyage of discovery. Helplessly, she began to turn into him, ready to become putty in his hands. He shifted his stance, welcoming her, murmuring her name.

Then a screech filled the forest and sent ice water running down her spine. At once she found herself backed up against the rock face, with Cope standing firmly in front of her, back to her.

"What the heck?" Her mind had trouble processing the sound except that it was terrifying. Her mind immediately summoned images of an animal being torn apart.

Then it came again. Cope swore. "Don't move, Renee."

"But what is it?"

"Nothing I've ever heard before. Just don't move."

That's when she realized he somehow held a knife in his hand, and now she felt that every muscle in his body was poised to spring.

"I'll take the mad flute player," she whispered shakily.

"You and me both."

She waited, hoping not to hear that bloodcurdling sound again.

Just as she became sure she couldn't stand the tension for one more minute, she heard the pounding of feet on the path.

"Here comes the cavalry," Cope remarked, but didn't relax his stance.

Mason and Maddie burst out of the shadows into the beam of the flashlight that now lay at Renee's feet. "What the devil was that?" Mason demanded.

"You heard it, too?" Cope remarked, sounding as if nothing were unusual about it. "Sounds carry well at night."

"No kidding," said Maddie, drawing closer. "That still doesn't say what it was."

"The others?" Renee asked as Cope stepped forward, giving her room to move.

"Denise, Bets and Carlos thought they could be more useful down there. Larry's still not getting around very well. He sure couldn't run if he needed to. But that still doesn't answer the question. I swear I never heard a sound like that before, and it's not like I haven't heard animals die in the night woods."

"It was unique, all right," Cope agreed. He bent and picked up the flashlight, using it to scan the woods around. "Whatever, it seems to be over."

"Small comfort," Mason remarked drily. "Well, if you don't need us, we'll head back to our coffee klatch. If you get the urge, join us. Bets went into town and bought some poppy seed bread and some pound cake, all of which are to die for."

The weather had warmed up, so Renee's hands didn't feel like ice as she accepted the flashlight back from Cope. "What's going on?" she asked.

"I wish I knew. That's why it wouldn't surprise me if Gray Cloud is indeed on a vision quest."

Renee thought about that, part of her rebelling at the entirely unscientific idea of a vision quest, but another part of her wanting to believe that Gray Cloud might get answers out of the ether.

"For sure," she said after a moment, "if this mountain talks, it'll talk to him."

He caught her hand and squeezed gently. "Feel safe to go down or should we stand guard?"

She hadn't done so for the last five or six days, and that weird death-scream didn't seem to require sleeping on the egg. There was so much richness in that rock wall that she seriously doubted anyone could do total damage to it. As for the egg... Denise had a thousand photos by now. Important details were recorded. So...

"Let's go down," she said. "I can't live on top of that egg."

"Unless you're trying to hatch it."

The humor blew through her like a healing wind,

and she laughed aloud. "Cope, you're the best medicine in the world. Like a pill for my obsession, or one for my too-serious nature. Thank you."

Smiling, he walked hand in hand with her down the slope. She made him feel pretty good, too, and he wasn't about to analyze it.

Stockman was reaching his limit. Haunting this damn mountain for weeks on end with an unclear purpose except to find a way to get the scientists to abandon the dig was wearing on him. He wasn't built for living in the rough indefinitely. In fact, if he had a choice he'd never use a tent again.

Darting away from the Bear brothers, leaving no sign behind, had been an amusing challenge for a while. Stockman could mess up a trail really good.

But Broadus was driving him nuts. The guy's original orders, to get these folks out of here before the place became some kind of historical site, had originally made sense. Get 'em to move on. Except they weren't moving on. The rockslide should have been enough, a second one should have finished it, but the damn people had called the cops, ruling out any possibility of another slide.

Broadus was beginning to dither. He had things "in the works" and needed the team gone. Except he wouldn't authorize anything that might get his hands dirty.

Not yet, anyway. Stockman was chafing and he didn't much care what Broadus's timetable might be. Enough of those damn fossils were starting to emerge from the rock wall that Stockman was convinced that they already had enough to get the place declared a historic site, and would as soon as they published their findings, or whatever it was they needed to do. He was just holding his breath for the day he saw park reps from the state out here looking around. Too late then, most likely.

Broadus didn't much care about the fossils. He just wanted to make sure the ravine was useless. No trail of curious visitors, no park guards, nothing like that. Obliterate it before…

Before what? Broadus's intentions were still unclear. All Stockman knew for sure was that that ravine couldn't remain even partially intact. It had to be rendered useless.

But the longer Broadus waited, the harder it was going to be to eliminate the problem. Nor did that really matter to Stockman. He wanted out of this place as fast as possible. The cat calls hadn't scared anyone. The rockslide had done nothing. In fact, the only person scared by this mountain seemed to be Stockman himself. Thank God he hadn't heard that flute again.

Indeed, Broadus seemed to be slipping steadily to the back of Stockman's mind. He was developing an obsession of his own: getting rid of those paleo-whatevers. Getting rid of the fossils. And he was rapidly passing the point where he cared if it looked like an accident.

He had to clean up whatever mess Broadus was worried about, collect his final check, already in a lockbox at a bus terminal, and get the hell out of here. The longer he stayed, the more likely it was that he would get caught doing something.

Pulling out his long-range scope, he settled belly on

the ground and watched the group gathering around their campfire. Cozy. Not for long, if he had anything to say about it.

Cope sat back, a little apart from the others, only half attending their conversation.

He was still trying to put pieces together in his mind, knowing he lacked information. He was used to that. You just had to move the pieces around until you could almost pick out the picture.

And he was getting worried. The rockslide could be perceived as an outright threat. The flute and the screaming animal were nothing but a scare show.

So what the hell?

The longer this dragged on, the more he feared that whoever was behind this would take drastic action of some kind. What's more, after all this time, he doubted the Bear brothers were keeping a really tight eye on anything. It was natural to relax, to begin to assume that nothing more would occur.

After all, even some ordinary pranksters could have jimmied that rock loose just to cause a scare.

But the feeling of being watched seldom lifted. The strange sounds out of the woods might mean nothing or might mean everything. Someone was trying to scare them off.

The certainty was growing in him, and along with it a strong feeling that he'd been lax. He'd been too quick to rely on the Bear brothers for the kind of work even a trained Marine could slip up on if it went on too long without results.

He'd spent his time with Renee, thinking to protect

her if there *was* a threat, but now he was beginning to believe he'd failed her.

Those fossils meant everything to her. What if they were getting in someone else's way? He couldn't imagine how. A takeover of tribal land wouldn't be easy, not these days. They'd need a damn good reason.

Or maybe they just wanted the fossils gone. How would he know? The reason didn't matter. The growing conviction that this was taking too long, that someone was moving slowly for a reason, worried him.

He needed to stop sitting on his can. He had no one else to rely on, not even really the Bear brothers. He was sure they'd been trying to do what Gray Cloud had asked, but they were young and with time, interest waned.

He needed to do some prowling on his own. Maybe he'd find something the brothers had overlooked. Or maybe they were dealing with someone who was good at covering his tracks. Cope was also good at ferreting those people out.

Eyes half-closed, watching the dancing flames, half listening to the chatter, he waited. Some instinct inside him was awakening. Warning.

Between one breath and the next, the horrible screech they'd heard before tore down the mountain, bringing with it visions of blood and evisceration. God!

Just once, but it froze everyone around the fire. Then came a distant, almost inaudible sound of chanting, as if some ceremony were taking place higher up.

"This mountain gives me the creeps," Maddie said, standing. "I'm sleeping in town. I keep waiting for the whole thing to just collapse on me like an avalanche."

Pretty much everyone seemed to agree with her.

Soon the crew were packing up their backpacks, apologizing profusely to Renee and looking downright sheepish.

"It's okay," she said to them. "Camping out here wasn't part of the original plan. Better if you go sleep where you feel safe."

"You, too," Cope said. "I can keep an eye out here."

She shook her head. "Wild horses couldn't drag me away, pardon the cliché. I want to know what the hell is going on out here. I wish Gray Cloud hadn't disappeared."

Cope wasn't sure what Gray Cloud was supposed to do about any of this. Maybe if he'd gone on a vision quest he'd learn something up there. Maybe not. Cope himself was betting on human problems.

There was, thought Cope, something exceedingly lonely about watching the others drive away to town. He wasn't usually prone to such feelings, but for some reason he was feeling it now. Maybe because they'd all become buddies.

What really bothered him, however, was Renee's refusal to leave. He wasn't one to question her judgment. He had the sense she wouldn't take it well, might even consider it sexist. He just knew he'd feel better if she were safe. He knew he could take care of himself, and probably her, but another person in the equation made it all more difficult.

It wasn't that he didn't want to be with her. Far from it. He was feeling an attachment grow, at least on his part, and if he had half a brain he'd bail before he messed up and brought her grief.

Because he didn't trust himself anymore. No, he didn't have PTSD, at least not bad PTSD, like so many of his fellow troops, but he did have it in spurts. And during those times he had a temper that rivaled Mount Vesuvius. Who needed that?

It was weird, too, to feel like he couldn't trust himself. It had taken him some time to get past denial and admit that raging bull was him, and that it would keep on happening from time to time. No isolated incident.

Tugging him gently from his dour thoughts, Renee reached out and took his hand. He welcomed her touch, let it pull him back to the man he wanted to be, not the one he feared he might be.

He wanted to get up and walk around that mountain, looking for any evidence that someone else might be up there. It was dark, and the chances he'd find anything were zip, but the need for action was growing in him.

Still, it could wait till morning when light should help him considerably. He honestly didn't want to leave Renee down here by herself while he wandered in the darkened woods. If somebody did have ill intent of some kind, she'd be unprotected. And the niggling feeling of being watched was strong again.

Someone out there was interested in something. More than interested. Renee kept calling her fascination with the fossil egg an obsession, but he felt the true obsession belonged to the unknown watcher. What was in it for him? If he wanted to steal some fossils, a few were almost ready to come out of the rock. Including the egg.

But that didn't fit with the rockslide…unless they'd picked up a new groupie. He doubted that, though. There was ineptitude behind all this, from the noises in the night to the rockslide. Deliberate ineptitude, maybe?

That chanting from upslope had caused more discomfort among the team than anything so far. He couldn't say he blamed them. Animals could make really uncomfortable sounds at night, but the idea of a group of people chanting somewhere up there in the dark?

Sinister horror movies were bound to come to mind.

Renee spoke. The chanting from up the mountain had nearly died away. "I wish my team could feel safe here. They ought to be able to. Digging fossils out of rock isn't usually a death-defying task." But despite her words, she glanced over her shoulder toward the mountain, toward the place from which the chanting had seemed to come.

"That mountain is huge," she remarked a minute later. "Up close like this it's impossible to tell. I mean, we're sitting two thousand feet up its flank right now. It's so deceptive, but I suspect the real problem is that our minds can't really encompass something so huge."

"You're probably right. We keep cutting them down to size." That stirred a memory for him. "A buddy of mine took his daughter to the shore, and out on this pier was a place you could feed pelicans. So his older child, a boy, wanted to feed the birds and my buddy gave him the necessary two bucks to get a few fish. Then he said to his daughter, 'See Tommy feed the birdies?'" He laughed. "God, the way he told the story. His two-year-old daughter absolutely refused to believe the pelicans were birds. She kept saying 'no birdie' then pointing to some crows and saying very definitely, 'birdie.'"

Renee started laughing. "So the pelicans were too big?"

"Too big for my buddy's daughter, at any rate. At

least that's what he figured out must be going on, and I think he was right."

"I agree with you," Renee answered, still smiling. "What a great story. Well, I guess I'm having a pelican problem with this mountain. It's so big it could be crawling with dozens of people and we'd never run into any of them. Reminding myself of that isn't easy."

"Maybe we should drive east one day soon so you can get a look at it from the foothills."

"I'm not sure that would help," she said wryly. "The farther we drove, the smaller the mountain would look."

"True." Then, unable to stop himself, he leaned toward her, ignoring the warning creak of the camp chair as he did so, and kissed her on her surprised mouth.

"You know, gorgeous, we've got the camp to ourselves tonight."

She drew a long tremulous breath and he could hear the longing in it. "The watcher…"

"You're still feeling him, too?" It was almost enough to flip his mood on a dime. But then he shoved the watcher away. "He can't see through the tent."

He was pleased to see the smile dawn on her face in the flickering firelight. He spared a glance at the fire, decided it had burned down enough to be safe in its ring for a while, then got up, still holding her hand.

She looked up at him, reading his face, he supposed, then rose to join him.

In an instant the entire night changed. The air grew thick with hunger; passion seemed to hum through the very earth. The whisper of wind in the trees sounded like an encouraging song.

His heart accelerated, shortening his breaths, as he led the way to Renee's tent. He was through arguing with himself and trying to ignore the overwhelming need he felt for this woman.

He no longer cared about anything except these moments, now, with her, and that he make them the best moments possible. More, he wanted to stamp himself on her body, her mind, her heart. To make a place for himself in her life that reached beyond some fossils.

Given her obsessions and her career, he didn't even know if that was possible, but he was past caring. If the next hours were all he had, he'd embrace them fully.

Because even as he unzipped her tent flap and let her enter first, he knew he was never going to forget this time with her.

Renee's baggy work clothes gave way to a figure he'd only imagined before. The orange glow of the fire outside penetrated the tent just enough to paint her almost golden, like a goddess.

She didn't wait for him to undress her, almost as if she were making a commitment to the experience ahead. He liked that. He liked it a whole lot. He waited, watching the last piece of clothing drop away until her pants puddled around her work boots.

For the moment he ignored that, instead drinking in her perfection. Small, rounded breasts, not too small but just right. Their curves drew him but he held himself still, taking in her swanlike neck, her strong shoulders and arms, all flowing downward to a tiny waist above smooth, flaring hips. And the secret thatch between her legs, calling to him.

Her legs, too, showed athleticism. This was a lady who used her body and he approved wholeheartedly.

Dropping to his knees, he knew he had to finish the

job. He felt her hand grip his shoulder to steady herself as he reached for her boots, and the touch shot through him like lightning.

"Damn, you're perfect," he muttered as he struggled with laces—really, she double-knotted them?—and at last freed her from the weight of her boots. Then her trousers and undies, tossed carelessly into a canvas corner.

When she stood barefoot, he just wanted to start kissing her from her toes on up, but he felt her push his shoulder. "Your turn," she said almost breathlessly. "Cope…"

How could he ignore that plea? He had nothing to offer to compare with what she had just shown him, but since he didn't, he tossed his garments away as quickly as he could. Including the damn work boots.

Then, naked, he started to reach for her, to claim her. Too late.

She astonished him by dropping to her knees, gripping his buttocks tightly with both hands, and burying her face in his groin. Then, all she did was inhale, as if she wanted his scents to fill every corner of her.

Never had anyone done anything so sexy to him before. For a while he could only stand, letting her magic flow over him even as she seemed to be stealing the strength from his legs.

Then hunger could be denied no longer. Moving carefully, he released himself from her hold and urged her down on her sleeping bag. Propped on his elbows over her, he muttered, "You are a witch."

A breathless laugh escaped her; then he began his journey of exploration, learning every inch of her with his hands, his tongue, his lips. She made soft sounds as his hands trailed over her but he was getting past the point of hearing much except the thudding of his heart, which reached right to his groin, making him feel heavy, hot and hard.

Every inch of her felt like satin, tasted like woman, but when his hand slipped between her thighs into that nest of curls, he felt warm moisture and felt her arch toward him.

Ah, man, he wanted to hold back, to put her on the pinnacle and keep her there until she could stay no longer, but his plans were becoming fuzzy, giving way to the deeper urges that held no thought except pleasure.

Then her hands skimmed his back, reaching down to his buttocks, trying to pull him closer.

Not yet…not yet…but the hammering in his blood took over, the pulse in his groin defeated every resolution, and he slid into her silken glove as if it had been made just for him.

Somewhere between pulling her own clothes off and feeling Cope's hands and mouth on her, rational thought had completely deserted Renee. Her brain seemed to shut down, leaving room only for her heart to leap and hammer, and her nerves to tingle with yearning, for an ache to build between her legs until she needed pressure down there more than she had ever needed anything.

She forgot if she was breathing, didn't hear the sounds that escaped her. The entire universe seemed to be whirling inside her toward an explosion of colliding stars. Want and need became the same thing and focused themselves on Cope.

All too soon the colliding stars joined in an explosion that turned the world white. Renee barely felt Cope shudder to his own completion as hers swept her away.

Cope had gone to get his own sleeping bag, and when he returned he zippered the two together. "Don't move," he said to Renee. "Enjoy the mood."

"What about you?" she asked.

"I'm fine. Enjoying myself. Relax."

As if she were capable of anything else. Her limbs seemed to have turned to warm honey, and her mind and heart were still awash in the amazing experience they'd just enjoyed.

She watched him ease out of the tent for the second time, wearing only his jeans and untied boots. A touch of chilly air crept in behind him.

Weren't men supposed to be sleepy after sex? she wondered dreamily. Of course, it wasn't as if she had a whole bunch of experience. Maybe the guy who had fallen asleep on her had just been bored with her. He was her only sample, so how would she know?

Stretching languorously inside the warm sleeping bags, she then rolled onto her side and waited, her mind rummaging through her sex with Cope as if trying to engrave every moment in memory. She hugged herself with happiness and hoped there'd be more with Cope. He'd shown her places she'd never dreamed existed, but apart from the sex, she liked everything about him. So understated. So funny at times. Yet at moments she glimpsed the man who could be dangerous if he had to be. But so gentle and kind with her, and never crossing any of those invisible professional lines…until tonight. What a wonderful crossing it had been.

Eventually—it really wasn't forever although it felt

like it—he returned, leaning in to place a plate inside, then following with two mugs.

"Hot chocolate," he said. "Or at least the instant stuff someone brought. And a plate of cookies. Chocolate chip, I think, but in the firelight I suppose they could be ants and not chips."

She laughed. "I'm sure they're chips. Besides, it's impossible to go camping without ingesting a few gnats or ants."

She pulled her arm out of the sleeping bag to take one of the cups he handed her.

"With any luck it's still hot, so don't burn your mouth. If you do you won't be able to taste the ant chip cookies."

Moving carefully, he slid into the sleeping bag attached to hers, then placed the plate between them and reached for his own cup.

"There," he said with satisfaction. "Now we can hug or talk, or whatever pleases you."

"You please me," she answered forthrightly. "That was wonderful beyond words. And eventually I'd like a repeat." When had she become so bold?

"You can bet on it," he answered warmly. "We gotta keep sending the kids to town at night."

A quiet laugh dribbled out of her again, but died quickly. "They were scared, Cope."

"That awful scream was bad enough," he answered, "but that chanting? Ghosts anyone? And I don't believe in them."

"I know exactly what you mean." She sipped cocoa, feeling suddenly chilled. By the mention of ghosts? "It's eerie, but there's got to be a natural explanation.

Maybe Gray Cloud *is* on a vision quest up there, and maybe he's not alone."

"I thought vision quests were solitary."

"Like I actually know? I've heard there are different ways of doing them, though. Customs vary, I guess."

"Well, I have to admit I wish he were around," Cope said presently. "I'd like to ask him about these sounds. I suspect he knows these mountains better than anyone."

"I wouldn't be surprised. From what my cousin tells me, he takes being the guardian very seriously."

"Gray Cloud doesn't strike me as the kind to take important matters lightly. You said your cousin met him when she was researching the wolves up there?"

"Yeah. She's a wildlife biologist, and she'd heard rumors of a wolf pack on Thunder Mountain. You know they introduced wolves to Yellowstone?"

"I remember."

"Well, this was a long distance from there. She was hoping to find out if they were a migration from Yellowstone or from south somewhere. Mexican gray wolves have been steadily moving this way, too. Anyhow, she wanted to get a bead on whether there were wolves, if so how many, was it a viable pack…and if they needed protection."

"Okay."

"Mercy said that when she initially met Gray Cloud, he really didn't want her on the mountain. He warned her it was sacred, that the mountain was alive and she could get into trouble…"

"Whoa," he said. "How did she take that about the mountain being alive?"

"She didn't believe it. At least not at first. I think she believes it now, though."

"It would be easy to do, especially right now. And the wolves?"

"Oh, they exist up there. She found a den with pups just in time to save them. Someone was trying to get rid of them all. People have funny ideas about wolves. Funny odd, not funny ha-ha."

"I got that." He fell silent. "We hate them but I'm not sure why. They tend to be shy, they avoid people, and if they take livestock it tends to be something sickly... or a very bad winter."

"The fear runs deep. I've never done any research into the subject, but I seem to remember people didn't always live in fear of wolves."

"I think you're talking about European peoples."

She laughed. "I guess so. I don't think most Native Americans considered them a problem, but then I'm getting out of my area here. I'll just leave it that Gray Cloud wanted to protect them, and he wasn't sure my cousin's research wouldn't expose them to trouble."

"Did it?"

Her answer was dry. "By the time Mercy found them, they were already in trouble."

He held a cookie out for her, encouraging her to take a nibble. She bit into it, then tried to lick the crumbs from her lips.

"You can do that forever, and I'll watch," he said. "How many wolves are up there?"

"Nobody's sure. They aren't seen often, and Gray Cloud's people don't want any of them collared with tracking devices. They apparently need quite a wide range, though, so there may only be one or two packs up there, and whether those packs are small or large is anyone's guess."

"You have an interesting family," he remarked, then let the subject go, allowing them to finish their cocoa and eat the cookies.

The nights still grew chilly, but not as cold as they had at first. Nevertheless, Renee found it a treat to cuddle in the joined sleeping bags with Cope. Not only did he hold her comfortably, but he was practically a furnace, heating the interior of their cave pretty much by himself. Her fingers and toes no longer felt cold at all, nor did his hands when they began to roam her again, a silent invitation she was more than ready to accept.

Curling into him, as new as the experience was, still felt utterly natural to her, as if it were a place made just for her. His hands ignited fires all over her, causing her heart to accelerate, her breaths to shorten, her entire body to bow toward him.

And when she reached out with her own hungry hands, she heard him draw sharp breaths and felt a deep shudder run through him. How powerful it made her feel when her touches drew a deep groan from him.

In those minutes he was hers. She felt it all the way to her soul. Hers. As she was his. The sense of belonging was almost as overwhelming as the desire that flowed hotly through her, at once weakening her and strengthening her.

Dimly she realized that this night was changing her forever. She would never see or feel the same again. And she was loving it.

They were both damp with passion and breathing heavily when he lifted her over him. As her legs spread, ready to receive him, she felt the ache of needing to be filled, the ache of needing to become one.

Then he slid into her, holding her close, rocking

her with a gentleness that almost frustrated her until the rhythm took over and swept her away on the rising tide of excitement.

Then at last galaxies exploded around them, surrounding them in a cocoon of heat and light.

When she collapsed on him, his shudder and groan hurled her over the top once more.

Heaven.

Chapter 13

Cope rose just before dawn. Much as he didn't want to climb out of the best nest he had ever enjoyed, he realized the beginning of the day could bring threats. Something wasn't right on this mountain, and from long experience he knew he'd better at least have his boots on. Nothing could slow a guy down faster than having to run barefoot across rough ground.

Moving as silently as he could, he dressed and carried his jacket outside. The fire was little more than glowing embers, the brightest thing in the predawn.

After he pulled his jacket on, he headed for the stack of dried wood the team had been steadily collecting and built up the fire. He knew he could make coffee on the propane stove, but a little general warmth would be welcome, too.

He wondered if the watcher he kept sensing on and

off was enjoying his time hiding in the woods. Probably not. He wouldn't dare build a fire or brew coffee, the fire because it could be seen for miles, and the coffee because the aroma would perfume the forest.

Cope took a small amount of satisfaction in imagining the guy's discomfort. He probably had to drive to town to…

Cope had just been about to settle into a camp chair while the coffee perked when the thought struck him. He needed to call the sheriff. Somebody hanging around in town like this guy might have drawn attention.

Unlike the rest of the county, Conard City wasn't a place a stranger could disappear into. It wouldn't be long before he'd be noticed and people would start wondering.

Of course, he might not be a stranger. He might well be a local, hired to do something out here.

But whose cockamamy idea had that screaming animal and the chanting been? Sure, it had unnerved the team last night, but it hadn't unnerved Renee. Or him. So if he had wanted to clear the place out, he'd failed.

The huge question still remained, though. Why should anyone give a damn?

He picked up a stick to stir the fire a bit and told himself to stop chasing his tail. All would be revealed in good time. It always was. He just hoped it was revealed before anybody got hurt again.

He wondered if the egg was still okay, and if maybe Renee would be willing to try to dig it out faster. He didn't know why, but he was beginning to feel that time was short. Short for what, he didn't know.

He hated situations like this, where you couldn't

identify the enemy and, worse, didn't know why there was an enemy to begin with. He could count on the fingers of one hand the events that made him feel someone wanted this dig shut down, but none of them added up to a clear picture he could work with.

Man, it just might be some nut who had a thing against fossils. Maybe someone who believed that evolution never happened and that people really had once ridden dinosaurs. Or whatever. He wasn't clear on that line of thinking.

He could understand people not liking the idea of evolution, but being afraid of knowledge? If they pulled those fossils out and someone dated them to sixty-five million years in the past, it wouldn't matter to those who believed the world was only six thousand years old. Evidence could be easily dismissed, especially if you didn't understand the science behind it.

Nor would that egg or anything else they'd found affect many people outside the paleontological world.

But if they turned that rock wall itself into a protected historic site, or a museum... Well, he guessed that could chap someone's hide, although he didn't know if the tribe would approve any such thing on sacred ground.

As far as he could see, anything Renee found probably would be shipped out. In its wake it would leave a bunch of tumbled rock that a few fossil hounds might want to pick through...if the tribe permitted it.

So where was the hassle? It was apparently enough to make someone want to sabotage the team, but not enough to make them want to kill. Not yet, anyway.

Weird.

The coffee smelled ready so he got himself a cup

and moved the pot farther from the heat. The sunrise was about to begin, one of those special sights where rays streamed outward from the sun, rather than a smear of pink and orange across high clouds. Must still be dust in the air.

Just as the first sliver of sun, looking like molten gold, lifted above the distant horizon, Renee emerged from the tent. Fully clothed, including her jacket, she stretched widely, looked at the sun and said, "Wow." Then she looked at Cope with an almost impish smile, adding, "And double wow."

He laughed and rose, going to give her a huge bear hug. "That's triple for you, lady." Then he kissed her long and deep, a reminder of all they had shared. Unfortunately, it awoke the male parts of him that he didn't want aroused right now. Morning. People coming. Things to do.

He released her reluctantly, feeling her hands slip from his back.

"You can do that again anytime," she said, her lips slightly swollen.

"I'll take you up on that offer. Come on, coffee's ready, and when you're ready I'll rustle up some breakfast."

She took her camp chair and happily accepted the coffee he handed her. "You know what's good?" she asked.

"Tell me."

"Some of that instant hot chocolate in a cup of coffee."

"Sold," he said immediately, and went rummaging around in the box of nonperishables. Soon he had both their cups topped with hot chocolate and the flavor, he decided, was a great idea.

It was a time of day when parts of the world woke quickly, and other parts seemed to take their time. Birdsong had been issuing from some of the trees since first light, but now with the sunrise, the chorus grew bigger. The sun's rising happened so rapidly when seen against the horizon that it was impossible to believe that it was the same sun that drifted across the daytime sky. Right now, it was almost possible to feel the earth spinning on its axis.

Reaching out, he clasped Renee's free hand and felt her squeeze back.

"Any bright ideas this morning?" she asked.

How quickly she returned to work. No mooning about, no discussion of the night before. He respected that about her. He'd been in enough tight places that he knew the importance of being able to shift gears quickly.

"None," he admitted. "There's not enough to go on. I can't for the life of me figure out why anyone would care about this dig enough to cause problems. Clearly someone does, but I'm left wondering if it's some juvenile who needs a little counseling, or something more worrisome."

"The slide," she said.

He nodded. "You're right. There was nothing childish about that. There was certain intent. Whether it was vandalism or something worse, I can't imagine."

"It isn't adding up," she agreed. "Nothing is. It doesn't make sense to do things that seem designed to scare us off but not to hurt us. And that crazy chanting. I don't care that it made everyone nervous—if that was supposed to drive me away, it missed the mark by a mile. Even that awful scream didn't do that. Or the flute. It's beginning to feel like a Halloween house of horrors designed for kids."

That was it exactly. But the point? He wished he could ferret out the point of all this. "You heard anything from Claudia?"

She shook her head. "Nothing beyond that she had to take care of some business and would be out of pocket for a few days. Not long, she seemed to indicate. Why? Do you think she knows something?"

"Knows? Not about this crap. Not yet anyway. Maybe she went on the vision quest with Gray Cloud."

"I hope they get some visions," Renee muttered. Then, because she couldn't do anything else, she sipped her chocolate coffee and watched the day's birth.

Cope sat there holding her hand, wishing he could carry her into the tent and hating the feeling that he was blind. In all, nothing that had happened seemed intended to seriously hurt anyone. But he had a growing feeling that if they didn't clear out, someone *would* get hurt or killed.

"I feel like a mouse being toyed with by a cat."

Renee's head nearly jerked as she turned it toward him. "You, too? I didn't want to say it because…" She bit her lip and with it bit back the ensuing words.

Cope had no such qualms. "Because at the end of the game the mouse dies."

Her lips compressed. What could she say to that? She'd been trying all along to convince herself that no one meant any serious harm to her or her team, but as this dragged on, the stupid things that were happening were beginning to feel more like a warning. A serious warning.

The sun was now high enough that looking at it could be dangerous. Like everything else around here, Cope thought. Benign at the outset and then…maybe not so benign. He couldn't escape the feeling that they were simply waiting for a shoe to drop.

"I think," he said slowly, hoping he wasn't about to tread on her feet but knowing that was the last thing he should worry about, "I think that we ought to get the team to stay away for a few days."

He felt her tense. The stiffness reached him right through their clasped hands. "Do you know how tight my schedule is? I've got to get an awful lot out of here before it starts snowing again. Given that this is Wyoming, before we know it it might be too cold to work anymore, snow or no snow."

He understood that. "I'm not trying to screw up your work schedule. I know you have deadlines to meet… for your grant, right? If you want it to be renewed so you can continue work next year and maybe save this site, you have to produce, don't you?"

"Yeah." Her tone was short, sharp. "Photos won't do it. Not at this point. We need to start releasing some important fossils from that ground, and not just the egg."

He twisted a little, trying to read her face. Unfortunately, it looked as if it was of a piece with that rock wall. Unrevealing. "Why isn't the egg enough?"

"Depends on what you're looking for. The egg alone is a great find. It'll come to rest in a museum somewhere if the tribe doesn't want to shelter it in a museum of their own. But it's the other fossils I need as much, for my theory, or it's just another dinosaur egg, Cope."

He understood. But he also understood something else. "If we appear to send the team away for a while, then the problem will be partly solved for whoever is doing this. Only two people left to deal with."

"You're thinking you could draw him out?"

He could see the wheels working behind her lovely eyes. "Maybe. Or maybe he'll think we're closing down the dig and just go for what he really wants. Then we know."

She nodded slowly, closing her eyes as she thought. Golden sunlight bathed her face, and he found himself thinking that she should always be out in the sunlight. Its warm touch magnified her beauty.

"I'm worried about them," she said. "The team. I've been worried since Larry was hurt. No one thinks it was intentional, and given the crazy things that have happened since, I have to agree. But what if this person does something worse? What if we don't just get scared off? Maybe it *would* be better to have everyone stay away, at least for a little while."

It had to be her decision, so he said nothing, merely continued to hold her hand while the day aged.

Stockman watched from a distance through his high-powered scope. From time to time he caught sight of the twin brothers slipping around the ravine like they thought they might actually creep up on something.

Then there was the damn lady scientist and her college professor lover. The others had skedaddled at the sound of the chanting last night, but not those two.

He'd told Broadus they weren't scaring off, but Broadus didn't seem worried. "I just need a little more time to wrap up my business."

Stockman was growing increasingly annoyed. He was beginning to wonder why Broadus had hired him at all. Sure, he'd been given a general outline, but nothing Broadus had him doing right now seemed to fit that outline.

Here he was, twiddling his thumbs, doing dumb things to try to scare some folks away from some damned fossils. In fact, he felt stupid about the whole thing. A rockslide intended to do no harm? Spooky sounds in the night?

This wasn't his style at all. He liked to move swiftly, clean up whatever the problem was, then move on. He didn't necessarily have to kill anyone—in fact, he vastly preferred not to—but Broadus had hired him and now had him hamstrung in these damn woods just as the freaking mosquitoes seemed to be coming to life.

There was no rhyme or reason to it. If Broadus wanted the fossils for himself, all he had to do was say so. There were lots of ways to take care of that. If he wanted the dig shut down and the fossils gone for some reason, that was easy to take care of as well.

This damn show was somewhere in the middle and wasn't making a lick of sense. Maybe Broadus was stupider than he seemed. Maybe *he* didn't know what he was doing. Although when Stockman thought about it, he figured that given how much money Broadus seemed to have, he couldn't be a total idiot.

Still… Stockman sighed heavily. He was running out of patience. If something didn't happen soon, he might just take out that whole damn wall of fossils himself. He had pretty high confidence in his AR15 to do enough damage to make the whole site worthless. And if he took a few scientists out at the same time, so what? Damn woman was running around like a mother duck with her ducklings in tow. Except she didn't seem to feel very protective of them.

Broadus had better make up his mind what he wanted, soon, or Stockman might just take matters into his own hands.

In fact, the more he thought about it, the better he liked the idea. A little mayhem might make those sacred lands profane forever. He liked that idea as well.

A dust cloud rose in the sky toward the south, suggesting that the others were returning. Renee saw it and leaned forward. "Here they come." Yes, indeed, and she still hadn't decided how to handle Cope's suggestion. The rockslide had given her cause to offer them a chance to leave with a good grade, but these last things, the strange screaming, the chanting... They didn't really seem threatening, did they? Except the chanting had caused her stalwart crew to spend the night in town. That combined with the death scream had been enough.

She wondered if they'd even want to work during daylight. Then she remembered all she had discussed with Cope, primarily the sense that this was ratcheting up somehow. Whoever wanted them gone seemed to be getting a bit impatient.

Nothing deadly, but getting worse, to judge by last night. That could be a recipe for disaster.

The car pulled up, disgorging Maddie, Mason and Bets. They were carrying white bakery bags and a drink tray of tall plastic cups.

"Pastries for everyone, and lattes from Maude's diner if you want them."

Cope and Renee exchanged looks. "Lattes?" he said. "Without coffee grounds?"

A gale of laughter greeted that remark. Soon they were gathered around the fire, everyone eating doughnuts or Danish in one hand and holding tall lattes in the other.

"Denise and Carlos stayed with Larry," Mason explained. "Frankly, I think after the weird noises Larry's afraid to come out here."

"Maybe he should be," Renee said bluntly.

That silenced everyone. Then Maddie said, "Aw, c'mon. Just because the chanting and that screaming made us want to sleep in town?"

"Not because of that," Renee answered. "Mostly because whatever is going on here seems to be increasing. I don't want to see anyone else get hurt."

"But why…" Mason's voice trailed off.

"Someone wants us gone from here," Maddie said quietly. "That's what you think?"

Before Renee could answer, Mason spoke angrily. "I'm not going to let anybody drive me off with some spooky noises. For heaven's sake, Renee, this is too important."

"It's apparently important enough to someone else that they didn't care if they hurt someone. I hate to say it, but I want you guys to stay away from the dig."

"For how long?" Maddie asked, almost sounding like she wanted to cry. "I've been looking forward to this for months."

"Hopefully not long," Renee answered. "But we've got to figure out what's going on here before we move ahead. I don't want to be worrying myself sick about you guys. So you're getting a brief holiday. At least I hope it's brief."

Well, that threw a wet blanket over the morning's mood, Renee thought. Anger and weariness warred in her. Anger that someone wanted them out of here, and weariness from worrying about what she couldn't see or touch. Even when she tried to ignore it, the worry was at the back of her mind, mostly for her team. With the exception of Claudia, they were young, and even at her not-so-advanced age of thirty-four, they seemed terribly young to her.

As the thought of Claudia crossed her mind, she asked, "Has anyone seen Claudia?"

Bets, Maddie and Mason exchanged looks. "No," Bets said. "Last time I saw her, she said she had some research to do. You haven't heard anything?"

"Not a peep." Renee shook her head. "I wonder what she's trying to find out. I know we need her to come up with the composition of the rock around the fossils. There are so many of them, and they all seem extremely well preserved."

"That's probably it then," said Maddie. "You've known Claudia for a while, Renee. She can get her head lost in rocks like the rest of us do in clouds."

It was a valiant attempt at humor, but Renee noticed that the three of them were beginning to look toward the path up the mountain, as if waging internal battles about what they should do.

Cope hadn't spoken a word since the discussion about whether to remain had begun. He'd polished off a doughnut and pretty much finished his coffee, listening intently, but silent. She wished he'd let any of them know what he was thinking. He'd been the first to suggest she keep the team off the mountain. Was he changing his mind?

"This has been too weird," Mason said presently. "None of it is making sense. First, we almost get flattened by a rockslide that someone caused, and now we're being treated to creepy sounds? Where does that get anyone?"

Maddie spoke. "It got us to go to town last night rather than stay out here. Anyway, I'm sure Renee has been chewing all of this over and over and I'm not sure the three of us have a darn thing to add. It's weird. That's about it. Someone wants us to move on? Probably. But who and why? I mean, maybe some members of the tribe don't agree with Gray Cloud and the other elders. Maybe they want the entire place left untouched."

It was possible, Renee thought, but it didn't seem likely judging by what her cousin had told her over the years. For one thing, Gray Cloud and the other elders were highly respected and liked. For another, no decision would have been made without a lot of discussion and a general agreement among the people. The tribe was not in any way, shape or form a dictatorship. When there was disagreement, a compromise was sought.

When a decision was made, everyone followed it because community was more important than the individual. Or so Mercy had said. Regardless, there could be malcontents anywhere who might not follow the usual rules.

But damn, it didn't feel like that was what was going on here. The Bear brothers would surely have caught wind of something like that.

"The point is," she said finally, "we don't know

what's going on or how serious it might get. Larry was hurt. Maybe accidentally, but given the rockslide that fell on him, he's lucky all he has is a broken leg. What if that happens again and it's worse? I just don't feel like playing Russian roulette with you guys."

"Well, then," Maddie said briskly, "let's go free that egg before something happens to it. Then we can decide if the rest of us should even be out here in the daytime."

Renee was given no opportunity to argue or tell them to just go to town, per her instructions. Without another word, they picked up their backpacks and started up the path.

Renee looked at Cope. "I think I've just been overridden."

"While the sun is up, anyway. Let me bank the fire, then we'll go keep an eye on the mutineers."

"Truth is," she said, "I'm a bit touched. They're devoted to saving that egg, and not just because of me, I'm sure. They understand how priceless it is."

"They wouldn't be here if they didn't. And I'm with them. Let's get the egg out before anything happens to it. Then we can work our way through everything else."

"I wish that Denise had come. She makes the most amazing sketches."

He looked over at her as he finished piling ashes and sand on the fire. "I think we can do pretty well with rulers for scale and photos, don't you?"

Of course they could, and she knew it. She also knew that he was trying to cheer her up.

If she thought about last night, she could brighten with remarkable rapidity. Facing today cast her down. Someone wanted to get rid of them, and she seriously doubted it was because they wanted the fossils. Maybe it was one of those metals Claudia had mentioned, although she said that one in particular was hardly worth the trouble to minc without a rich vein.

But who knew what they might uncover as they dug? On impulse without a word to Cope, she went to the supply tent and found the Geiger counter.

"Good thinking," he said as he saw it. "Want me to carry something for you?"

She shook her head. "You're not my pack mule, Cope."

"Maybe I'd like to be."

In that instant she lost her breath. Looking into his blue eyes, she saw fires as hot as lava.

"Later," he murmured. "Now let's go save an egg."

Cope was fairly impressed with the three interns who had gone up to free the egg. They had plenty of reason by this point to consider this job potentially dangerous, but they wanted that egg saved as much as Renee did.

Dedicated. He liked dedicated people. And he didn't at all like the crap flowing around this site. It was almost as if they were dealing with a lunatic, but what difference did that make? Lunatics could be dangerous, too. No, what was bothering him was the obscurity of purpose and direction. Like someone couldn't make up his mind what exactly he really wanted.

That worried him as much as the opacity of these efforts. Plan be damned. As scattershot as the events they had experienced were, it remained that at any instant the inscrutable could make itself deadly. That worried him as much as anything. In an instant this could go from some kind of insanity, some kind of game, to death.

He carried Renee's pack over her objections, which left him no hand to seize and hold hers. He was also carrying two tool sacks and a decent digital camera. To make up for Denise, he guessed.

They could only have been five or ten minutes behind the others, but Maddie and Mason were already working with the tips of their trowels around the egg. Bets was occupied with supervising, watching closely and telling them which way their trowels might do damage.

Renee had wanted to pull it with more delicate tools, but that opportunity was gone. Or maybe not, but they had no way to know, and that egg had to be gotten safely out of here.

Whatever was going on, Renee had been willing to sleep up here to protect the egg. By herself if necessary. So the heart of any solution would be to get that egg clear before anything happened to it.

At this point, however, for all he knew, removing the egg might prove to be a catalyst for further trouble. He'd have given a whole lot for some additional information to figure this out.

But Renee was headed upward, her students were up there, and all he could do was try to protect them.

Stockman finally had it out with Broadus, the dithering boss who was driving him nuts.

"I'm not dithering," Broadus objected angrily. "I have to get my ducks in a row."

"What row?" Stockman demanded. "You've had me out here for months skulking in the woods doing crazy things because you don't want anybody hurt, but you want them out of here. Do you have any idea how crazy that is? Do you even know what you're doing?"

"If you'd been any better at what you do, you'd have arranged that landslide so we didn't have cops crawling all over it. I don't want the cops involved, Stockman. I need the veneer of respectability for what I'm doing."

"What's respectable about driving a bunch of scientists off a sliver of mountain? Are you afraid of what they'll find?"

"They won't find anything but fossils," Broadus said angrily. "That's not the issue. The issue is that I don't want it to become a historic site where nobody can ever do a damn thing again except gape. Are you reading me?"

Stockman had read this all before, but it was no help. "Who cares? You can always get that reversed. You must have the power to do that. The friends."

"Whatever friends and power I have, I have them only because I don't abuse them. I need you to remove the problem without drawing legal and law enforcement attention to the place. I hired you because you're supposed to be good at covert activity. Instead, the first thing I hear is that you have the sheriff crawling all over the place. That was not a part of the plan."

"Do you have a plan? Because nothing is working. They're going to uncover those fossils and it'll be too late."

Broadus grew ominously silent. Then he said the words Stockman had been waiting for. "Whatever it takes. But you'd better not have the FBI and BIA all over the place."

The FBI. Stockman didn't need a reminder about them. Just his rotten luck, he got one anyway.

"It's Native American land, you fool," Stockman said. "They have jurisdiction on capital cases. So if you decide you have to kill someone to get this done, make sure you do it in a way that'll look accidental because the Feds will get this tied up in knots for years. Hell, they might even get *you*."

Stockman ground his teeth and wondered why he'd ever let himself get involved with this jerk. He usually had better discretion. The Feds? No. Absolutely not.

His job had just become a hundred times harder. "You should have told me more when you hired me, Broadus. I need more information to plan well. You waited too long. Now it's going to be a mess. You better hope I don't drag you in."

"If you do," Broadus said in a frigid voice, "I have alternatives for taking care of you."

Yeah, right, Stockman thought as he disconnected the satellite phone call. Nobody had ever been able to take him out, but a guy like Broadus? He'd be easy to remove.

Never mind. He had his marching orders. Whatever it took, preferably without committing a major crime that would get the attention of the Feds.

Swatting at the mosquito that bit his neck and waving a cloud of gnats away from his face, he started thinking. There was no real plan, only some goals. Okay then. He'd plan and Broadus would have to live with it.

The egg was released from the rock just as the afternoon light began to wane. Renee lifted it reverently and placed it in a metal case lined with foam. Running her fingers over it, she expressed her awe. "Not only did we get a whole egg, but the shell cracked open in such a way that we have the entire fetus in here. This is amazing!"

Cope watched the geeks geek out over the egg while he kept pacing the cliff edge, watching, listening, for anything out of the norm. Once he thought he'd caught a flash of reflected light from way back in the woods, but only once. It could have been a bird carrying a prize for its nest. Still, the skin on his neck was crawling.

"Let's get that egg down from here," he said, not caring if he was sounding like a man giving orders.

Renee as usual didn't heed him. She looked into the cavity left by the egg and just purred. "Look what's back in there, guys. This find could keep us busy for the rest of our lives. I can hardly wait..."

"Egg. Now," Cope said even more firmly. "We can't do any more in this light and you know it. Tomorrow is soon enough." If they had the chance.

As if the breeze were talking to him, or Gray Cloud's mountain, he felt warning growing. Danger lurked, more danger than at any other time in this dig. Gone was the possibility that the intent was to scare them off.

In Cope's mind the certainty settled as it had on other missions in other places: danger. Life-threatening danger. "Forget the goats, forget the medical care and get the hell out of this town."

He hadn't realized he'd spoken aloud until Renee touched his arm. "Cope? You okay?"

"Get that egg down from here now. No ifs, ands or

buts. Then a group of you are taking it to town immediately. Do I need to ask the sheriff to escort you?"

He could barely imagine what might be showing in his face, but he saw the change in Renee's expression. She was looking at a stranger. Well, too bad. Some things were more important than others, and right now his screaming instincts couldn't be ignored. The very atmosphere of this mountain had changed.

He met her stare steadily, feeling his face settle into stone.

"Okay," she said after the merest hesitation. "Come on, guys, let's wrap it and get down to camp."

He accompanied them down, wishing all the while that he had his M4 in his hands. God, he felt naked. His knife was useful, but only at close range. He didn't know whether he'd be dealing with one person or a group. And he didn't know if he'd get close.

His hands fell into the position of carrying his M4 at the ready, and he forced himself to drop them. No point wishing for what he didn't have. He knew that from long experience.

He'd manage.

They got the egg. To Stockman it had been obvious nearly from the start that that was the fossil most important to the paleontologist woman. What was her name? Renee. Yeah, Renee Dubois.

Well, they got it out of there. He suspected that one item would draw a lot of attention, and quickly. His time had run out. He had to shut down that mess before Broadus's worst fear came to pass: that it became a historic site and attraction.

Stockman didn't pretend to understand since it

was already on Native American land and couldn't be touched, but he'd been around the world enough times to know that it didn't matter who owned it: money could take it. Money and power.

Taking care, he began a sweep of the area while he tried to figure out the best way to shut the whole thing down. Those Bear dudes weren't anywhere in sight. Maybe they'd stopped patrolling. Possible, since nothing physical had happened since the landslide. Sounds were nothing, however creepy. Not threatening. Not the kind of thing you needed security to protect you from. Maybe in that regard, Broadus hadn't been so stupid.

But here he was, and with the egg removed time had to be getting short. That whole rock face was filled with fossils and he had no idea which ones were truly important. But he had some ideas about how to make them all useless.

"You should go with them," Cope said as the team piled into their car with the well-protected egg. "Keep an eye on your prize."

She looked at him. "And leave you here all alone to face whatever it is you're expecting tonight."

He kept his face straight. "What are you talking about?"

"You can be revealing sometimes. Or maybe I'm just getting better about reading you. Anyway, you're expecting trouble. You can blame that suspicion on how eager you were to get the egg out of here."

Maddie, at the wheel, gave a couple of cheerful toots on her horn, then hit the rough road at daredevil speed. Renee winced. "I hope there's enough foam in that case."

"That fossil isn't exactly indestructible," he reminded her.

No, it wasn't, but she was troubled that they'd had to pull it quickly from the matrix, leaving questions to piece together later. Angry that they'd exposed other pieces that might be just as valuable to the elements that could damage them. Maybe it was time to shoot some plaster into those holes.

He took her hand, pulled her toward him, then cupped her face, looking deeply into her eyes. "I'd love to sweep you off your feet and take both of us far from here for the night but…"

"But?" she asked, battling the hazy fog of desire he'd unleashed in her.

"But I want to do some scouting first."

"The Bears are doing that."

He shook his head slowly. "Not the way I can. You should have gone to town, Renee. But since you didn't I'm going to ask you to stay right here by the fire and nurse that shotgun that Mason brought along to scare away menacing wildlife. You do know how to use it?"

"Of course." She bit her lip. "But we're not talking about menacing wildlife."

"And maybe I'm just paranoid. Will you do that for me?"

She nodded, hating it. But he was right. She wasn't trained to move through the woods hunting someone, and he was. He didn't need to be worrying about her, so she'd sit here and guard the home fire, such as it was. Anyway, she had a whole table of fossils to pore over. Not very exciting, but important nonetheless. So until the light failed her…

"Okay," she said, emphasizing her nod. "But don't do something stupidly brave, Cope."

Stupidly brave? he wondered as he melted into the woods. Didn't the two words go together?

He'd noticed a distinct lack of the Bears and wondered if they'd taken up a post somewhere, or if they were only coming by occasionally. Or maybe Gray Cloud had taken them off guard duty. The two men must certainly have something to do with their time. Like jobs.

He started with a wide circle around the ravine. If someone were trying to maintain concealment while watching them, he would spend most of his time well out of any possible line of sight. He could move in for a look-see without leaving any hard-to-remove signs that he'd been there, such as boot prints twisted into the ground, cigarette butts, whatever. Even a candy wrapper.

Steadily he wound the circle inward, moving quite silently on the pine-needle floor of most of the forest, avoiding branches that would crack under his feet. The waxing moon provided just enough light, even under the trees.

Suddenly he smelled something not of the forest. Lifting his head, he closed his eyes and drew the air in through his nose. Body odor. Fresh. It had the stale smell of someone who hadn't bathed recently.

Smiling to himself, Cope pulled the knife out of his belt holster and followed the guy's stench. He couldn't be far away now or the piney woods would have swallowed his odor, expunged it and freshened it.

Allowing for the way the air stirred, he followed the

guy's smell as best he could. Sometimes it just disappeared. Then it would come back strongly. It seemed he was heading for the rock wall.

Was he planning another slide? Well, that wasn't going to happen on Cope's watch. A bigger slide could do considerably more damage. It wasn't even difficult to imagine that it could shut down Renee's work indefinitely.

At this point it didn't matter what this guy was up to. Cope needed to stop his mischief. Later would be time enough to find out his reasons.

He knew he was closing in. He could feel it. Right now he'd have been glad if one of the Bear brothers had materialized out of the shadows to help. Extra bodies were always welcome.

But no one materialized. Halting often to listen, Cope soon heard the sounds of some rustling of some kind, and then the all-too-familiar and sickening sound of a large-caliber bullet being racked into an AR15. The guy was getting ready to shoot. But what?

Hurrying as fast as he could without giving himself away, he tried to get close without finding the guy turned around and facing him with that loaded weapon.

The forest almost seemed to hold its breath. Then the crack as the rifle fired, and there was no mistaking that the bullet ricocheted off rock. He knew that sound all the way to his soul.

Was the guy going to shoot up the fossils? How much damage could he do with a three-shot limit to his bursts? Plenty.

Then Cope saw him. Saw that he was aiming carefully, as if it weren't just enough to shoot the rock, as if he had picked out specific targets.

Cope's mental calculations happened at the speed of light. Just as the guy was about to shoot a third bullet, Cope got close enough to leap, knife in hand.

The fool hadn't hooked the strap of his weapon around his shoulder properly, so the AR flew a few feet away before landing on gravel. Cope gave it no thought as he landed on the guy and gave him a solid punch to the solar plexus.

Gasping for air that he couldn't draw, the guy's eyes widened, reflecting moonlight. Cope socked him again, then put his knife to the guy's side.

"Don't move or you'll get this in your spleen."

For an instant, everything froze. Cope wished for some lock bracelets, for another body to help out. What was he going to do, hold this guy all night?

But then the man rolled suddenly beneath him, breaking free, kicking Cope in the side of his head the instant he got to his feet.

Cope felt the world try to spin into darkness, but he fought it down as he reached his own feet and took off after the running man.

At least he didn't have his AR15 anymore. But heaven knew what other weapons he might be carrying, and Renee was down there. Alone.

Forgetting any need for silence, he took off like a bat out of hell without any concern for his own safety.

Renee. She was the only thought on his mind.

Renee heard the pounding feet coming her way. She immediately checked the shotgun to make sure she had a shell in the chamber, then held it tightly, getting ready. At least with a shotgun she didn't have to worry all that much about her aim.

She might know how to use the gun, but that didn't mean she was capable of hitting a target dead-on.

Her nerves tightened even more as she waited. God, she just wanted this to be over with. To have her whole team safe, and this miscreant, whatever he was up to, unable to bother them anymore.

Then he burst out of the shadows into the firelight and froze when he saw her shotgun. After a moment, the grungy-looking guy said, "You won't shoot me."

"Just stay where you are or you'll find out."

He hesitated, shifting from one foot to the other, looking back up the path down which more pounding feet were coming. She hoped it was Cope.

"I'm gonna leave," the guy said, evidently deciding whoever pursued him was a bigger threat than a woman with a gun. He took two steps toward the road when Renee pulled the trigger.

He froze.

She didn't know if she'd missed him purposely or not, but she had. Regardless, now he was afraid to move.

Ten seconds later, Cope appeared at a dead run, kicked the guy in the back of his legs and knocked him to the ground. "Rope?" he said.

"Plenty," she answered. Still holding the shotgun, she went to the box that held nylon rope. She handed a coil to Cope, who proceeded to hog-tie the guy. He wasn't going anywhere.

Cope looked down at him. "What the hell were you doing up there?" he demanded.

"Following orders, dude. Just following orders."

Before Cope could question him further, the cavalry began to arrive. Claudia and Gray Cloud came in the same vehicle. They took in the situation and soon Gray Cloud was on his sat phone calling the sheriff and Jake Madison. "We need help."

Chapter 14

Three nights later, after a busy day at the dig site, the group sat around the fire sipping cocoa and coffee and talking about what they had learned.

Claudia and Gray Cloud had basically uncovered the issue. Gray Cloud hadn't gone on a vision quest at all. Instead he and Claudia had entered the bowels of the courthouse and begun viewing enough microfiche and film to kill their eyesight.

It took a while for Gray Cloud to uncover a pattern of relatively recent land purchases around the tribal land and along the base of Thunder Mountain. It had taken Claudia even longer to dig around into mineral surveys to find what she needed. As she was doing so, Gray Cloud had gone to talk to Earl Carter, a lawyer, and his son, Judge Carter. The talks had been revealing.

There was indeed a rich vein of promethium along

the lower slopes of Thunder Mountain, rich enough to mine. There was, however, a problem. Some property owners didn't want to sell. Among them was the tribe, who counted its piece as sacred land.

The mining company, headed up by a guy named Caron Broadus, was trying to keep a lid on the reason for their purchases, talking about a resort. As they accumulated more and more property from ranchers who were having a hard time, and as those who wanted to keep their land unthinkingly sold nearly forgotten—and they thought useless—mineral rights, they got closer and closer to the reservation land that held the strongest vein of promethium.

But the tribe remained adamant in its refusal to sell.

Hence, the right of eminent domain entered the picture. Once the mining company owned enough mineral rights around the sacred land, it could claim the tribe's land for mining.

A dirty trick, but a legal one.

The fossil dig had thrown a big wrench into the plan. If that land became a protected historical site, there wouldn't be any mining at all. The first thing Broadus decided to do was stop the dig. If that didn't work he'd probably planned to try to grease a lot of palms to get around it, but that wasn't an infallible way to get what he wanted once the area held a different kind of treasure.

Stockman proved an interesting character who claimed he'd never been able to figure out what Broadus was up to, he'd never wanted to hurt Larry, and the only thing he was going to shoot the night Cope found him was fossils. Destroy the site.

It was convoluted and they all talked it over, trying to organize the craziness in their heads. They supposed it made sense.

"But to think they were going to get rid of us with some spooky sounds," Maddie scoffed. "I think we're tougher than that."

"What they needed," Claudia said, "was time to make their eminent domain case airtight. We were interfering with that. So scaring us away one way or another seemed smart."

"Dumb," said Larry, who was getting around much better on his walking cast.

Along about nine, the group decided to head into town. Some wanted to play darts at Mahoney's. Others wanted a piece of pie from Maude's diner, and they all planned to sleep in more comfortable beds at the motel.

"I can take just so much sleeping on the ground," Bets said, and Maddie agreed. Soon Renee and Cope were once again alone.

"I have the feeling," he said a short while later, "that they're trying to give the two of us some space."

"Space for what?" she asked, then her cheeks flamed as she realized. "They can't know?"

"That we're lovers? I've learned over time that something like that tends to show no matter how hard you try to conceal it."

Renee put her face in her hands. "Eeps," she said. Then giggled. She really wanted to enjoy another night with Cope.

"But first," he said slowly as her hand reached for his, "I want to get a little bit serious."

She stared at him. He was going to tell her that he enjoyed the fling but he didn't want her to make more of it than it was. Except she feared she already had.

Still, he hadn't promised her a damn thing, and she had only herself to blame if she expected more.

"Don't look like that," he said softly, and reached out to run his finger along her cheek. An instant shiver ran through her. "I'm not ditching you."

"Oh." She wasn't sure that made her feel any better. She'd probably made a juvenile mistake with her heart.

"No," he said. "The thing is… I want to date you."

"Date me?" She was having trouble connecting her disconnected thoughts. She thought he was dumping her and he was saying something else.

"I think you know what dating is," he said drily. "And I'm serious. I realized you don't know me all that well yet, but I want you to know that never, ever, not once in my life have I felt about a woman the way I feel about you. I don't want to lose you without at least taking the opportunity to win you first."

Win her? Her heart quickened. She pretty much thought she was already won. "Cope…"

"Shh," he said. "You don't have to answer. Just think about it. And just don't say no. Dating is a try-out, right? You should have the time to make up your mind about me."

She swallowed hard, her mouth going dry. "I think it's already made up."

He looked down. "That bad?"

"That good."

His head jerked up. "What are you saying?"

"You idiot. Of course I want to date you. Of course I don't want to lose you. You'd better be prepared to stick around until you're sick of me."

A slow smile dawned on his face. "That'll never happen."

"You don't know me that well, either. So yes to the dating, but at some point I might get impatient and want more."

"Sweetheart, you can have as much of me as you want. Forever."

The he rose, lifted her right out of her chair and carried her into her tent. "Forever's a long time," he murmured.

"Not long enough," she answered.

Bliss. She could almost feel the mountain's blessing.

* * * * *

Don't forget previous titles in Rachel Lee's Conard County: The Next Generation series:

Conard County Revenge
Undercover in Conard County
Conard County Marine
Conard County Spy
Conard County Witness

Available now from Harlequin Romantic Suspense!

SPECIAL EXCERPT FROM

⬡ HARLEQUIN®

ROMANTIC suspense

*When Elissa Yorian first met K-9 cop Doug Murran,
she never expected she'd need his professional help.
But as soon as someone attacks her, Doug is on the case,
and he's having a hard time not making it personal.*

*Read on for a sneak preview of the next book
in the K-9 Ranch Rescue miniseries,*
Trained to Protect
by Linda O. Johnston.

"I just wish I had some idea who it is, and why."

"Yeah, me, too." Doug had a sudden urge to take Elissa into his arms, hold her tightly against him, maybe attempt to cheer her a little by kissing that alluring yet sad mouth of hers…

But of course he wouldn't do that. Never mind that he felt attracted to her, or that he wanted to fix things for her. He had plenty of reasons not to get involved with her other than as a civilian who needed help. But she did happen to be a civilian who needed help.

A vision of his uncle Cy's face flashed in his mind, encouraging him and Maisie to become cops like him— and to act like professionals at all times.

"Anyway," she said, "I'll be working at my local hospital tomorrow and Sunday, both as a nurse and doing therapy dog work, so I won't be home much this weekend. Then I'll head back up to Chance on Monday to give my first therapy dog training class. I'll call you then and maybe we can catch up on what's going on here and there."

"All right," Doug conceded. What else could he do? He might be concerned about this attractive, dog-loving civilian, but he wasn't even a cop in the jurisdiction where she lived who could theoretically give her orders—or at least conduct some of those patrols and drop in on her sometimes.

And he clearly wasn't convincing her to do something else—except to walk her dog along with a neighbor. Some of the time. Without additional protection at night.

"Well, be sure to keep in touch." He recognized that his words had come out in a tone of command, which appeared somehow to amuse her.

He wanted to kiss that smile right off her lovely face... but didn't.

He motioned for Hooper to join him at the door, where he removed his dog's leash from his pocket and snapped it on his collar. "Let's go," he told his well-trained partner.

Peace also came to the door to see them off. While they stood there, Elissa petted both dogs. Then, to his surprise, she leaned toward him. "Drive carefully," she said, and planted a soft and swift kiss on his lips before backing away. "And I can't thank you enough for all your help."

You just did, he thought, but all he said was, "You're welcome. Be careful, keep in touch, and we'll see you next week."

Don't miss
Trained to Protect *by Linda O. Johnston,*
available October 2018 wherever
Harlequin® Romantic Suspense books
and ebooks are sold.

www.Harlequin.com

Need an adrenaline rush from nail-biting tales
(and irresistible males)?

Check out **Harlequin Intrigue®**
and **Harlequin® Romantic Suspense** books!

New books available every month!

CONNECT WITH US AT:

Facebook.com/groups/HarlequinConnection

 Facebook.com/HarlequinBooks

Twitter.com/HarlequinBooks

Instagram.com/HarlequinBooks

Pinterest.com/HarlequinBooks

ReaderService.com

H HARLEQUIN®

**ROMANCE WHEN
YOU NEED IT**

SGENRE2018

LOVE
Harlequin
romance?

Join our Harlequin community to share your thoughts and connect with other romance readers!

Be the first to find out about promotions, news, and exclusive content!

Sign up for the Harlequin e-newsletter and download a free book from any series at

www.TryHarlequin.com

CONNECT WITH US AT:

Harlequin.com/Community

 Facebook.com/HarlequinBooks

 Twitter.com/HarlequinBooks

 Instagram.com/HarlequinBooks

 Pinterest.com/HarlequinBooks

ReaderService.com

 **HARLEQUIN**®

**ROMANCE WHEN
YOU NEED IT**

THE WORLD IS BETTER WITH

Romance

Harlequin has everything from contemporary, passionate and heartwarming to suspenseful and inspirational stories.

Whatever your mood, we have a romance just for you!

Connect with us to find your next great read, special offers and more.

f /HarlequinBooks

🐦 @HarlequinBooks

www.HarlequinBlog.com

www.Harlequin.com/Newsletters

Ⓗ HARLEQUIN®

A *Romance* FOR EVERY MOOD™

www.Harlequin.com

SERIESHALOAD2015

Reward the book lover in you!

Earn points from all your Harlequin book purchases from wherever you shop.

Turn your points into *FREE BOOKS* of your choice
OR
EXCLUSIVE GIFTS from your favorite authors or series.

Join for FREE today at
www.HarlequinMyRewards.com.

Harlequin My Rewards is a free program (no fees) without any commitments or obligations.

MYR17